THE LEAF READER

THE
LEAF
READER

EMILY ARSENAULT

SOHO
TEEN

Published in the United States by Soho Teen
an imprint of
Soho Press, Inc.
853 Broadway
New York, NY 10003

Library of Congress Cataloging-in-Publication Data

Arsenault, Emily
The leaf reader / Emily Arsenault.

1. Fortune-telling—Fiction. 2. Supernatural—Fiction. 3. Missing children—Fiction. 4. High schools—Fiction. 5. Schools—Fiction. I. Title
PZ7.1.A78 Le 2017 DDC [Fic]—dc23 2016042097

ISBN 978-1-61695-907-4
eISBN 978-1-61695-783-4

Interior art by Emily Arsenault and Ross Grant

Interior design by Janine Agro, Soho Press, Inc.

Printed in the United States of America

10 9 8 7 6 5 4 3 2 1

To Al Chute

SEARCH CONTINUES FOR MISSING GIRL

COLESBURY DAILY
March 12

Police boat teams and divers—along with about a hundred volunteers—continued their search for Andrea Quinley yesterday, scouring the Whitfield River and its surrounding woods.

"We're working well together and we're staying positive, but it's been forty-eight hours now. As time passes, our concern grows," said Colesbury police chief Robert Swindon during a brief press conference on Thursday afternoon.

The sixteen-year-old girl, a junior at Colesbury High School, has been missing since Tuesday. Andrea's parents say she was last seen at her home that morning. Andrea complained of a cold and stayed home from school. Her mother left for work at 9 A.M.

The last phone call on Andrea's cell phone, made at 10:50 A.M., was to her friend and classmate Matthew Cotrell. Matthew was in class and did not pick up. When Andrea's father returned from work at approximately 3:30 P.M., his daughter was not home.

That evening, Andrea's blue Toyota Tacoma was found abandoned off Barton's Notch Road, at one of the Whitfield River scenic areas. Her cell phone was found in the front seat of the truck.

Charles Quinley, Andrea's father, says Andrea often enjoyed fishing and hiking along the Whitfield, both with her family and friends and on her own.

"It's possible she felt better later in the day, saw that the snow was starting to melt, and decided to get some fresh air," Quinley said. "Or, knowing Andy, I suppose she might have been playing hooky."

Andrea is well known in the community for her impressive performance on the Colesbury girls' basketball team—the young forward had just begun playing on the area All-Star team, and last year was designated by the *Connecticut Courier* as the state junior varsity MVP.

Authorities fear Andrea may have slipped on the rocks near the river. There are no signs of foul play.

CHAPTER 1

/

Back when Andrea Quinley went missing, I never thought it would have much to do with me. Sure, it affected everyone in Colesbury in a *things-like-that-don't-happen-here* sort of way. Andrea was a year ahead of me in school and friendly with me—as she was with just about everyone. And I was, of course, as sorry as anyone else that something terrible might've happened to her.

They feared the worst about the river, but they didn't find her. Andrea's story went national on the sleazy *Martin Report*—not surprising since Mitzie Martin is partial to stories about pretty, missing teenage girls. Then spring came. Mitzie's camera crews left. And then summer stretched and simmered along and no one found anything. The HAVE YOU SEEN ANDREA? signs on all of the shop doors faded and curled at their corners. There were no more vigils or fundraisers. The newspaper articles about her became infrequent, then stopped altogether.

School started again. My junior year. Andrea would've been a senior. But everyone started to think of Andrea Quinley as old news. Sad and disturbing old news, yes—but still old news.

Surely those people who had been close to her still thought about her every hour of every day.

But the rest of us—reluctantly, guiltily—settled into the idea that she was gone.

I know I did.

And I know I never thought she'd appear in my tea leaves.

CHAPTER 2

"If you can't get rid of the family skeleton, you may as well make it dance."

Ms. Platt read this quote to us in English class sometime in the fall of last year, back when I was a sophomore. It's from George Bernard Shaw.

I loved it. I can relate to the whole skeleton thing.

I don't have just one skeleton—a single, secret thing I'm ashamed of. I have more like a chorus line of skeletons rattling casually around me, always: Creepy house. Foul-mouthed grandmother/guardian. Absentee mother. My brother's reputation for "drug issues," whether that's deserved or not.

I'm so painfully, obviously not your typical Colesbury material, it's almost laughable I'd ever tried. I'd learned by sophomore year that I was never going to be embraced as a soccer girl or a student leader. I'd spent most of middle school and ninth grade trying to pretend it was possible—joining clubs I didn't like and babysitting like a madwoman to try to afford the kind of clothes most of the Colesbury golden children wore. By tenth grade, I was ready to try something new.

I couldn't pretend anymore. I had to make my skeletons dance. If I was going to have to be creepy, I figured I may as well find a way to make it interesting.

It was around then that I found the book about tea-leaf reading in my grandmother's dusty shelves. It was a stinking, yellowing thing from the sixties: *Cosmos in a Cup: A Guide to Tea-Leaf Reading*. On the cover was a girl with hippie hair staring googly-eyed into a teacup while tiny stars swirled above her head. G. Clara claimed it was never hers. She said it came in a box of books she got for a dollar at a tag sale. G. Clara never cops to anything hippie.

Tea-leaf reading is a kind of fortune-telling, I learned from the book's introduction:

> *The art of tea-leaf reading—or tasseomancy—is an ancient one. The practice spread from the Orient to Europe with the trade and consumption of tea.*
>
> *Of course, it borrows much from other ancient forms of divination. Throughout human history, people have sought out patterns or signs to help them forecast the future: in sand, bird formations, stars, entrails.*
>
> *Tea-leaf reading has become less commonplace since the invention of the teabag. Still, it is one of the easiest and most accessible forms of prophecy. All that is required is a teacup, water, loose tea, and an open mind.*

After you drink a cup of tea—with loose tea, not a teabag—you leave the last bit of liquid and tea leaves at the bottom of the cup. Then you flip the cup over on its saucer and turn it around three times counterclockwise, concentrating your thoughts on the cup. When you turn the cup right-side up again, you look at the images formed by the clumps of tea leaves. It's a little like spotting pictures in the clouds. Someone might see a penguin where someone else might see an ironing board.

Cosmos in a Cup had a long "Symbol Key" toward the end, arranged alphabetically:

> *Wagon: A positive change is coming.*
> *Wall: Resistance or misunderstanding. Also: a physical or mental barrier.*

Wheel: A journey with a positive outcome. Often a metaphorical journey of discovery.

Window: Consider looking at things from a different perspective. Also: psychic ability.

Wolf: Envy, within oneself or from one's associates. Can also signify a greedy or vicious adversary.

Wreath: Sometimes signifies a ceremony to come—a wedding, a graduation, a funeral. Also: a symbol of loss, grief, or death.

I started studying the symbols sometimes before bed. I found it weirdly relaxing. And it seemed related to another interest I'd had for a long time: dream interpretation. I'd always liked the idea that your brain—or maybe the universe—could be trying to tell you secrets with little signs or symbols here and there. Tea-leaf reading allowed for that possibility when you were awake, too. Why not give it a shot?

Then I started to try some readings on my friend Carson at the Clover Café, the downtown coffee shop.

"I THINK I SEE a goat, Carson. A goat can mean you've got hidden guilt about something."

Carson didn't look up from his homework. "If you think I'm going to bite that easily, you're wrong."

I squinted at a blob of tea leaves at the very bottom of his cup. A few larger leaves had clumped into a lopsided sort of U-shape, with a few smaller leaves poking out of one end (feathers?) and a single pointy one sticking out the other (a beak?). "But I also see a rooster. A rooster means arrogance."

"Wow, Marnie. Tell me how you *really* feel. You know, it sounds like I've got a barnyard sort of cup this time. Do you also see a pitchfork? A manure pile?"

"No." I tried not to sound exasperated. "I see an archway. I don't remember ever seeing that in my book, but if I had to guess, I'd say it means a new beginning."

Carson tried to meet my gaze over his laptop, but I couldn't quite see his eyes through his overgrown black bangs. Lately he'd been experimenting with hair growth—on both his head and his face.

"Unfortunately, I don't believe in new beginnings," he said.

I rolled my eyes. "Okay. How about it's the entranceway to the campus of an Ivy League university?"

"Perfect." Carson began to type again. "The tea leaves are probably telling me to get back to work. Maybe they're trying to tell you the same thing?"

"I don't have much homework today," I grumbled. "I'm going to do it after dinner."

I was about to get my jacket on and abandon Carson then and there, but Leah Perry and Morgan Gorse came up to our table. They were two drama nerds who hung out at the Clover Café sometimes.

"What're you guys doing?" Morgan wanted to know.

"I was reading Carson's tea leaves," I admitted.

Carson blushed, but Morgan and Leah wanted their own readings.

IT PROBABLY WOULD'VE ENDED there if I hadn't seen an image of a boat in Leah Perry's teacup. A boat usually symbolizes a big windfall, and I'd told her so. Three days later, she won a huge scholarship from a national essay contest. I was as surprised as Leah was. Had I gotten lucky, or had I sensed a real sign in her cup? I wasn't sure. Meanwhile, Leah told everybody I'd made a spookily accurate prediction, and then all of her drama friends wanted a reading.

And it went from there. They even paid me . . . Well, sort of. A latte or a cocoa for a reading. I don't actually like tea that much. Besides, if I'm drinking something else, it keeps people from asking me to read my own cup in front of them. Ever since Leah and her friends graduated, though, I'd had only a few regular "clients."

◈

"DON'T YOU FEEL LIKE a little bit of a fraud?" Carson once sniffed at me. "I mean, don't you feel like you're pretending?"

I *did* feel like I was pretending, at least at the start. I admit that. But whenever you start on something, it always feels a little like pretending, right? If you let that stop you, you might never try anything new.

And maybe Carson could stand to loosen up and try something new himself. From the time I met him, when he moved to my neighborhood in the seventh grade, all he's ever cared about is getting into Yale. Most of the time he talks and acts like he's already there. Twice a week he drives down to New Haven and does his homework in one of the coffee shops there. Now that we're juniors—now that his grades are more important than ever and he has to start thinking about his application next year—he's becoming a monster.

I don't see him as much as I used to, but that's okay. I'm happy with my decent-enough grades and my tea readings and my pretending.

CHAPTER 3

October 6

"For this reading, I want to focus on relationships," Cecilia announced as she flipped over her cup. "*Only* relationships."

"Okay." I shrugged. Cecilia never wanted to do a reading about anything else, but I decided it was best not to point that out. "Relationships" for her means guys, even if she doesn't know them.

"There's a guy I was way into last year," Cecilia said, rotating her cup in its saucer. "I'm still sort of interested. But after this one party I was at a few months ago, he didn't really want to talk to me anymore."

Both seeker and diviner should be relaxed and mindful when the seeker drinks his cup of tea. The diviner's job is not simply to interpret symbols from a book. Both seeker and diviner are responsible for capturing a glimpse of the future in the energy of the present moment.

The diviner should consider his role to resemble that of a photographer. He is patient, waiting for the right moment, the right glimpse of the seeker's self and energy. If both seeker and diviner are appropriately attentive, the "snapshot" produced in the cup can be remarkably clear and remarkably accurate.

I'm not sure if Cecilia and I are the sort of people the author of *Cosmos in a Cup* had in mind when she wrote about "seekers" and "diviners." But in any case, Cecilia is both my most regular and most unlikely "seeker." She and I were dissection partners in biology last year. We didn't have anything in common and never talked about much besides flatworms and starfish guts. Until she got wind of my readings. She told me that her late great-aunt used to give her tarot card readings. We started meeting at the Clover Café nearly every Monday afternoon.

"I'm not sure if I should keep bothering with him. Maybe I just don't have a chance." Cecilia handed me her cup and I looked inside.

It's important to take a moment to examine the whole cup, to look first and get a feel for what's in front of you, before announcing anything to the seeker. Some of the formations might require a little bit of studying before they become recognizable to you. Some might be recognizable right away. Nonetheless, the diviner should always consider what he sees before he speaks.

"Hmm," I said. "Well, in the present I'm seeing what looks like a fence. So there might be some kind of barrier. Something getting in the way of the relationship—or the kind of relationship—you want to have."

Cecilia was meticulous about never revealing her mystery crush, although in the past, the crush changed nearly every week. If I dug deep enough, I could probably determine who it was from the other details. They were usually football or basketball players. But it seemed to me, lately, that she kept coming back to this one particular guy who wasn't into her at all.

"Well, the fence is running almost to the middle of the cup," I continued. "So whatever the problem is with this guy, I don't think it's going away soon. You may want to ask yourself why he didn't want to talk to you after that one party. Did something happen at the party? Or was it *around* then that you guys stopped connecting somehow?"

Cecilia leaned forward and widened her eyes. Sometimes her face reminded me of a Disney princess, all eyes and pointy chin.

"Oh, *something* happened at the party," she said gravely, then nibbled at the enormous blueberry scone she'd bought along with her tea.

Cecilia has a talent for making every story seem dark and dramatic, even something dumb, like a person being insensitive about someone else's hair, or when someone gets mad at a friend for throwing up in her car.

"What?" I asked. "What happened?"

"I'm not sure if I can explain it very well, without saying stuff that's not really for *me* to share."

Cecilia likes to tease me with her bits of gossip. I try not to care too much. The popular kids used to be more interesting to me back when I used to worry about how I might become popular myself. But when you get this far into high school and it hasn't happened yet, you kind of learn to cut your losses.

"Unless you think it somehow got in the way of possible romance between you and . . . you and, uh, the guy, there's probably no reason for us to talk about it," I offered.

Cecilia sighed. "I guess you're right. But I've started to wonder. I think maybe he's embarrassed that I know about it, and it's ruining my chances."

"Embarrassed?" I repeated.

Had a drunken football player peed his pants or something? I tried to shake off my curiosity. I didn't want to be the sort of person who wanted to *know* whether or not a football player peed his pants.

"It was a prank. Oh, never mind. He probably isn't interested, and I guess I'm just looking for another way to explain it. Kind of pathetic, right?"

I gazed into the cup for a moment. There were two little blobs attached to each other by just a couple of specks in the middle; the lower blob was slightly smaller than the one above it. A vase or an hourglass.

I bit my lip and thought about what my book had said about each symbol:

Vase: Good health or fertility. Alternatively, a secret admirer.

Hourglass: Time might be running out for you to finish a particular project or endeavor. Alternatively: Imminent peril.

"Deeper in the cup, near the bottom, is a vase," I said. "Maybe we should focus on that."

Cecilia sighed. She had done this enough times to know that the images deeper in the cup indicate stuff that's going to happen further in the future, while the edge of the cup is closer to the present. "What's a vase mean?"

"An admirer," I said. "A secret admirer."

Cecilia looked skeptical, folding her thin, freckled arms.

"Now, I'd be worried about this if it were near any negative symbols. But near it is a little round thing that looks to me like a balloon. A balloon is a pretty positive thing. It usually means good times. Or taking worthwhile risks. So I think this secret admirer is going to be someone you never considered before, someone outside of your circle. But you'll probably be happy you gave him a chance."

Cecilia tapped her nicely manicured nails on the tabletop. "Hmm."

That balloon could've easily been a horseshoe crab or a wineglass or nothing at all. But I figured, why not keep things fun and float this secret admirer idea? Now, sometime around Christmas, maybe some poor sap who liked Cecilia Daly would be given an unlikely chance.

"Hey, Cecilia," I heard someone say behind me.

I whipped around. Matt Cotrell was standing there, wearing his famous Hello Kitty T-shirt, tight over his chest. It seemed to me he wore that shirt more since Andrea had disappeared. I wondered if it had been a gift from her or something.

Tall, dark-haired, and cute despite his overgrown eyebrows and sleepy expression, Matt was a senior basketball player who'd been on my school bus back in the old days—in middle school, when Colesbury's golden children are too young to have cars or even have friends with cars. I was sure he didn't know my name anymore, if he ever had.

"Oh. Hi, Marnie," he said. His voice was a little tired, like his mind was somewhere else. *On Andrea, always?* I wondered.

"Matt . . . you're here!" Cecilia exclaimed. She turned to me. "I told him about you, Marnie." She glanced back up at him. "Do you want to join us and see what it's like? You don't mind, do you, Marnie? Matt, get yourself a chair."

"Well, I don't know . . ." I began.

"I do want to," Matt said, dragging over a chair. "Cecilia's told me about this thing you do. Do you charge anything?"

"Uh . . ." I glanced at Cecilia, suddenly tongue-tied.

"Of course she doesn't, Matt. Look, if you really want a reading, you go up and order some kind of black tea, like Earl Grey or Darjeeling. No flavored teas with little fruit chunks in the teabag. Stuff like that can mess up the reading. And make sure they give you a round white cappuccino cup, not a mug. And they'll give you the hot water in a separate little pot if you ask. That helps."

Matt turned to me, scratching at a tiny hole in the shoulder of his T-shirt. I wondered if this shirt would make the cut when he packed for college next year.

"Is that right?" he said.

"Yes," I said, staring self-consciously into Cecilia's teacup.

When Matt returned to our table with his steaming water and white cup, Cecilia said, "I'll let Marnie tell you the next part. I have to pee."

Before either of us could say anything else, Cecilia had disappeared into the back area of the coffee shop. Matt stared at me, waiting.

"Um, so, you want to tear open your teabag and pour about a half teaspoon of the leaves into your cup, and then pour the water over it." I was talking too fast, as if what I was saying embarrassed me. Maybe it did. "Much more than that and it just forms a big clump and you can't get much of a reading out of it."

"Can I put sugar in?" Matt asked, flicking a sugar packet against his palm.

"If you feel like you have to," I said. "But go easy on it. Stir it in good so it dissolves. And then you'll have to wait for longer for the leaves to settle. After a minute or two, when most of the leaves settle at the bottom, you can drink it. All but the last little bit at the end."

Matt raised his eyebrows, then shoved the sugar packet in his jacket pocket. I could tell he found me amusing, maybe not in a good way.

As Matt sipped his tea, I explained to him the basics.

"When you look inside a teacup, you're supposed to think of the handle as symbolizing the person whose reading you're doing. Images that appear close to the handle are especially important. They signify emotions or events that will affect the subject very deeply or directly."

Matt nodded, so I continued. "Then, looking at the rest of the cup, you can do a little fortune-telling. You think of the outer rim as the present or the very near future—the next day or so. Further down the sides of the cup is a bit further into the future—maybe a couple of weeks, give or take. The images at the bottom of the 'bowl' of the cup are the furthest in the future: several weeks or maybe much longer."

I could feel Matt's eyes on me, but his mouth was hidden by the cup as he drank. I had no idea what he thought of all this.

"This isn't the only way to read the leaves," I said. "There are different ways to do it. I'm not strict about the timing part of it. It helps me to read a little more . . . freely, I guess."

Matt sipped his tea. "Is it true you learned this from your grandma?"

If Matt didn't know my grandmother, this might lend my readings an air of legitimacy—an inherited, time-honored art. But no. G. Clara teaches at Colesbury High, and everyone knows she is not a Wiccan or a gypsy or anything exotic.

"Uh, not exactly. I found a book about it on her bookshelf."

I didn't explain that G. Clara is a mild hoarder, which is why we could have such a thing lying around our house for years without any of us being aware of its existence or its contents.

Matt took a couple more sips. Just when the silence was about to become unbearable, Cecilia came bounding back to our table.

"How're you two doing?" she asked.

"Great," Matt said. He gulped down most of the remainder of his tea so fast I was afraid he'd slurp down all of the leaves and leave me with nothing to read.

"I left just a little, like you said," Matt told me.

"Okay. So you see the leaves floating at the very bottom?"

He nodded.

"Then you can swirl that little bit around a few times. Then put the cup facedown on the saucer."

Matt did as I asked.

"And rotate it around three times counterclockwise," Cecilia added before I could. "This is the part where you're supposed to concentrate on the questions you have for the reading."

Matt nodded and turned his cup, which made three long, shrill squeaks against his saucer.

"Now you tap the cup three times," I said. "And then you pick it up. You can look at it first before you give it to me, if you want."

Matt glanced at it momentarily, and then handed it to me. I looked inside and stared at the teacup for a while. Most of the cup was overwhelmed by a single image—a sort of animal whose tail started at the edge of the right side of the cup, and whose body curled around into the bottom. Its pointy ears could've been interpreted as a Doberman's, perhaps. But the length of the figure and the bumps on its back made me think it was maybe something else: a dragon.

I remembered the wording of the tea-leaf guide on this symbol because it was so stark and offered only a single interpretation.

Dragon: Self-delusion. A dragon appears powerful, but breathes smoke and fire into its path, clouding its own vision and judgment.

"This is really interesting," I said slowly. "I think I see a dragon here. Well—a dog or a dragon. But I'm leaning toward a dragon."

"Where?"

I pointed into the cup.

"See the head here? With the mouth open? And then the body all along here? I'm thinking it's probably too long to be a dog."

"Unless it's a wiener dog," Matt said. "I love those little wiener dogs. But . . . is a dragon bad?"

"Umm . . ." I glanced into the cup, trying to decide how to explain. "It doesn't have to be. It's something you can, uh, learn from."

"You know what?" Cecilia said. "I told my mom I'd call her if I was going to be late. I'm gonna go outside for a sec."

We both watched her flit out of the Clover Café's front door.

"So what does a dragon mean?" Matt sounded impatient.

"It represents self-delusion," I admitted.

Matt sat back in his chair. "Oh."

I let him process that for a moment.

"Well, that's kind of a relief," he said with a little smile. "I thought you were going to say it stood for death and disease. Or failure."

I smiled back, unsure if this was supposed to be a joke. "No, the dragon almost always means that one thing."

"What would a dog mean?"

"Usually a dog represents a friend."

"A friend?" Matt stared at me. *Uh-oh,* I thought. Why did I admit that? Of course his mind would immediately go to Andrea. But as Cecilia knew, or at least I hoped she knew, tea-leaf readings were supposed to be for fun. I never tried to make predictions about really serious things.

"It can be literal, too," I hurried to say. "It can really mean a dog. A dog is one of a handful of symbols that can be taken literally *or* symbolically. But I think this is a dragon. Now, it's interesting that the dragon stops before the middle of the cup. Are you doing early decision for college? Maybe it has something to do with your college applications?"

"Like I'm deluding myself that I can get into Dartmouth?"

I laughed, then hesitated, again unsure if he was kidding. "Um, are you applying to Dartmouth?"

Matt shrugged. "I'm not sure yet. My dad wants me to. But I wouldn't say I have any delusions about it. I don't really want to go there."

"It's probably something you're not even thinking of," I said. "Something that won't occur to you until it reveals itself to you in a month or two. That's how self-delusion works, right?

"So you shouldn't worry about it too much. This is just for fun, you know?"

Matt slumped back in his chair and nibbled his thumbnail.

"Would you like to know what else I see?" I said, trying to lift the mood. "That dragon—dog—whatever—isn't the only thing in the cup."

"Okay." Matt stretched in his chair, then absently rubbed the sparkly hearts on his chest.

"I see an oblong shape . . . that can mean a letter . . . like, an important communication. News of some sort."

Matt perked up. "A letter?"

"Um, yeah. But letters are quite common in cups. Almost any oblong figure can be a letter. It's small, though. Maybe not something terribly important."

The image was really fuzzy and could've been anything, but I was desperate to steer the reading away from anything that could be interpreted as relating to Andrea. Leaning hard on the college thing was the only way I could think of, since I didn't know much else about Matt besides basketball.

"I think it must have to do with college," I suggested.

"Is it good or bad, though?" he wanted to know.

"Oh. Um, I see a small flower near it, so it's probably good." I gripped the handle of the cup and stared in again, looking for something else to talk about. That stupid dragon-dog was all I could see, really. I was staring at it so hard that I didn't notice Cecilia had come back inside.

"You guys? I have to go," she announced apologetically. "My mom needs me to watch my little sister while she runs out for something."

"See you later, then," Matt said. I gave her a little wave. "You see anything else?"

As he shifted in his chair, another image did pop out at me. The dragon was curled around something. At first it looked shapeless, but now I saw it was a fox. It was so close to the dragon's mouth, it looked as if the dragon were about to swallow it whole.

"A fox," I said.

Matt laughed. "None of this is sounding very good. Cecilia didn't tell me how harsh your readings are. She's always been kinda sunny about it."

I wondered exactly what Cecilia had said to Matt about my readings. Hadn't he observed that Cecilia is kind of sunny about *everything*? Or maybe it was wishful thinking on Matt's part? Maybe he just wanted me to say something encouraging about Andrea.

"A fox can mean trickery," I said, hoping this wouldn't relate too directly to Andrea. "But I think in this case, it means a trickster. A sneaky person."

"What makes you say so?"

"I don't know," I confessed. "Just the way he was hiding in there. I almost didn't see him." I handed the cup back to him. "Usually a tea-leaf reading isn't for deep into the future. Usually a few weeks. You probably just have some rough weeks ahead. I wouldn't worry too much about it."

Matt put his cup into his saucer and sighed. "I appreciate your honesty."

"Any time," I mumbled.

"Can I ask you kind of a random question?" Matt asked.

"Yeah?"

"Isn't your brother Noah a friend of Jimmy Harmon's?"

I tried not to look surprised. Thanks to his little "problem" last year, people usually avoided talking about Noah with me; even Carson never mentioned him. But Jimmy Harmon . . . that startled me. Jimmy Harmon, who used to spend hours and hours at our house. Who played Magic cards with my brother in middle school. Who said the word *pussy* at the table one time when G. Clara let him stay for dinner. Jimmy Harmon whom we didn't really know anymore. I hadn't thought about him in years. He dropped out of Colesbury High in tenth grade.

"Um. Well, they were friends when they were kids. They haven't been close in the past few years."

"Why's that?" Matt wanted to know.

I shrugged. "You know, Jimmy got kinda messed up—"

The second I said it, I was sorry. Sorry for bringing up *messed up* at all.

Noah's kinda messed up, too, would be a fair response. Jimmy was a dropout, rare for Colesbury, but Noah's overdose and resulting stint in the hospital made him pretty scandalous as well.

Matt didn't go there, thankfully. He just twisted his sugar packet in his hands, looking thoughtful. Maybe, because of Andrea, he understood a little about *messed up.* In some form or another.

"When's the last time you or your brother saw him, anyhow?" Matt asked.

"Oh . . . I don't know," I said. "Quite a while, probably."

"Have you seen him in the last, say, six months? Has your brother?"

I didn't want to admit how little my brother and I actually spoke to each other these days.

"No," I said firmly. I wanted to end this conversation. And it was the truth. I hadn't seen Jimmy and I doubted my brother had. Since rehab, Noah barely left the house or talked to anyone. He was taking a couple of community college classes, but only on G. Clara's firm insistence.

"Why do you ask?" I said.

"Just curious." Matt shrugged. "He sort of disappeared, didn't he?"

"I guess. He never liked Colesbury."

"People say he went up to Lyndham . . ." Matt pulled on his black athletic jacket, yanking its neon yellow zipper tight over his chest. "Do you want a ride home?" he asked, surprising me. "It's raining."

"No," I said automatically, then corrected myself. "No thanks. I like the walk. It's, like, the only exercise I get."

It was partially true. The real reason was that I don't like people to see where I live, if I can help it. Probably most people know anyway, but it's best not to remind them.

"I've got my umbrella," I added. "And I like the smell of rain."

Matt shrugged and let it go.

The peeling paint and general disrepair of the house was embarrassing enough. The weird spray-paint art my brother put on the toolshed this summer made things even worse. The house screams *trashy* from the outside.

I can't say that the inside is much better, really.

WHEN I ARRIVED I saw that Noah had added a new bucket to our fireplace to catch the leaking rain. Actually, it was a red plastic dollar-store mixing bowl. Since G. Clara doesn't cook, it was a good choice for this purpose. The living room had its usual chill. Noah was on the couch, watching some Animal Planet thing about snakes and flipping through a textbook. He was wearing an old Red Sox sweatshirt over his T-shirt and sweater. Our house requires a little extra layering, even in the early fall.

"You walked home?" Noah asked.

I was surprised by the question. It was almost a greeting, which was rare for Noah these days.

"Yeah. It wasn't too bad, though."

"From the coffee shop?" Noah looked up from the television, actually appearing a bit interested. "A reading?"

"Yeah."

Noah tossed the textbook on the couch. "Do you really like doing those?"

I was tongue-tied for a moment. Noah had never asked me about my readings before. I'd always assumed he thought that it was a lame thing to do and therefore not worth discussing. But he'd never said as much.

"Sometimes," I said. "How was your class?"

He shrugged. "Community college is like high school, except with a few old ladies in every class. Not for you. I'd recommend you aim a little higher."

I decided not to remind him of my plan to attend college far away from here. That might offend him and shut him down.

"When's the last time you saw Jimmy Harmon?" I asked instead.

Noah returned his gaze to the television. "What?"

"Jimmy. Jimmy Harmon. When's the last time you—"

"He doesn't live in Colesbury anymore, Marnie. Why would I have seen him?"

"Where does he live now?"

"Last I heard, Lyndham. With his cousin, or something. Why are you asking?"

"Just wondering."

The fleeting trace of warmth was gone from Noah's face now, replaced by the same blank mask that had become familiar to me over the summer.

"We're not friends. We haven't been in a long time. That'd be like me asking you about Amy Swanson."

Amy Swanson was the girl I did cartwheels with in third grade. We both had the same discounted pink jacket from Marshall's. We thought we were the coolest, and we were insepa-rable until middle school. Then she joined the junior marching band. The Colesbury Marching Band is the closest thing our high school has to a cult, so we don't talk anymore.

"Aren't you curious, though?" I asked Noah.

"Marnie." Noah yawned and stretched. I couldn't tell if he was bored or just trying to look bored. "You're gonna learn next year, after you graduate. There will be a lot of people you'll probably never see again. And you won't care. Or at least, you shouldn't care."

He sounded like an old man, as if he had been out of high school for decades, rather than a recent graduate. And I was using the term "graduate" loosely, since after OD'ing in April, Noah had gone to the hospital for a while, then had to make up his final credits in summer school.

"I'll take that under advisement," I said, and went to my room.

I opened my laptop and clicked onto Facebook. Carson was on there all the time, probably stalking his rivals for valedictorian or something. I don't ask a lot of questions, because I don't want to know. But I knew he'd message me if he saw I was on, too.

What's up? he wrote, within a minute.

Not much. Just did another reading with Cecilia. Things got weird, though. Matt Cotrell showed up and she made me give him a reading, too.

Carson's response took longer than usual.

Uh-oh. I'd be careful what you say to him. Did he ask you about Andrea?

Carson used to talk about Andrea Quinley all the time. He had a big crush on her, I think, although he'd never admit it. He acts like crushes are beneath him, for now. He says that when he gets to Yale, he'll "pursue accomplished and career-driven women."

Lots of people had crushes on Andrea. Not just boys. She wasn't exactly what you'd call pretty. You'd maybe call her handsome. Or maybe something more neutral, like *attractive*. She was big and bulky like a guy but with a sweet porcelain face.

She was super polite to the lunch ladies and chewed tobacco. For real. And she was always smiling—half laughing at something or other, even though she wasn't very funny herself.

She was a sort of puzzle. If you liked her, did you like girls or guys? It was hard to say. Maybe a little of both. I'd never mentioned this to Carson, though. He was smart enough to see it. If he wanted to see it.

I tried not to let the conversation get too serious, I typed. *I don't know if I succeeded.*

I'm sure you did the best you could. Under duress.

Carson is much nicer over a computer than in person. If I didn't know him over Facebook and Snapchat, I probably wouldn't be able to stand him anymore.

Thanks. I should go. G. Clara left me a Tuna Helper I'm supposed to cook.

So rogue! Enjoy.

Carson and I call G. Clara a "rogue" since she's nothing like what a home-ec teacher is supposed to be. She's taught home ec at Colesbury practically since the dawn of time. "Family and Consumer Science" is what they're supposed to call it now, but since they called it home ec when G. Clara started, she still calls it that. She doesn't cook or clean much in her real life; she orders a lot of takeout and brings the occasional box of junk to the Salvation Army to make more room for new tag sale finds she'll recycle out a couple of years later. She says "shit" a lot in class and gives answers during tests—which she wrote sometime during the Reagan administration and hasn't edited since—if kids ask nicely enough. But she has tenure and home ec teachers can be hard to find these days, so the Colesbury High administration doesn't seem to care. Only slackers and special-ed kids—and the occasional girlie girl like Cecilia—take home ec anymore, anyway.

The no-cooking, no-cleaning thing isn't because G. Clara doesn't care about us. It's that she didn't expect to practically raise and support her grandkids like her own. She wanted to be retired by now. She gets pretty tired by the end of the day.

If I were a better granddaughter I'd probably do more house-cleaning. I used to do a ton—back in those middle school days when I was desperate to be like everyone else. But then, early on in ninth grade, I was cleaning the bathroom and found a small mushroom growing out of the space between the tub and the loosening linoleum floor. I sat for a long time staring at that mushroom, so small and yellow and delicate, and then cried.

After I'd picked it and tossed it outside, I concluded that none of us could really keep up with the house. It's full of mildew and spiders and mushy spots on the ceiling where old, wet leaves are stuck up on the roof. It is quickly and inevitably sinking back into the earth. We're all just hoping it holds on till Noah and I get jobs or go away to college, when G. Clara can sell it (or at least the lot it's standing on) and move into a sensible little condo like other single ladies her age.

In the meantime, I do the dishes and laundry but leave the bathroom spiders and the kitchen moths alone, like G. Clara and Noah do. Homework and fortune-telling are probably more productive uses of my time, anyhow.

CHAPTER 4

I was walking by the river in the cold. I don't know why, because normally I hate the cold. That's why I'm going to go to college somewhere warm. Somewhere far from here. California or Arizona.

Everything was frozen. Why was I here? I coughed and sputtered along and then it started to snow. Hard. The wind drove the sharp little flakes right into my face. I looked down at my clothes and realized I was wearing only jeans and a tank top, with no shoes. But somehow I couldn't feel the cold. Was I numb?

I walked faster because it was all I could think to do. But the sound stopped me—the sound of a twig snapping. And then I saw its snout poking out from the tree in front of me. Then he showed his whole self: a red-brown fox, mangy and thin.

I jumped away. His mouth opened and I saw his yellow teeth. He didn't step closer to me, though. Just smiled a slight, cunning smile.

I knew foxes didn't eat people, but I was afraid of his face, his gaze. I'd read once that you should make lots of noise at black bears; it scares them away. But a fox? What do you do with a fox? Scream? Wave your arms? Tiptoe away? Avoid eye contact? Say shoo?

I wanted to turn and run, but my feet wouldn't move. And somehow, he wouldn't let me look away.

CHAPTER 5

October 8

"You shouldn't eat that stuff," Carson said for maybe the millionth time since we'd started high school. "It's probably full of weird preservatives."

He was referring to my chocolate pudding cup. G. Clara doesn't pack me a lunch, but sometimes she leaves me snacks on the kitchen table along with lunch money.

"I don't want to hurt G. Clara's feelings."

Carson snorted and finally looked up from his book. "Your grandmother's a tough old bird. Everybody knows that."

"She has her tender moments, though," I said.

Instead of returning his attention to his book, Carson stared beyond me.

"I think Matt Cotrell is coming over here," he said softly.

"Matt . . . ?" Before I'd finished repeating the full name, I felt a finger tap my shoulder.

"Hey." He was wearing a set of shiny Mardi Gras beads and squeezing an orange as he spoke. His eyes were fixed on me; he didn't even seem to notice Carson. "I wanted you to see something, Marnie."

"Okay," I said.

I was still uneasy about the reading I had given him. I'd felt things had ended awkwardly. And I'd never dreamed about a reading before.

Matt pulled out his phone and waved a picture in front of

my face. It was a photo of a dog—a little terrier, like Toto in *The Wizard of Oz*.

"Not a wiener dog, but kind of close," Matt said. "I go running almost every day. Yesterday, I found this dog near the parking lot at Whitfield Park."

"You *found* him?"

"Yeah. He seemed to be lost. He had a leash attached."

My heart seemed to beat a little faster. I wasn't sure why. As far as coincidences went, it wasn't that surprising. Everyone walked their dogs in Whitfield Park. "Did he have a tag?"

"Nope. A collar and leash, but no tag."

"You going to call the pound?" I asked. My eyes flicked to Carson. He was staring up at Matt with a look I couldn't quite place.

"We left a message," Matt said with a shrug. "In case someone calls looking for him. But we're not sure we want to put the poor guy in the pound." He smiled. "I've almost got my dad convinced we should keep him if we don't have any luck with that."

"Uh-huh," I said, trying to keep the *and-you're-telling-me-this-because . . . ?* tone out of my voice.

He absently lifted one of his strands of Mardi Gras beads—a purplish pink one—and twisted it in his fingers. I watched him, wondering about his habit of wearing girlie things. Was it to say, *Look at me, I'm so masculine and cool, I can wear this stuff just for laughs?* Or did he genuinely like sparkles and beads and Hello Kitty?

"So you were right about the dog in the tea, is what I'm saying," Matt finally said. "Kind of awesome."

An amused squeak came out of Carson, who promptly buried his face in his book. The title was *Constitutional Law: Cases, Comments, and Questions.* I was embarrassed for both of us.

I let Matt's gaze catch mine. "It was a dragon. Not a dog."

He looked surprised. "I was giving you a compliment. If I were you, I'd stick with a dog."

I didn't like his dismissive tone—as if a "compliment" would make me forget what I'd actually seen. "You saw it as a dog," I said, "but I saw it as a dragon. A dragon and a fox. I remember it pretty clearly."

Carson cleared his throat. "I think I'm going to go buy myself an ice cream."

"Go ahead," I said, and he dashed away.

I noticed he headed for another table, not the snack stand.

"I'm glad he took off," Matt said. "Because there was something else I wanted to talk to you about. Kinda . . . privately."

"Oh. Um. Really?" For a second, I allowed myself to think that Matt maybe liked me. Was he going to ask me to hang out or something? Without the teacups? What would I say?

"Yeah. Aside from the dog, you said you saw something like an envelope."

"Oh. A letter, yeah."

"I think that's interesting."

"Oh? Why's that? Did you get a letter recently, too?" I said doubtfully.

Matt drummed the table with his hands, then glanced fitfully around the cafeteria. "Um. No. I just . . . wish I'd asked you more about that."

"It was a tiny thing," I said quickly. "Just a blob, really. It could've also been—"

Matt interrupted. "Maybe we should do another reading."

"About the letter?" I said.

"Well, just, Cecilia says you'll sometimes do readings for a very specific question."

"Sometimes," I mumbled. "Sure."

"Do you need to know what the question is, exactly, to do that kind of reading?"

"Well, no. I guess not." I couldn't figure out why he was being so evasive. But maybe he'd taken the sudden appearance of a dog in his life as proof positive of the accuracy of my readings. I wasn't sure how I felt about this, since *I'd* called it a dragon.

"Are you free Friday, then?" he asked. "I don't have practice."

"I think so. But at the coffee shop they're always setting up for their Friday concert then. It can be annoying. Hard to get a seat."

Matt thought about this. "Can we go to your place?"

"Umm." I sucked in a breath. I preferred not to have Matt at my house to meet the spiders and the weevils. Or worse, run into my brother when he was in the wrong mood.

"Or mine?" Matt suggested.

"Okay," I said, before I had a chance to think about how weird that might be. "Let's do that."

ONCE I WAS HOME, I got on Facebook. This time, I didn't wait for Carson to notice me there. I could see he was on, so I messaged him right away.

Thanks for abandoning me like that.

Carson wrote back within seconds. *What was I supposed to do?*

Matt wants me to do another reading. At his house this time.

It took Carson nearly a minute to reply. *Interesting.* And then after a few more seconds, *Maybe he's trying to seduce you.*

Shut up, I wrote back.

Seriously, maybe it's his weird way of asking you out?

This was the sort of thing Carson wouldn't usually say to my face. He tries to be encouraging on digital formats, even if he finds it difficult in person.

I wonder, Carson wrote, before I had a chance to respond. *Did he ever go out with Andrea?*

They were just friends, I typed back. *That's what everyone says.*

Carson took so long to write back that I wondered if he'd stepped away from his computer.

I don't want to say he doesn't like you, he wrote, after a couple of minutes. *I'm not saying it's impossible. But do you think he REALLY believes in your tea-leaf readings, or is this just a cry for help, or something of that nature?*

Typical Carson. I rolled my eyes as I typed, *Sorry. Have to go. G. Clara calling.*

CHAPTER 6
October 9

The fox again.

I don't know how long we'd been standing there, but it must have been a while, because his back and head were coated with a thin layer of snow.

He blinked, and I was able to take a step away from him. Then another. He turned away from me and took a few steps in the opposite direction.

In my effort to avoid eye contact with him, I stared at the snow where he'd just been.

And then I saw a dark blot of blood, spreading in the snow.

"MARNIE?"

The red disappeared into black as I opened my eyes.

"Marnie, are you okay?"

G. Clara stood in my doorway, squinting in the light of the hallway.

"Yeah," I mumbled, sitting up.

G. Clara was wearing the red plaid robe that Noah had gotten her two Christmases ago. It made her look like a grizzled old lumberjack lady. Her gray-white hair looked beautiful on her shoulders. Most of the time, she wore it pulled tight.

"You were crying," she whispered.

"No, I wasn't."

"In your sleep, then. Bad dream?"

G. Clara looked so tired. I wanted her to go back to bed and not to worry about me.

"Uh. Not that I remember, G. Clara."

"Are you sure, Marnie?"

I rubbed my eyes, then buried my head in my pillow. "Yeah, I'm sure. I'm sorry I woke you up."

"Don't be sorry. Sleep tight."

G. Clara slipped back into her room, and I heard her bed-springs creak. In the silence that followed, I heard a couple of soft, stockinged footsteps, and then the subtle squeak of the hinges of Noah's bedroom door. Noah had apparently heard me too and was about to head down the hall himself.

I wondered how loud I'd been, to awaken the whole household.

And all of this over some tiny leaves that had simply, coincidentally, arranged themselves into a shape that looked just a little like a fox.

Tiny leaves, I told myself, as my eyes drooped closed. Tiny leaves from a teabag at a teabag factory. Just for fun.

CHAPTER 7
October 10

It wasn't until I arrived at Matt's that I wondered how lame it looked for me to bring my own teapot and cups. But I'd worried that his parents wouldn't have any cups that were the right shape.

While the tea steeped, Matt slapped a sleeve of Oreos on the countertop between us.

We sat face-to-face on wooden stools. Both of his parents were still at work.

"The leaves don't ever really answer a direct yes or no, if that's the kind of question you have," I said. "All I can do is interpret the images they give me."

"Understood." Matt pulled the Oreos open, took two, and then offered me the package. I shook my head. I love the cookies but hate the cream center. I didn't want to peel apart the layers in front of Matt or have to figure out where to toss the round flap of filling.

I poured a cup for each of us, enjoying the sound of the liquid trickling into the teacups. Normally, at the Clover Café, that sound was drowned out by the buzz and whir of the espresso machine. Here, against the silence of the empty house, it made this tea feel calmer and somehow more official. Plus I loved using my own pot and cups. They were small and rounded at the bottom, with silver trim and tiny pink rosebuds.

I watched Matt sip. He grimaced a bit at the first bitter taste. With his muscular build and his athletic look of determination, he looked odd drinking out of my delicate floral teacup. I averted my eyes and took in the room. The kitchen island was a shiny black granite—so shiny I didn't want to put my hands or elbows on it. The whole place smelled faintly of new paint, as if it had recently been remodeled.

When Matt was finished, he didn't wait for instructions. He swirled the last of the tea around and flipped the cup onto the saucer.

"Concentrate on your question while you turn the cup," I said. "Do it slowly."

He seemed to be holding his breath as he twisted the cup. *Squeak. Squeak. Squeak.* He even remembered to tap the cup three times. Then he lifted it and handed it to me without looking first.

I studied it for a minute, extra careful to absorb it before saying anything. "Over on this side of the cup is where I'm seeing the clearest image," I told him. "It looks like an arm to me."

I tilted the cup toward Matt, but he didn't seem to want to look.

"And the thing about an arm . . . it's one of a handful of symbols that can have different meanings depending on what direction they're pointing. This arm is pointed upward. So that can mean seeking. Seeking answers."

Matt folded his arms. "That's kinda conveniently vague, isn't it?" he said. "Of course I'm seeking answers. Why else would I be having you do this?"

"I'm just telling you what an arm *can* mean. I'm not trying to scam you."

"Oh." Now Matt seemed apologetic. "I didn't say you were."

"If I were a scam artist, don't you think I'd at least charge you a buck or two?" I stopped, realizing how snippy I sounded.

"No one said you're a scam artist," he said. "Listen, you should've heard Cecilia going on and on about you at the last party. She said that sometimes she gets chills when you tell her something you see in the teacup, because sometimes it connects to something in her life you couldn't possibly know about."

"Oh." My neck prickled at this statement. I wondered if Cecilia really meant this or was just being dramatic to get people to listen to her.

Matt watched me, appearing to weigh my reaction. "So that seemed like something I ought to try for myself. Um, with my situation. You know what I mean?" He didn't wait for an answer but unfolded his arms and reached out for the cup. "Can I see where you see the arm?"

I tilted the cup toward him and pointed.

"I don't think that's an arm," Matt said softly. "I think that's a knife. See the handle?"

A knife. I could sort of see it, but I didn't really want to go there. Not with Andrea Quinley looming over this reading.

"I hadn't thought of that as part of the same image," I said slowly. "It's a little separated."

"What would a knife mean, though? Danger? Violence? Is someone in danger?"

Knife: Antipathy, revenge, or fear. Alternatively, an upcoming surgery or other medical procedure.

"A knife often means fear," I told him.

"Am I afraid?" Matt asked, forcing a fake little laugh.

But I could tell he wasn't kidding.

"I don't know," I said gently. "*Are* you?"

Matt was silent for a moment, then he put the teacup back in its saucer. "Where'd you get these cups?" he asked.

"My grandmother picked them up for me at a tag sale," I said.

He fiddled with the cup, looking at it from different angles. He looked so sad that I was starting to feel ashamed of myself, though I wasn't sure what for.

"Matt," I said slowly. "I don't know if I ever said how sorry I am. About everything with Andrea. I didn't know you that well last year, and—"

"Don't worry about that." He pushed the cup and saucer in

my direction. "Nobody knows what to say. Saying nothing is as good as anything."

I thought about some of the weird things people said to me after Noah's pill incident. Like, *I'm sure it was just an accident.* Always, I wanted to reply, *I'm not sure. And I know him pretty well. So how can* you *be sure?*

"I know what you mean," I said finally.

It came out hoarsely, almost a whisper. Matt gazed at me for a moment, then nodded a little. I picked up the teacup and peered inside again. Aside from the arm, I thought I saw a brush. And then I saw something behind the brush—closer to the handle—that made me jump.

Another fox. My pulse quickened. I'd never seen a symbol appear twice in a row in someone's cup like that before.

"What is it?" Matt asked.

I handed him the cup. "Do you see the fox near the handle?" I pointed to the image.

"Oh. I guess I do, yeah. That's weird. Didn't last time . . ." Matt didn't finish his sentence.

"Last time I saw a fox, too. Yeah."

"And you said a fox was a trickster."

"Possibly," I said. "Very few symbols have only one meaning."

Matt thought for a moment. "I think I want to show you something."

"Uh, okay."

He abruptly hopped off his stool and left the room, leaving me alone for a couple of minutes. I breathed in the new kitchen smell, then took apart and gobbled an Oreo, tossing the filling into the garbage disposal. Matt returned with a piece of paper and handed it to me. It was still warm from the printer.

"This is a message I got," he said. "An email. A few weeks ago."

It was addressed to Matt, but the sender's address was a long string of numbers and letters.

The email said:

*I want you to know I'm still out here. I feel all alone and wish
I could call. I wonder how much you know? Love, Andy.*

After reading it, I handed it back to him.

"What do you think?" Matt demanded.

I took a breath.

"Andy?" I said. "You called Andrea Andy, I take it?"

"Some of us called her that. People who knew her when we
were little."

"You got this over the summer? And did you tell the police
or anything?"

Matt nodded. "Yeah. My parents went to the cops with it, and
they took it seriously. But now they're pretty sure it's a hoax."

"What's made them think that?"

"Well, they tried to trace it, for one. They said whoever sent it
was pretty good at hiding the origin of the message. Apparently
there are ways to hide your IP address, various servers you can
put a message through that will eliminate that information."

"Is it possible Andrea would've done that?"

"Not really. She wasn't—isn't—all that tech savvy. Unless
she has someone helping her. Since the email actually says
very little, and since my name was mentioned in the papers
and the stories—you know, about her last phone call and all
that—the police think it's a fake. They said I was a likely target
for these kind of hoaxes."

I hesitated. I'd forgotten about Matt being the last person
she'd called. He hadn't picked up because he was in Mr. Bernier's class. Mr. Bernier *hated* cell phones. He went ballistic
if one went off during a test or a quiz. I wondered how many
times Matt had asked himself, *What if I'd picked up? What if
she'd called a little earlier? A little later?* No wonder he was taking
this message so seriously. He was probably wondering if it was
a second chance.

I bit my lip. "How would a random hoaxer get your email address?"

"Well, I had an open Twitter account back then, and I had my email address on it. I mean, I've taken it down since. The police officer thought maybe that's why this 'hoaxer' chose me in the first place. Because I was the easiest of Andrea's friends and family to harass. No one else had their email address or phone number on display. I'd put it up for some stupid reason like a year ago, telling other basketball camp guys to keep in touch and send me pictures from the summer. Also, a lot of people referred to her as *Andy* in all the press about her disappearance. Her brother, her mom."

I turned the information around in my head. "But does this sound like Andrea to you? This note?"

Matt sighed and stared down at the paper. "It's hard to say when it's so short."

"Well, is there anything here that's like her style, her way of saying things? That would prove to you it's her?"

"If she really was alone and desperate somewhere, would she think of that?" Matt folded the paper carefully. "Proving it's her? I don't think so."

Alone and desperate somewhere. How sad to have to think that of your best friend. I could see why Matt might find it hard to dismiss the note as a hoax, not if there was even a tiny possibility that Andrea was reaching out to him and him alone.

"Did she normally email you?" I asked stupidly. What she *normally* did probably wasn't relevant in this situation.

"No. She always texted. That was one thing the police pointed out. Emailing me was kind of random. Maybe easier to do anonymously. Again, indications of a hoax."

"Did the police try to track her phone or anything like that? I mean, when she first disappeared?"

Matt shook his head. "She left her phone in her truck that day."

"Oh. I guess I remember that. I forgot. That wasn't like her, huh?"

"I don't know. A lot of things she did around then weren't like her. In my opinion, anyway."

We were both quiet for a moment. It felt to me like he wanted to say more, so I waited.

"We walked together by the river a lot around then. Even when it was cold. She wanted to get out of the house. Away from her parents." Matt picked up his teacup, cradled it with both palms, and stared into it. "The last time was two days before she disappeared. It was a Sunday and she disappeared on a Tuesday. And she said some strange things to me that Sunday."

"Strange?" I repeated.

"She said she'd been wondering what it would be like to drown. She said, 'They say it's a painful way to die, but the pain is short, and then it's calm.' It seemed like a fair enough thing to wonder about, but then she said, 'And I deserve a little pain anyhow.' When I asked her what that meant, she was like, 'Don't we all? Here in this little suburban bubble? What makes us think we don't deserve to suffer, ever?'"

Matt turned the teacup this way and that. I wondered if he was looking at the fox or hoping to find other symbols for me to interpret. He looked up. "Doesn't that sound to you like something someone pretty depressed would say?"

I sucked in a breath, unable to meet his gaze. Now I understood—or at least thought I understood—why Matt kept seeking out my company and my opinion. Because of Noah. Not Noah and Jimmy Harmon, necessarily. Just Noah. Carson had guessed there was something a little desperate about Matt's interest in me. It seemed Carson had guessed right.

I'd learned how to ignore people's funny looks since Noah's incident. Shit like that doesn't go down very often in sunny Colesbury. But there I was, the sister of the pill popper. Was it an accident, or was it on purpose? Either way, my brother was damaged and I was damaged by association. It was one thing to *say* you were depressed. But my brother was the CHS kid who had most recently and most visibly *acted* on it.

So maybe I was an easier person to approach with such a question, easier than Matt's perfect friends. And possibly Matt hadn't come to me because of my readings after all. Possibly he asked for the readings to have a chance to talk about Andrea in this way. With someone who could possibly relate, if only just a little.

"What do you think?" he pressed.

"Maybe," I said. "It would depend on how well I knew them. It kinda depends on the person. Some people say stuff like that all the time and it doesn't mean anything."

"*I* thought she was depressed," Matt said, more firmly now.

"Okay. Did anyone else think so?"

His head drooped. "I'm the only one who really said it. Her parents, her dad in particular, doesn't want to admit anything like that about her. He acts like it's crazy talk. Andrea was a star athlete, popular girl, smart cookie, everything in the world to be happy about."

"I'm sure lots of people see her that way."

"Sure. But he *lived* with her. He *had* to see it, even if he wanted to ignore it. That's what annoys me. He liked having people think she was perfect. Even after she disappeared. But *I* know the kinds of things she was starting to say. And *I* know she meant them."

I paused for a little while. "So, why? *Why* was she depressed?"

Matt shook his head. "I don't know for sure. All I have are guesses. But I knew Andrea pretty well. We were never *together*, you know? But that doesn't mean I didn't know her."

Good friends but never in *that* way. Like everyone said. Like Carson and me.

"I get that," I told him.

"I figured you would," Matt said. "I knew her better than almost anybody. And I could tell something was off. I can see why her parents don't want to see it that way. It maybe makes it harder for them. But it still doesn't change what I saw in her."

I nodded, uncertain what to say.

"The Andrea I knew before then wouldn't have said something like that."

I wanted to say *I get that, too,* but wasn't sure if that were true. Instead, I was silent. As Matt had mentioned, silence was safer.

"Sometimes I think I'm going a little crazy wondering about this. Did I really think a teacup would help me? Is that how crazy this whole thing has made me?"

"I'm sorry," I said, though I wasn't sure what for.

"It's not your fault. You're only doing what you do. I just keep wondering if I should write back."

"Oh," I said. "I see."

"So would *you?*"

"Umm, well. I don't know. What do your parents think?"

Matt rolled his eyes. "Obviously I'm not satisfied with what they think."

"What do your friends think? Like, what does Phoenix Long think?"

Phoenix Long was another close friend of Andrea's. Also on the girls' basketball team and as cool as her name. The female half of the charmed redheaded Long twins. Phoenix and Payson: athletic, smart, and blessed with rich parents. I'd had a study period with Phoenix once, but I'd never spoken to her. She always looked like she was deep into either her homework or her phone and never much wanted to talk to anyone. But I knew she was also pretty good friends with Cecilia.

"Not many people know about this," Matt said, lowering his voice. "And no one was as close to Andrea as me. Not even Phoenix. So it doesn't matter what anyone else thinks."

"So you want someone to tell you to write back, basically."

Matt shrugged. "I guess I do, yeah."

"Then write back." I dumped my own tea, which I'd not even sipped and didn't plan to, in the kitchen sink. "How about that?"

"Is that what you would do? Tea leaves aside?"

"Yeah," I said, rinsing my cup. "Write back and see what happens. Why haven't you already?"

"Because you're not supposed to encourage hoaxers," Matt said. "Because maybe it's some psychopath."

"Maybe. But do you really think so? If it's a hoaxer, it's most likely just some ass. And if you write to him a little more, and that reveals itself, you at least won't have to wonder anymore."

"Maybe." Matt picked up his keys. "Now, can I drive you home? We can talk about it more in the car."

"No, thanks. I mean, I don't need a ride."

"Come on." Matt jangled the keys, trying to tempt me—like I was a dog who was supposed to jump and yip at a jangling leash. "Let me. What is it, two miles? More?"

It was probably more. Carson had begrudgingly dropped me off here, but I hadn't made a plan for getting back home. Before starting my long walk, I decided to stop being chicken and ask Matt one other thing.

"Why were you asking me about Jimmy Harmon the other day?"

Matt stopped shaking his keys. "Because I thought your brother was his friend."

"Yeah, but I mean, why did you want to know?"

"I've sort of wondered about him because he had a connection with Andrea before she went missing."

"A connection?" Now we were getting somewhere.

"Well, you know." Matt smiled. "The kind of connection a lot of people had with Jimmy Harmon. At least, that's how it started. Then after that they were kind of friends."

"The kind of connection . . . What?"

"Weed, Marnie." Matt sounded a bit impatient. "She bought weed from him a couple of times."

"Oh," I said, feeling dumb. I had known that Jimmy sold weed but hadn't considered it the only thing about him.

"I just assumed you would know that. With your brother."

Yes, now I understood perfectly. Because of who my brother was, I was apparently supposed to know about all of the illicit habits of all of Colesbury High. Like I didn't have enough other shit to think about.

"Right," I said. "Got it."

CHAPTER 8

October 11

Cecilia asked me to meet her at the Clover Café on Saturday.

When I got there, I was surprised to find her sitting at a table with Phoenix Long.

"Phoenix was here when I got here," Cecilia explained.

"She caught me buying a cupcake," Phoenix admitted. "I was just gonna run in and out for one, but Cecilia came in and caught me in line."

"Phoenix is addicted to sugar," Cecilia said.

"Cecilia, you don't *understand*, hon," Phoenix said. "I'm actually addicted to sprinkles." She smoothed down the ends of her long, red-brown hair at her shoulders—nervously, as if checking to see if the hair was still there, and still the same length.

"Cecilia talks a lot about your readings," she said. I studied her face for some sort of smile or judgment but found none. Her eye makeup was perfect—black liner and mascara framing the deep green of her eyes. Stark without being overdone. "I'd ask for one, but I just got coffee and I kinda hate tea."

"You can stay and watch her do mine," Cecilia offered.

Please, no, I thought.

Phoenix was already standing up, though.

"Umm, nah. I mean, I'm sure it's sort of a private thing. Am I wrong?"

"No," I said, at the same time Cecilia said, "Yes."

Phoenix smiled. "You two can work it out. I'm going to have a private moment with my cupcake. See you tonight, Cecilia."

"She's nice," I admitted, after Phoenix had gone. I tried not to sound surprised.

Cecilia shrugged. "Sure. Anyway, I was just thinking of getting a little booster reading. Because something's happening that I want to ask about."

"No problem," I said. "I wasn't doing much today anyway."

"There's a party at the Longs' house." Cecilia paused before continuing. "And I'm just going to go ahead and tell you it's Payson Long I've been mentioning in the readings. He's the relationship I want to know about."

"Oh," I said, unsure if I should try to hide my surprise. Maybe the reason Cecilia had been so cagey about her crush was because Payson was Phoenix's brother. That could get complicated, given how tight she and Phoenix seemed.

I suppose I had been expecting Cecilia's crush to be one of the neckless but spirited football players everybody worshipped in Colesbury. On the surface, Payson *almost* fit that description. He was a prized member of both the football and basketball teams, which basically made him Colesbury High royalty. But he didn't seem to care about much, including himself. He wasn't as cocky as the other jocks. His grades weren't great, and he was a little unkempt. His red hair often hung in his face, half hiding his perpetually bored expression. He rarely said anything that wasn't sarcastic. You got the feeling he did sports because someone (his parents, probably) thought he should, that he'd much rather be doing something else most of the time, though *what* else was unclear. I'd heard he drank a lot.

"You said last time there was a wall between him and me," Cecilia reminded me.

"Well, I said there was a *fence*, a barrier blocking you from the kind of relationship you want. It might be a barrier you're putting up yourself, for all I know. I didn't say he didn't like you, or anything like that."

"Can you see him and me together?" Cecilia wanted to know.

I tried to imagine the bubbly Cecilia with the bubble-bursting Payson. *Pop!* Was the first word that came to mind.

"You mean, according to your last tea leaves?" I asked.

"No. According to real life."

"Maybe," I said. "Yeah, sure. In a cute, unlikely couple sort of way."

"Unlikely," Cecilia repeated dully. "That word has come up in my head, too."

"Unlikely doesn't mean impossible," I said, unsure if I should pretend to be optimistic about her love interest. Maybe the "fence" that blocked off her relationships was more complicated than I'd considered. Maybe she chose someone unlikely because deep down, she didn't really *want* a boyfriend for some reason. Or maybe, deep down, there was an intelligent instinct trying to protect her from her own bad taste.

"I hear you've been spending a lot of time with Matt," she announced suddenly.

"Oh. A little. Uh, Cecilia? Are you going to order yourself a tea?"

"I don't know." Cecilia sighed, getting up and leading me to the counter. "I'm more in the mood for a cappuccino."

"But . . ."

"I'm demoralized. You're right about me and Payson. I don't think I need to do another reading. There's a barrier, and I don't feel like climbing it."

"Oh! Don't be demoralized," I said. It felt weird to see Cecilia this down. "I didn't mean it like that."

Cecilia shrugged, and we stood behind the counter together. "So . . . you like Matt?"

"He's a nice guy." I almost wanted to add: *That day he walked in here while I was giving you a reading—that wasn't a coincidence, was it?*

She nodded vaguely.

"I wonder how much he's really interested in getting his tea leaves read," I added. "Seems he kind of has another agenda. He wanted to ask me about Jimmy Harmon, the first time we talked. You know who Jimmy Harmon is, right?"

Cecilia bit her lip. "That kid who used to push weed around the school?"

I wasn't sure it was accurate that he *pushed* it. That made it seem as if all the Colesbury kids were so lily-white that they would never even have heard of weed if greasy old Jimmy hadn't brought it up. But I didn't exactly want to defend Jimmy, either.

"Why would Matt ask you about him?" Cecilia pressed.

"That's what I was wondering. My brother was his friend a long time ago. I think he thought we knew him better than we do. Maybe Matt thinks I'm, like, connected to Jimmy. Or in that kind of a crowd."

"Oh." Cecilia laughed a little. "I don't think anyone thinks that. Matt didn't say anything *specific* about Jimmy, then?"

The guy behind the counter interrupted us, asking for our orders. I asked for a small coffee, and Cecilia got a complex beverage involving foamed milk and mocha and shots of caramel. When it was finally made and paid for, Cecilia tapped her paper cup to mine.

"To unlikely pairings," she said.

CECILIA OFFERED ME A ride home, but I felt like walking. I took the long way home, looping around by the river and detouring onto Seymour Street. That's where Jimmy Harmon had lived, where his mother still lived, as far as I knew. The Harmon house was the most run-down on the street, a yellow ranch with its paint chipping away and its lawn overgrown. When Noah was friends with Jimmy, G. Clara never let Noah play at Jimmy's house.

Too many crazy boyfriends, she'd say of Jimmy's mother.

Back then, G. Clara would say sometimes that Jimmy had been dealt a tough hand. His mother had dropped out of Colesbury High herself as a teenager after she'd gotten pregnant with Jimmy by an older guy. That older guy had gone to jail when Jimmy was a little kid—for what, G. Clara would never say. But it must've been something pretty bad, because Jimmy's mother never got over it. She drank a lot. She was lucky, though, according to G. Clara, that she had a roof over her head at all. Her grandparents owned this dumpy little house and let her stay in it with her son.

These were the reasons why G. Clara told us we should be nice and patient with Jimmy, back when he was a kid. Because even then, he was hard to like. On the playground he called other kids names like *lardass, retard,* and *numbnuts.* He'd laugh at kids who cried easily or fell off the monkey bars—a loud, rasping laugh with his big, crooked front tooth sticking out. I remember Noah telling me Jimmy once peed in another kid's backpack because the kid had stolen Jimmy's favorite pen. Noah would tell me these sorts of stories with a mix of disgust and awe. As they neared high school age, though, and Jimmy's antics got bolder and nastier, Noah's awe seemed to fade. Eventually, they stopped hanging out altogether.

As I walked back toward home, I thought about Matt's email and about the police's conclusion that the letter was a hoax. Then I thought of the foxes I'd seen in both of Matt's teacups. I wished I'd looked longer and harder at the fox the second time. Had I *wanted* to see it again, for some reason? Because I'd been dreaming of a fox? Because I thought Matt himself was a little tricky like a fox?

Whatever else you wanted to say about him, Jimmy was definitely a trickster type. Sometimes, when we were kids, he'd take Noah's and my old toys—or other random household objects—and hide them in comically unexpected places for us to find. We'd discover an armless Barbie lying with the butter knives in the utensil drawer. Or G. Clara's Buddha paperweight peering out of a soup bowl in the dish cabinet. Tickle Me Elmo was hunched over in the breadbox, his mouth crammed with Doritos.

Was Jimmy, somehow, the fox in Matt's teacup? Could *he* be the one torturing Matt with odd emails? Had Matt been trying to imply that, or was I imagining things? I wasn't sure what reason Jimmy would have to do that, but obviously there was a lot about both of these guys that I didn't know.

On the other hand, why else would Jimmy's name have come up at all?

When I got home, Noah was on his laptop and watching a show called *Caught on Camera*.

"This week on *Caught on Camera*," the show host growled. "Fatal attraction. Watch some of the worst amusement park accidents ever recorded."

I cringed.

"Where'd G. Clara go?" I asked Noah.

"Tag sale, she said."

Thankfully, a commercial came on before they showed any of the deadly footage.

"Noah, can I ask you something?"

"Sure."

"Do you know for sure that Jimmy Harmon is living in Lyndham?"

Noah sucked in a breath. "For sure? No. That was just the last thing I heard about him."

"Well, is it true that Jimmy sold weed to Andrea Quinley?"

His face darkened as he flipped through the cable stations. He checked back to see if his *Caught on Camera* had started up again. "Jimmy sold weed to a lot of people," he said. "Everyone knows that. And I don't know any more about it than anyone else does."

"But is it true about Andrea?"

Noah rolled his eyes. "Probably."

"Did he *like* her?"

At that, Noah sat up and hurled the remote control at the fireplace. It flew across the room and shattered against the stone wall above the hearth. I flinched, staring at him in disbelief as the remote's batteries rolled along the hardwood floor and under the couch.

"What's wrong with you?" I whispered. My voice shook.

"How the hell would *I* know, Marnie?" He kept his eyes on the screen. "The guy was half out of his mind by the time we were in high school. You *know* I avoided him, so I don't know why you keep asking me about him."

I swallowed. "Matt Cotrell keeps bringing him up."

Noah snapped his laptop closed and stood up with it, making like he was going to leave the room. "Matt Cotrell. Friends with that Andrea girl, right?"

"Yeah. He's this basketball player—"

"Whatever," Noah interrupted. He paused at the door. "Whoever he is, you probably should tell him to go fuck himself. If he wants to know where Jimmy is, he probably ought to go find out himself. He's probably asking you who he can get weed from. Ever thought of that? I bet he's wanting to know if he can get it from *me*. Or even you."

I shook my head. "Nobody would ever think I'm dealing weed, Noah. I'm too much of a nerd."

Noah was silent for a moment. I knelt and gathered the remote pieces and batteries.

"Tell him," Noah repeated, "to go fuck himself."

I put the plastic and batteries on the coffee table.

"Okay," I said softly, and retreated to my room.

"Well, that went well," I mumbled to myself, sitting on my bed. What the hell was it about Jimmy Harmon that made everybody so sensitive these days? And when had my brother turned into a person who grunted and threw things and wanted to watch footage of people falling out of roller coasters?

I thought about when we were little, when G. Clara used to take us to Forest Wonderland—the crappy, rundown amusement park in the town next to ours. It was closed now, and they'd moved the beautiful merry-go-round into a mall somewhere. Noah used to make fun of me for always sitting on the stationary horses instead of the ones that went up and down. I was so chicken when I was little, I was afraid of accidentally letting go and flying off the carousel. Eventually, Noah convinced me to go on a moving one with him. I'd held tightly to his shirt. Now, considering what Noah was watching, I'd say I was smart to be cautious.

Not that I was about to go out and tell Noah that. I felt trapped in my room now—trapped by Noah's inexplicable anger and poor taste in television. I considered messaging Carson. Not that I was sure what I would say.

Before I could even type a word, though, I heard my cell phone buzz. Someone was texting me.

I looked at the phone. Matt.

I replied to that email, like you suggested.

And she wrote back.

CHAPTER 9

Andy, is it really you? Where are you?

That's what Matt had written back to the first Andrea message he'd gotten.

The response he'd received wasn't much:

I can't say. But need to talk to you. Need to ask you something and can't come home till I get an answer.

I stared at the words on Matt's iPhone.

We were sitting across from each other in a tight, uncomfortable plastic booth at the Main Street Dunkin Donuts. It was Matt's idea to come here. It wasn't very far for me to walk, and we weren't likely to be overheard by anyone we knew. No one hung out here but older folks from the Eastside Village apartments for retired people.

"And you already wrote back?" I said.

Matt nodded. "But just two words: *What's that?* Still waiting to hear back on that."

"Uh-huh," I replied.

It seemed like a good strategy to me—to let Andrea, or whoever was writing the messages, take the lead. Don't give this person much to work with, in case he or she is a fraud.

"The whole 'need to ask you something,' thing," I said uneasily. "Does that sound like Andrea to you?"

"It's not specific enough to *not* sound like her."

"But don't you think it sounds a little . . . manipulative?"

Matt opened the orange juice he'd bought to justify our presence in the booths. After taking a sip, he grimaced. "Who says Andrea was never manipulative?" he said.

"Okay," I replied. "What're you going to do now, then?"

"Well, wait. To start."

I nodded. Matt sipped his juice again. I began to wish I'd ordered something, to have something to keep my hands busy.

"Well," I mumbled. "Here we are. *Waiting.*"

Matt stared out the window at the parking lot. I realized I shouldn't have said *we.* I admired the shiny finish of Matt's black car. I wondered if he washed it, or had it washed, every week. It seemed like a weird thing to pay attention to, given all of the sad things happening in his life. I wondered how it was that I was starting to like Matt when there was so much I didn't quite get about him.

A red compact car buzzed into the lot, coming to rest right next to Matt's car. Matt jumped a little as the balding driver got out.

"You know who that is?" he said, turning to me.

"No." I squinted, following Matt's eyes. The man was tan and muscular, with a slight limp. "He looks familiar, though. Does he work at the—"

"Andrea's dad," he whispered.

I tried not to stare as Mr. Quinley walked into the doughnut shop, jangling his keys. He smiled when he caught sight of Matt. "Hey there," he said. "Surprised to find you here. Nice to see you."

"You, too," Matt answered, matching his smile. I couldn't tell if he was forcing it or not.

"You a coffee drinker, Matt?"

Matt held up his orange juice. "Not really."

"Good idea. Stay off the stuff as long as you can." Mr. Quinley went to the counter to order. After he bought a big cup of coffee, he waved his keys in our direction. "Tell your mom and dad I said hello."

"Okay," Matt called weakly. But his smile had vanished.

WE SAT IN SILENCE as we watched Mr. Quinley drive away.

"I feel bad that I was just talking about Andrea the way I was," Matt said in a low voice. "Hey, sorry I didn't introduce you."

"He sort of looked right through me, anyhow."

"He's like that. More so now than before."

"Because of Andrea, you mean?"

Matt shrugged.

I'd seen Mr. Quinley around town and at the school over the years, knowing he was someone's dad, even though I might not have registered *whose* specifically. He'd been one of the coaches of the girls' softball league. My old friend Amy had made me join when I was around twelve. Mr. Quinley knew the names of all the most athletic girls; he'd kid around with them and chat with their parents like they were friends.

The rest of us he called "dear" or "kid." I remember him grumbling, almost sneering, at Amy when she'd repeatedly strike out, as if there was something morally repugnant about her clumsiness. Amy had masochistically stayed in the league all season. I had quit in favor of spending my Thursday afternoons watching TV and eating Cheetos.

"Were they close?" I asked Matt, thinking of what he had told me last time—that Mr. Quinley refused to admit that Andrea might have been having problems.

"They were until, like, a couple of months before she disappeared. When she started acting weird, I think things got tough with her parents. Did you know she quit basketball a little while before she disappeared?"

"No."

"Well, she did. I thought it was strange that her parents would know she did that—Andrea, the big star player—and not see that as a sign of depression or some kind of trouble. Like I was saying the other day. When I asked her why she quit, she said she just didn't feel like playing anymore. And when I asked if her dad was mad that she quit, she said something like, 'Wake up, Matt. Like my dad cares about anything I do anymore.'"

"Which means what?"

"I don't know for sure. But I know that with all of his knee surgery problems, he wasn't able to do a lot of things he'd done before. I guess he was focused on his own health issues more than Andrea and her brother and sister, for a little while?"

I hesitated before speaking. "Maybe she quit basketball to see if that would finally get his attention?"

Matt smirked. "Well, aren't you the psychotherapist?"

I shrugged. "It's the tea-leaf reading. I have to do a little psychologizing with it."

"I see," he said. "Have you been psychologizing me much?"

"Only a little."

He nodded. "So. You asked me why I was asking you about Jimmy Harmon. I should have given you more of an answer."

Surprised, I said, "Okay?"

Matt leveled his gaze at me. "He liked you, you know."

"*What?*" Of all the directions my mind had wandered, it hadn't gone *there*.

"That's what Andrea said," Matt continued. "That he'd talk about you sometimes. About how he liked you when you were kids, at least. That he'd go over to your house and hang out with your brother, and sometimes, if they were watching a movie, or were playing a game with three players or whatever, you'd join them. He thought it was cute how important it was to you that everyone play fair. He said he'd try not to act so crazy when you were around."

I could feel myself blush. "I must've been . . . I don't know . . . eleven . . . the last time anything like that happened."

Matt held my eyes. "Sure. But. In any case."

"He never even talked to me once I got to high school," I said, looking down.

"He didn't?"

I thought about this. Jimmy would usually give me a sort of

half wave, a *hey* in the hallway. Sometimes he'd ask me how I was, to which I'd usually reply, *Okay*. I'd never thought to wonder if this was more attention than he'd give others. Now that Matt was talking this way, it seemed quite likely. Generally, Jimmy antagonized people.

"I guess sometimes. Why would Andrea have told you that?"

Matt sighed and looked away from me again, out toward his shiny black car.

"She talked about Jimmy quite a few times, the couple of weeks before she disappeared. Mostly random stuff, but . . ."

"Yeah, but . . . ?"

"I wonder, if I tracked him down . . . if *someone* could track him down . . . if you would be willing to talk to him for me?"

"I'd think if it's stuff about Andrea, you'd want to ask him yourself."

He hesitated. "I'm not the sort of person Jimmy would want to open up to."

"And you think he would open up with me, because he thought I had cute pigtails when I was a kid?"

Matt plunked down his juice bottle defensively. "I didn't say it like that. Don't be gross."

"I'm *not* being gross."

"Okay. Suppose you were able to track him down. What exactly would you ask him?"

"I'd ask him why Andrea was so depressed."

"Do you think she would've told *him* that?" I asked.

Matt took a deep breath. "I'm not saying that I think she *told* him anything. I'm thinking he might know on a different level. Like he was the *cause* of some of her problems. She only started acting funny *after* she met him."

"Oh," I whispered, understanding better now. "Do the police know that she was hanging out with him a lot? Did they ever question him?"

"I know they know, because I told them. But Jimmy wasn't in town when she disappeared." Matt shook his head. "I feel like if he was supplying her with pot earlier in the winter, then maybe he started giving her something more serious around then . . . you know? Something like that? Maybe something she might have even used that day. Especially if she was thinking of hurting herself."

It seemed like a reasonable theory. But if Andrea had killed herself, why hadn't anyone ever found her body? I was sure Matt had thought of that before, but I didn't want to bring it up myself.

"I get it, Matt. But do you seriously think that if that was the case, Jimmy would admit anything to *me*?"

Matt was silent.

"I don't know," he said finally. His voice caught. "It was just an *idea*. Not a brilliant idea, but at least *something*. I need to feel like I'm doing *something*. Do you think you could ask your brother, or . . . talk to Jimmy yourself?"

I looked up at him. His eyes were glistening. I knew I was being used. But at least it was for a good reason.

"I guess I could talk to him," I said slowly.

Matt perked up. "Great," he said. "You want a ride over to his house right now?"

CHAPTER 10

There was no doorbell at the Harmon house. I knocked on the storm door twice. I wondered if anyone could hear me.

As I stood there on the doorstep, an old memory of Jimmy popped into my head. He must've been about eight years old. It was Noah's birthday party, and G. Clara had packed each kid a goodie bag with candy and neon bracelets and a few sour gumballs. Jimmy got into the bags and jammed all of the sour gumballs in his mouth. When Noah found him hiding in the coat closet, his cheeks were fat like a chipmunk's, with rainbow-colored spit oozing out of his mouth and onto his T-shirt.

I glanced down the street, where Matt's car sat parked four houses up. We agreed that it might look odd for me to arrive with someone waiting in the car. We also agreed he should stick around in case things got weird. According to Matt, Andrea thought Jimmy's mom's latest boyfriend was a nut job.

A woman opened the front door. Her face was familiar, sharp cheekbones and dark eyes that were pretty despite their sunken quality. She must have picked Jimmy up at the house a few times back when he used to play with Noah. I also remembered her long black hair, longer than any adult's I'd seen. Now it was streaked with white.

"Yes?" she said, apparently not recognizing me. "You're not selling cookies or anything, are you? Because I'm trying to watch the carbs."

"No, Mrs. Harmon. Not selling any cookies."

"Oh. Honey. It's been a long time since I've been a Harmon."

"Oh. I'm sorry. I used to be a friend of Jimmy's. I mean, my brother was, and—"

"Jimmy's not here, honey. He doesn't live here anymore."

I took a deep breath and nodded. "Where does he live?"

"In Lyndham. He was living with his cousin, till a few months ago. Have you talked to him on the phone recently, or anything?"

"Oh. No. See, I was hoping to talk to him, but—"

"Has he texted you, or anything like that?" she interrupted, looking hopeful.

"No," I admitted. "I'm probably not explaining myself very well. I haven't been in touch with him at all. I was wondering if you could tell me how to contact him."

"I can give you his number. But he hasn't been texting me back lately. I'm getting a little worried."

"Lindsey?" A deep voice demanded from inside the house. "Who is it?"

"A girl who knows Jimmy!" Mrs. Harmon called back.

A heavyset, gray-bearded man came up behind Mrs. Harmon and stared at me. "She told you he doesn't live here, I take it."

"Yes."

I stared into his wide, pink face and got the distinct feeling he wanted me to leave.

"All right, then," he said gruffly.

"Yes, I'd like his phone number," I said to Mrs. Harmon.

"I don't think he answers anyone's calls or texts anymore, hon. But you can try. Here. Why don't you come in?"

Despite her welcoming words, the man remained in the doorway, his face growing even pinker.

"Move, Tim," Mrs. Harmon growled. "She can't get by."

The man stepped back to let me into the kitchen, which looked clean but smelled catty. Mrs. Harmon tore a paper napkin from the roll on the counter and leaned down to scribble something on it.

"Jimmy's number," she said.

"Thank you." I mustered a smile before I took the napkin. "Can you give me his cousin's number, too? The one in Lyndham?"

"Sure. But he doesn't know where Jimmy is, either. I talked to him just a couple of weeks ago."

The man—"Tim"—stepped closer to me. I could smell his aftershave. It smelled a little like my dad's. I hadn't seen my dad in nearly four months, so it wouldn't be fair of me to judge how long Mrs. Harmon had gone without seeing Jimmy.

"His cousin's name is Trevor Waleski," she said, writing that on the napkin as well. "You want his address?"

"Oh. Well, sure."

"Why are you looking for Jimmy?" Tim asked.

"Because . . ."

Tim's eyes were a creepy transparent gray. They made me want to squirm. "We've forbidden him from selling anything while he's living in this house. That's why he left."

I nodded. *Now* I understood. He thought I'd come looking to score some pot. How the hell had I let Matt convince me to do this?

"Oh, I see. I just came to see *him*. Because he's . . . an old friend. I wanted to reconnect."

"Well." Tim sniffed. "Good luck with that."

"If you do reconnect with him, tell him to call his mother," Jimmy's mom said, handing me the napkin. "Can you do that? Or come by here again and tell me where he is?"

I was already backing toward the door. "Of course."

MATT'S EYES LIT UP when he saw I'd managed to get a phone number and address.

"How about we go tomorrow?" he suggested. "I'll drive."

"It sounds like we'll only be able to find the cousin."

"So you'll talk to the cousin," Matt said.

"*We'll* talk with the cousin," I corrected him. Why was he so eager to involve me? To shield himself from something? "We'll both talk next time. Or maybe just *you* will."

"Okay, both of us," Matt said quickly. "Because it looks to me like you're pretty good at this stuff. In the meantime, you want to come to a party with me tonight?"

CHAPTER 11

I tried hard to keep my mouth from hanging open as Matt drove me down the Longs' endless driveway. I think you could call the place more of an "estate" than just a home. The lawn was a startling green given that we were pretty well into fall. Maybe the grass got some kind of chemical treatment. Maybe it was shipped in from somewhere else. I wondered if Phoenix and Payson liked to roll down its pretty little hills when they were younger.

There was a white gazebo on the right as you approached the enormous brick house with white trim and pillars. But the cherry on top was the circular driveway, like in the fancy houses in the old British dramas G. Clara liked to watch sometimes.

I sighed.

"What is it?" Matt said.

I shook my head. "What a *place*."

"I know." Matt seemed to relax a little. "It's party central when his parents aren't around. We just hang out in the basement, mostly."

"Where are they now?" I asked. "I mean, the twins' parents."

"On a little cruise. They do it once a year."

"A *cruise*?" I wasn't sure why I was so incredulous. Maybe because I thought only old ladies and honeymooners went on cruises.

"Yeah. Their parents go away a lot. Especially since the second older brother, Will, went to college."

"Do they know the twins have parties when they're gone?"

"Probably. But they keep it simple. Just invite a few friends over. So their parents don't much care, I don't think."

"Oh."

G. Clara *never* went away, so I couldn't really fathom what I'd do if she did.

Matt rang the doorbell three times before the double doors opened and Payson's bulky figure appeared.

He gave us a quick once-over. "You should've just come in, man," he said.

"I don't just walk into other people's houses," Matt said. "Uh, Payson. You know Marnie? I told you she was coming?"

"Cool." Payson glanced at me before turning away from both of us, leading us through a gleaming white kitchen to some basement stairs. "Hi. Come on."

The basement was a wide, mostly empty expanse of gray carpet, with a couple of couches and a coffee table in one corner of the room, where most of the kids were already gathered. On the coffee table was a mess of red plastic cups. Only Phoenix sat outside of the group. She was cross-legged on the floor, knitting. I did a double take. Really, Phoenix Long, knitting? She held up her work to examine it. It was a multicolored, psychedelic-looking sock.

"Marnie!" a familiar voice called from the crowd at the coffee table. Cecilia hopped up from behind the wall of red cups, came over to me, and grabbed me by the arm. For a moment I thought she was going to hug me.

"Guys," she announced, "I'm going to take a break for a round or two."

"Whatever floats your boat," said Payson, leading Matt to the table. I was beginning to think he wasn't too happy Matt had brought me along.

Cecilia sat down near Phoenix. She tugged at my jeans so I'd do the same.

"So, Matt asked you to come?" Cecilia whispered.

My cheeks suddenly felt hot. "Um, yeah."

"Have you guys been . . . hanging out?"

I wasn't sure how she meant that, so I wasn't sure how to answer. Phoenix looked up from her knitting, throwing her long hair out of her face. "Matt mentioned to me he's getting into the tea thing, too."

Cecilia looked impatient. "Phoenix, are you going to play at all tonight?"

"I don't think so," Phoenix said, returning to her sock. "I've got to get up early tomorrow. Kids' Carnival Fundraiser, remember?"

Cecilia nodded. I watched Payson pour beer into the red cups formed in a circle around the table, with one in the middle. Gathered at the table were Payson, Matt, an underclass boy whose name I didn't know, and a tall blond girl whose name was Hannah . . . at least I was pretty sure it was Hannah.

"Is that a drinking game?" I asked.

"What else?" Phoenix muttered. I couldn't tell if her annoyance was at my stupid question or the game itself.

"It's called Chandelier," Cecilia said. "You want to try it?"

"Um," I said. "I don't think so."

Between my mother's and my brother's issues, I've always thought it a good idea for me to stay away from mind-altering substances. At least until my brain is a little more fully formed. But why hadn't I come here prepared with an excuse? What did I think this crowd did at their parties? Played Scattergories?

"It's kind of fun," Cecilia said. "And it's *really* easy to learn."

"I had a headache before I left and took some Tylenol," I said. "I don't think you're supposed to mix that with—"

"Don't worry about it," Phoenix interrupted. "Nobody's going to make you play. Our brother is only willing to buy Payson so much beer. The fewer people play, the drunker . . ." Her voice trailed off for a moment. "The drunker *some* people can get."

"I'm gonna hop back over there for a second," Cecilia said, a little sheepishly. "You mind?"

"Of course not," I said.

Cecilia joined the group as they started another round. The game involved bouncing a Ping-Pong ball on the table and into the cups. Whoever's cup it landed in drank their quarter-cup of beer in front of them. There was some other step involving the full cup in the middle, but I wasn't sure what that was about yet. Phoenix's needles clicked. I felt awkward. Payson seemed to take drinks and refill his cup more often than required, but he was the one doling out the beer from a bottle beside the couch. Either no one noticed or no one cared.

"Hey," Phoenix said to me. "You know how to knit?"

I shook my head. "No."

"I thought you might, since you're Ms. Sheehan's grand-daughter. Right?"

"Right. But no. She's never taught me. She knows how, but I guess I was never interested."

"You should ask her to teach you."

"Someday, maybe." I shrugged.

"I'm trying to learn as many skills as I can. Fixing my own car. CPR. Cooking. Sewing. Knitting."

"That's good," I said uncertainly, not sure where she was going with this.

"That way I'll be all set," Phoenix said. "In case of the apoca-lypse."

I couldn't tell if she was kidding. She put down her knitting, slipped an elastic band off her wrist, and pulled her long hair into a messy bun.

"Except in the apocalypse, there probably won't be any yarn stores open," I offered.

Phoenix smiled at me. "But I'd be able to unravel old sweaters and knit whatever I want, for whoever needs it."

"I guess you've really thought this out," I said.

"Did your grandmother teach you how to do that tea thing you do?" Phoenix asked.

Touché, I thought. I knew there was some sort of agenda at

play. Tea-leaf reading would be markedly less useful than knitting, in the apocalypse. "No," I said. "Mostly I learned it from a
book."

Phoenix nodded and picked up her knitting again.

"*Aww!*" someone at the table yelled. We both turned to see
Payson drinking the full cup of beer from the center of the
table.

"I'm sure it's fun," Phoenix said. "But I'm gonna ask you a
favor." She stopped knitting for a moment and leaned closer to
me. "Just be careful. With Matt, I mean. With what you say to him,
in those readings. You know what I'm talking about, right?"

She meant Andrea, of course. But I didn't want to say the name.

"Right," I said. "I've worried about that part of it, actually."

"I'm sure you have," Phoenix said, meeting my stare. "You're
smart. I'm just saying it because I don't know if Cecilia would
think to."

"Oh," I said, wondering on what basis she was calling me "smart."

Phoenix's needles clicked some more. Her bracelet flashed
as she worked. I recognized the design; it was one of those
zodiac bracelets that all of the basketball girls seemed to wear. I
couldn't see what her sign was.

"*Yes!* Drink up, Matty-boy!" I heard Payson yell, and then Matt
was the one drinking the big center cup.

"God," Phoenix muttered, knitting harder.

I stood up. "Would you guys mind if I walked around outside
for a while?" I asked her.

She looked up, but her attention was on the other kids, not
me. "Go ahead."

I headed for the stairs. They seemed particularly beautiful for
a basement. The actual steps were black, the steep risers deco-
rated with sage, black, and white panels in a zigzag design. As I
stepped outside, I took a deep breath and tried not to ask myself
what the hell I was doing here.

Making my way across the perfect green lawn, I noticed that
the gazebo was now lit up with little white lights. Either Payson

had flipped a switch before we'd gone down the stairs, or the lights were on a timer. I stepped inside and for a moment, I just stood there, relishing the rare sensation of being framed by little lights. I wondered if anyone ever sat in the gazebo or if it was mostly for decoration. I couldn't imagine Payson or Phoenix sitting in here. But maybe their parents were romantics and hung out on the benches in the summer moonlight, watching the fireflies.

I closed my eyes for a few moments. In the quiet a memory came to me.

Jimmy Harmon. With the colored bubblegum spit oozing onto his shirt. When he'd come out of the coat closet, he'd started to cry. Noah was yelling "*Jim-MY! GOD, Jimmy! Why'd you DO that?*" And G. Clara was just sighing and shaking her head. Why was Jimmy crying? I'd wondered. It blew my six-year-old mind, that you'd do something so crazy and then cry right afterward. But the more his tears flowed, all mixed with snot and colored spit as they dripped down his cheeks, the more trouble I had holding back my own.

"*He's sorry!*" I'd started to wail at G. Clara, inexplicably sobbing even harder than Jimmy was. "*He's sorry!*"

I shook my head, shaking the memory away. I'd never have remembered that day, if it weren't for Matt and what he'd told me about Jimmy.

He liked you, you know.

"Marnie!" I turned around at the sound of Cecilia's voice. "Wow, you look like a fairy standing in there."

"Don't I just?" I scoffed.

"Matt was kind of wondering where you went. And I wanted to take a little break. I like to play along, but I don't like to get too drunk."

I nodded. "I get it."

"You know, I wanted to mention something to you." Cecilia lowered her voice. "Um, you're the only one I've told how I feel about Payson."

"Oh," I said. "Not Phoenix, you're saying. I won't tell anyone. If you were worried about that."

Cecilia nodded. "I didn't think you would. I just—thought I'd say something. But, Marnie . . . do you want something to happen with you and Matt?"

In the past, I'd never thought it was really possible that someone like Matt could like me. Generally I limited my crushes to slightly freakish types like myself, as those were the only guys I really thought I had a chance at.

"I don't know," I said. I wondered what Cecilia thought of the idea of Matt and me together. Something about it seemed to make her uneasy. Maybe now she regretted telling him all about my readings.

Cecilia sucked in a breath. "You might be competing against Andrea's ghost. You know that, right?"

I shifted uncomfortably. "I don't know if we should be using the word 'ghost.' Andrea might still be alive."

Cecilia stared at the bright green grass. "Well, I know Matt likes to think so. They all do. But do *you* think she's still alive? Realistically?"

"No," I admitted.

"Okay then." Cecilia sat on the steps of the gazebo, off to one side, making room for me. I joined her there.

"He told me he never liked her that way, though," I said, sitting beside her. It felt petty, changing the subject from death back to the business of liking and not liking. But it was easier to talk about that.

"Oh." Cecilia looked at me skeptically. "And you believe him one hundred percent?"

"Well, that's what everyone always said. And I know they've both gone out with other people."

Cecilia took a breath. "Phoenix and I used to have kind of a different theory about Matt and Andrea. Or at least, Phoenix did, and I thought it made sense."

I didn't reply right away. I wasn't sure if this was a conversation

I wanted to have. But ultimately, I couldn't resist. "Why? What does Phoenix say about it?"

"Well, *she* was always skeptical that they were so close and neither ever thought of getting together, you know? Also, Payson sort of *did* ask Andrea out once a long time ago, and she turned him down, so Phoenix and I wondered if she had her eye on someone else. Someone she wasn't willing to admit."

I stared up at the darkening sky.

Cecilia didn't say anything for a moment. "I would just keep it in mind."

"Okay," I replied. "Thanks."

"Sure. You know, I may as well be honest with *you*. Since you've been honest with *me*. About what you think of the Payson thing, and everything."

"I don't really know him," I said with a little laugh. "You shouldn't take anything I say too seriously."

Cecilia gazed past me.

I turned to see Matt coming out of the house.

"Hey, Marnie," he called.

"Yeah?" I said, noticing a slight stagger in his step.

"Somebody in the house was asking for you."

"For me?"

"Yeah. Someone wants their fortune told."

I glanced at Cecilia and she shrugged.

"Someone?" I repeated.

"Yeah," Matt called, waving us in. "I was talking you up. Come back in, you guys."

CHAPTER 12

Matt and Cecilia stayed with Payson and me in the kitchen while the water boiled in the Longs' chrome teakettle. But after Payson had poured his cup, Cecilia steered Matt out of the room by the elbow. As she led him back down to the basement, I heard her say, "The readings are best one-on-one. Right? You know that."

We both knew the truth—that I was being asked to perform a ridiculous party trick, and Cecilia was trying to reduce my level of humiliation by removing any audience.

"Give it to me straight," Payson ordered as he handed me his mug.

I nodded and tried to ignore the strength of his breath. Something alcoholic, obviously, but I couldn't tell what.

"This isn't the shape of your typical reading cup," I said. "So I think I can just look at the symbols generally, without much of a timeline."

Payson shrugged and hooked his thumbs under his imposing biceps. "Okay."

"There's an ox image here. See? Near the rim. Kind of leaping toward the rim. An ox is usually a symbol of strength. This ox has something on its back, though. So what that represents is kind of open for interpretation."

"So what do you think?" Payson's tone was suddenly sincere for a moment, his expression curious. His wide eyes were a fierce bright green like his sister's, but more innocent-looking without the eyeliner. I could see, just for a second, why Cecilia might like him.

"Well. I'd say that you're strong, but you know this year will have more significant challenges. Getting into college, all of that. You're leaping into it with that knowledge. That it'll be harder."

Payson flashed a crooked smile. "Have you considered working for the school guidance department?"

I didn't reply.

"I see a pineapple here," I said after a moment, and pointed to the side of the cup.

"Actually, yes," he admitted, tucking his overgrown reddish hair behind his ears. "It really does look like one."

"Pineapples mean wealth and luxury. And friends with money. Whatever that means to you."

I wasn't going to touch that one. Payson seemed okay with it.

"And here near the rim is a . . ." I squinted. "Doughnut."

Payson looked at me in disbelief.

"A *doughnut?*"

I should have thought longer and changed my interpretation to a *wheel* or a *ring*—something a little more mystical sounding. But it was too late. I'd look even dumber if I changed my mind. Payson bit his lip. I wondered if he was trying to keep from laughing. He didn't speak for about a minute.

"And what does a *doughnut* mean for my future?" he asked.

Just like that, the warm-eyed fellow was gone, and the familiar old asshole slipped back in his place.

"Um, I guess I'd interpret it the same as an image of a pie or a loaf of bread or something like that. It's homey. A warm and cozy home, that sort of thing."

"Seems a stretch." Payson folded his arms. "A doughnut means I have a cozy home life?"

I got the feeling Payson was either uncomfortable or deliberately trying to make me feel so. Or both.

I locked my gaze on his. "Is it not true?"

"Well, sure, I guess it's true. Compared to some."

"Do you and your family have nice Sunday mornings together?"

"Sure." He shrugged. His lips curved downward. "But it almost never involves doughnuts."

"I didn't say it does. Sometimes the symbols are just a reminder of what you have. A reminder to appreciate it."

Payson rolled his eyes. "How very fortune cookie." He took the cup from me.

"I wasn't done," I protested.

"I think you've given me enough to chew on," he said, rinsing the cup. "I'm gonna go back downstairs. Are you coming?"

"Yeah," I murmured. I paused, watching him plod down the steep stairs, clutching hard at the railing. He was unsteady on his feet.

I remembered the reading I'd given to Cecilia before I even knew who her crush was. I'd said there was a "fence" between her and the guy. Now I could see that there was definitely some truth to that. Payson built a "fence" around himself by acting like a jerk.

I felt uneasy at the accuracy of this reading—more for myself or Cecilia, I wasn't sure.

"Payson!" Phoenix barked as soon as he reached the bottom step. "*What* have you guys been drinking?"

"Just the beer," Payson replied unconvincingly.

When I got down to the basement, I saw that Matt was lying on the couch, eyes closed, hands folded on his chest.

"That's such horseshit," Phoenix snapped.

I turned to Phoenix, caught off guard. *Horseshit* was so much folksier than *bullshit*. Like something G. Clara would say. I had to suppress a smile.

"Don't lie to me," Phoenix said. "Matt told me you guys were chugging on something else during the game. He just didn't know what it was. Last words before he passed out."

"I'm not passed out," Matt mumbled without opening his eyes.

"It wasn't Dad's bourbon, was it?" Phoenix asked. "Because if it was, I'm not taking the blame for that."

Payson whirled on his foot a little, lost his balance, and then grabbed the edge of the couch to steady himself.

"You want to hear about Marnie's reading, Phoenix? You want to know what she saw in my teacup?"

Cecilia stood up. "Payson," she said.

"Doughnuts! She saw *doughnuts!*"

"So?" Cecilia said.

Phoenix continued to glare at him, as if he was telling a joke she just didn't get. I was pretty sure the joke was me.

"Means something about what a great home life we have, how rich we are, and whatnot," Payson said, and then flopped down on the couch next to Matt's feet.

"All that from doughnuts?" piped up the underclass kid whose name I didn't know, who had been quietly sipping from a red plastic cup in the corner.

"All this doughnut talk is making me hungry," Matt slurred. He opened one eye. "Do you think they've got those glazed blueberry ones this time of night?"

"I'm sorry my brother's being an ass," Phoenix whispered to me.

"Why don't you get a reading, too, Phoenix?" Payson demanded. He was talking louder than he needed to, almost yelling. "I'll bet you'll get doughnuts, too."

"Oh my God, Payson," Phoenix murmured. "When are *you* gonna pass out?"

"Wouldn't *that* be convenient for everyone?" Payson roared, but then, as if on cue from Phoenix, he closed his eyes.

I could feel Phoenix's gaze. I could tell she was trying to decide what to say. I wasn't sure if it was going to be good, bad, apologetic, or scolding. I didn't want to wait and see.

"I think I'm gonna head home," I said.

"Oh!" Cecilia said. "Don't go."

"I really should. I told my grandmother I'd help her with . . . something."

As lame as it sounded, kids in Colesbury don't generally live with their grandparents. I've learned that many people assume that such a situation comes with special burdens and responsibilities. In a way they're not wrong.

Phoenix nodded solemnly.

"Text me later, okay?" Cecilia said.

I glanced at Matt. His eyes were closed again, too.

IT WAS DARK BY the time I reached the end of the Longs' winding, wooded driveway. But I liked listening to the crickets until I got to the main road. Then I walked a block to the 7-Eleven and decided to pop in for a soda. That's one thing G. Clara refuses to buy for us much.

While I was staring into the long refrigerator full of endless soda choices, I got a text from Cecilia.

Are you walking? I forgot you don't have a car! Why didn't you ask for a ride?

It's okay. I like walking, I texted back.

I selected a Dr. Pepper and got in line. After I paid I continued down Main Street, trying to walk and sip at the same time.

A couple of cars passed me, and then the street was quiet. Colesbury is so dead at night. Even on weekends. I wondered how, once I was older and had more cash, I would manage to keep myself from drinking a few sodas a day. As I passed the entrance to the elementary school and the unlit post office, I noticed someone's headlights were on me. They remained on me and didn't pass. I could hear the car's low engine purring behind me.

I hurried across the driveway in front of me, assuming they wanted to turn in there. But after I'd passed it, the headlights didn't budge.

I prayed they'd pass. They didn't.

I walked faster.

The turn for my neighborhood was about four blocks up.

Too far. I tried to breathe. I was afraid that if I ran, something worse would happen. I stopped for a moment, and then the car seemed to stop moving. I started walking again, and it inched forward. I walked as fast as I could and took the next right. A few steps onto that street, I took off running down the sidewalk, my heartbeat in my ears.

The car was no longer behind me.

It must have moved on down the main road. Still driving so slow? I wondered. I knew this street pretty well because it was near my old friend Amy Swanson's. So I could get home without going back to the main road. It would take only a few extra minutes.

When I could breathe again, I took out my cell.

"To what do I owe this honor?" was how Carson answered his phone.

"I'm walking home. It's dark. I got a little spooked. I wanted to talk to someone till I got home."

"You need a ride from somewhere?" he asked, now sounding concerned.

"No. Thanks. I'm almost home."

"Where are you walking from?"

"The Long twins' house. Matt invited me to a party there."

He paused for a moment. "I've always wondered when you were going to abandon me for the cool kids."

I smiled, grateful to have his voice for company. "You're the coolest kid, Carson."

"Your sarcasm . . . it wounds me."

"Funny how sarcastic *you* sound," I said, laughing now.

"Meta-conversation. My favorite kind."

"Shut up," I said.

"So how was the party?" Carson wanted to know.

I thought for a moment. "Beer-brimming."

"Okay. I could've guessed that. What else?"

"Umm, well, I'm not sure if anyone was having any actual fun."

"Are you and Matt hitting it off now?

"I don't know. I mostly hung out with Cecilia."

"But *Matt* asked you to the party, right?"

"Yeah."

"So, what does that mean, Marnie? Was it a date and then he ignored you?"

I hadn't thought of it that way. But he had a point. "No, I think maybe I ignored him. I was invited into the drinking game but I didn't play."

"I wonder what his deal is?"

"If you're thinking he's using me, you're probably right," I said.

Another pause. "Using you for what?"

I did my best not to be offended that Carson couldn't think of anything for which I could possibly be used. Instead I told him about our trip to Jimmy's house and our plans to search for him more tomorrow.

"Huh," Carson said. "Well, that should be interesting. You know, you should always be on the lookout for unusual experiences to write about in your college essay, and this might very well be yours."

"I can't believe you just said that."

"Believe it, Marnie. I'm actually a sociopath."

I turned, heading down the sidewalk that led to G. Clara's. I took a deep breath. I was almost home.

"What are *you* going to write about?" I asked.

I knew Carson had been worrying about this since the eighth grade. But we hadn't talked about it in a few months.

"Lately I'm thinking I'll write about when I volunteered at the nursing home. But it will have a quirky opening, because I'll start with the time I tripped and dropped that plate of brownies in the Bingo room. Do you think it would be terrible to change it to cupcakes, for dramatic effect?"

I didn't have the heart to tell him that sounded like a terrible essay. He would realize it eventually. He always did. He had a file full of "practice essays" he'd been writing since the start of high school.

I was at the end of our driveway now. My phone started buzzing.

"Cecilia's calling me," I told him. "I should pick up and see what's up."

"Okay," he said, and I switched over to the other line.

"Just checking to see if you made it home okay," Cecilia said. "Kind of a long walk, right?"

"I'm here now. Just got here." I paused under our front-porch light.

"You know, Cecilia. I'm going to be honest with you. Payson doesn't seem like the greatest catch to me."

Cecilia was silent.

"Cecilia?" I said. "Are you still there?"

"Yeah?"

"Do you see what I'm saying?"

"I guess. And Marnie? What I said about Matt; just remember that."

G. CLARA WAS WATCHING TV in the living room when I got inside.

"Did you have a good time, honey?"

"Yeah," I answered. I stared down at G. Clara's braided rug. I'd hated that rug for so long, because no matter what you did to it, it always looked dirty. Now, after being at the Longs' house, I hated it just a little bit more. Why couldn't we go to some cheap rug store and get one that didn't look like it was waiting to have a dead body wrapped up in it?

"What're you watching?" I asked.

"Oh, some stupid thing. There's this forensics lady, and her boyfriend is missing, and then the police come to her and tell her she has to help investigate this disembodied hand someone left on a doorstep wrapped up like a Christmas present, and then she's afraid it's actually her boyfriend's hand, but it turns out to be his brother's."

"Uh-huh." That sounded like a description of every show G.

Clara watches. Sometimes I think she makes this stuff up to see if I'm really listening. "G. Clara, was Payson Long ever in any of your classes?"

"Payson Long? No. I hear he's a real pain in the ass, though. Why? Did you see him tonight?"

"Both of them. Him and Phoenix."

"Oh. Phoenix. She was in one of my classes last year. Polite. Speaks very well. A little intense, but in a good way."

"What do you mean?" I asked.

"Well, she works hard. Takes things seriously. I've never had a baking student make such a perfect pie crust before."

Of *course* Phoenix took home ec classes. When the apocalypse comes, she'll be the one making the cupcakes.

"I think it was pretty rough on her when that Andrea girl disappeared," G. Clara said, after a moment. "They were best friends."

I wanted to point out that in fact *Matt* and Andrea were best friends. Not Phoenix and Andrea. But it seemed an insignificant point, in light of what G. Clara was saying. Andrea was gone now, so what did it matter, degrees of friendship? They were *all* friends with Andrea. Maybe that was what made me so uncomfortable at their party—not so much the drinking or the tea-leaf reading gone awry, but the unspoken grief.

"It's a terrible thing," G. Clara added.

"Yeah," I agreed. "Well, have fun with your show. Good night."

"Good night, honey."

My cell phone buzzed with a text before I even got to my bedroom.

Matt.

Why did you run off?

Tired, was all I wrote back. It was true.

Still up for tomorrow?

Apparently he wasn't drunk or sick enough to forget our plans.

I guess, I wrote back. I knew I was letting myself be used, but

I didn't have to sound jazzed about it. Maybe if I were a little smarter, I'd have told him no. But my curiosity was winning out against my dignity.

I was curious about a lot of things. If he really believed some parts of my tea-leaf readings. If he really thought he knew something about Andrea's disappearance that the police didn't. If he liked me in spite of Andrea's ghost.

CHAPTER 13

The fox was several feet from me now—limping toward a vague source of light beyond the trees.

I looked behind me. In that direction, the forest was darker and thicker. But the fox was headed toward a streetlamp, or a house.

He turned and gave me a long-tongued, doggy grin. He tipped his face upward and snapped at the falling snowflakes, as if trying to taste them.

I stepped over his blood and followed him, at a safe distance. He was small and seemed harmless. But in the back of my mind I knew he was hurt. I felt sorry for him, yes. But he could still be rabid.

CHAPTER 14

October 12

"Sorry about the bourbon incident last night," Matt said after his GPS told us to take the next exit. He hadn't said a word on the drive until now. "Payson and I got a little carried away."

The GPS lady interrupted with directions, saving me from having to reply.

"Did you have any fun at all?" Matt asked. "Or do you think we're all jackasses?"

I wondered if Matt was fishing for my *real* opinion of himself and his friends. Or if he just wanted my reassurance that I thought they were all as cool as ever. His eyes were tired and expressionless, and I suspected he wasn't feeling great after last night. I doubted he was up for a real conversation.

"Well . . . all of you? No."

"Just Payson?" Matt said, turning to me for a moment and forcing a smile. "I feel like he was smarter when we were younger. He's *still* smart sometimes, if you catch him at the right moment."

I sniffed, wondering what moment that might possibly be. "Maybe it's actually true, all that stuff in the news about football," I said. "And what happens when you get knocked in the head a few too many times."

Matt was silent. Maybe I'd said too much. Since Matt didn't play football himself, I hadn't thought much of the comment. But Payson was still his friend, after all.

"Maybe," he said finally.

"What's up with him and Phoenix?"

"I don't know. Do you and *your* brother get along?"

I shrugged. Good point. I had no idea what was going on with Noah and me most of the time. "Payson seemed to get all bent out of shape when I mentioned doughnuts."

"I think he was bent out of shape before you ever came inside. Seriously. I wouldn't take it personally."

The GPS interrupted to tell us we'd "arrived at our destination."

Matt parked on the side of the road. "Looks kind of run-down," he said. He stared up at the dark-green duplex towering above us. I thought it looked kind of nice, compared with G. Clara's house. It still had most of its last paint job, at least. And no graffiti.

"Don't be so judgey," I said. "He's a young guy. It's probably his first apartment or something."

"Do we text him and say we're here?" Matt wondered aloud. He'd talked to Jimmy's cousin, Trevor, earlier in the morning, right after he picked me up. It was a short conversation. Trevor said that he didn't know where Jimmy was living now, but that we were welcome to come and chat if we really wanted to. Now that we were here, I wondered exactly what Matt was hoping to find. Did he *really* think Jimmy was the key to Andrea's disappearance? Or was he picking on Jimmy because it was easier than thinking about other possibilities?

"Let's go wild and ring the doorbell," I suggested. "He said he's in number three?"

Matt nodded. We hopped out of the car and climbed the stairs. I rang before either of us could second-guess ourselves or chicken out.

The guy who answered was tall and skinny, with a gruff expression. But what I noticed most was the long, full black hair that rested on his shoulders. Hair so beautiful that I wondered if he'd blown it dry and styled it.

"Hey, Jimmy's friends," he said in a dry voice. "Come on

up. I'm making a cake for my girlfriend's birthday. It's in the oven."

"What kind of cake?" Matt asked, following. I fell in line behind them.

"Chocolate. German chocolate. I'm not sure what makes it German, but that's what she likes, so that's what I'm doing."

"Smells good," I said, and I meant it. "You do a lot of baking?"

Trevor grunted as he led us into his kitchen. It was small but clean, with an ugly brown linoleum floor.

"More than I used to. The girlfriend likes it. I don't know what I'm doing, but I know how to put an egg and some oil into a cake mix."

"Marnie's grandma is a cooking teacher," Matt offered. I glared at him. I thought the goal was to avoid looking like naïve little Colesbury kids. He wasn't going in the right direction, talking about our grandmas.

"You're lucky," Trevor said. "Now, you want to talk about Jimmy, right? I gotta ask, how close were you?"

"Well, my brother was his friend," I said.

"And so was my friend Andrea," Matt added.

"Andrea? The one who disappeared?"

I could see that Matt was studying Trevor now. "You know about her?"

Trevor turned toward the oven. "Of course. A police officer came and talked to us about her. But we didn't have much to tell him. Andrea only came here a couple of times. In, like, December. Two or three months before she disappeared."

"She came here twice?" Matt asked. "Why?"

"Just hanging out with Jimmy. It kind of made my girlfriend nervous, because Andrea was a minor, and we were worried they'd be smoking together. Not good. Could get us all in trouble, big-time."

"And did they smoke pot together here?"

"No, I don't think so. But my girlfriend was always worried about it. Oh . . ." Trevor turned back to us, sheepish for a moment. "You know Jimmy sells—"

"Yeah, pot," Matt interrupted. "We know."

"Well, Becca found his *other* stash."

"His other stash?" Matt prompted.

"Pills. He was starting to sell pills, too. Oxycodone. Also a little Molly, I think. That was when we decided he couldn't live with us anymore. He could've gotten us all in trouble. Because say the police had some reason to come here, find Jimmy's stash. In *our* apartment. She was afraid we could all be considered, like, accomplices or whatever."

I wondered if Noah ever had a "stash." Or if he still did.

"Do you think Jimmy was using, too?" I asked.

"Probably. I don't know if it was Sullivan pushing it on him, or what."

"Who's Sullivan?" Matt asked.

"Oh. Sorry. He was Jimmy's pot supplier." Trevor's eyes narrowed.

"You kids aren't looking for trees, are you?"

"Trees?" I repeated. It was clear he expected us to understand his drug slang. I had the feeling he didn't believe we were friends of Jimmy's at all. He probably thought we were wannabe clients.

"Uh. Pot," Trevor clarified.

"Oh," I said. "No."

"We just have some questions, that's all," Matt persisted. "About Andrea and Jimmy."

Trevor continued to slouch and stare at the temperature dials. "Yeah. Well, so did the police. I'm not sure there was much to the relationship, though. They were hanging out some a few months before she disappeared. Not around the time of her actual disappearance—we'd kicked him out by then. I think she was just stringing Jimmy along anyway. One of the times she was here, I heard her say she thought Sullivan was cute. And I thought that was kind of mean, I guess. Because Jimmy obviously liked her. And then here she is, playing dumb, telling him how cute his sleazy supplier is."

I watched Matt. He was growing red and breathing through his nose. "Are you sure?" He stopped for a moment, clearly trying to sort out his thoughts. He'd been thrown by that remark, that Andrea thought Sullivan was cute. "Um, are you sure that they weren't hanging out anymore in the month or two before Andrea disappeared?"

"Well, that's how I remember it. Jimmy was gone—in New Jersey, I'm assuming—like, a whole two months before the police came around here wondering if we knew something about Andrea."

"So the police know that she was here once," Matt said, his voice tight. "Did they go talk to him in New Jersey?"

"I think they tried, but couldn't find him. You know, *I'd* say he disappeared just as completely as Andrea did. But he wasn't a minor like her. He wasn't some Colesbury darling like her. And *he* told people he was leaving. But that was a couple months before she disappeared, see? So the police *did* want to talk to him, but I think they probably know he couldn't have had much to do with it."

"I don't know about *that,*" Matt mumbled.

I cringed inwardly. I wondered what the hell he was thinking, saying this to a member of Jimmy's family.

"And he didn't tell you where, specifically, he was going in New Jersey?" I asked, jumping in before Matt could go on. "What he'd be doing there, who he'd be with?"

Trevor didn't seem offended. His eyes remained on the stove. Maybe he was stoned, himself. "You have to understand—he was kind of mad at me, so he didn't communicate much." He paused. "I hated that we had to kick him out, but I didn't have much choice. It was him or my girlfriend. And *he* was the drug dealer, after all. There are things I can ask of her, as my girlfriend. But living with a drug dealer isn't one of them."

"Sounds fair," I said.

Matt was silent, looking at the linoleum floor. It was clear to me that he wasn't getting what he wanted out of this little visit. But what *did* he want?

"So after he took off," Trevor continued, "I know he went back to Colesbury for a little while, even though he hates it there. No offense. But his mom was only able to let him stay a few days, because her boyfriend wanted him out. Same reasons. No drugs in the house kind of a thing. That guy acts all self-righteous about this sort of shit, even though he used to be a huge drinker himself. I don't know. Not my business."

He put on a pair of oven mitts with Santa Clauses on them, opened the oven, took out his cake, and stuck a toothpick in it. He frowned at the toothpick when it came up clean.

I glanced at Matt, whose hands were at his sides, clenched into fists.

Trevor was oblivious. He sighed and closed the oven door, then straightened. "Anyway, I guess he rented some cheap mother-in-law apartment somewhere in Colesbury. Not sure where he got the money for that, but I can guess. Then next thing I know, a few weeks later, he sends me this text saying he's headed to New Jersey with a new girlfriend."

"Andrea?" Matt demanded.

I shot Matt a pleading glance. *Shut up.* It seemed like he might start to get combative. I needed to get him out of there.

"No. Of course not." Trevor scowled at him. "What the fuck? Some girl he met in New Haven, he said. I don't know. As I said, he was kind of mad at me, and kind of mad at his mom. Both of us kicked him out on account of significant others, I guess. Probably he felt discarded. But you know, if it bothers you, get a real job and quit dealing weed, for God's sake. I gotta look at it that way."

"When was that, when he said he was going to New Jersey?" Matt asked.

"Umm . . . sometime in the spring, I think. Early spring, maybe? But since then, he never texts back. The texts go unde-livered. Maybe he got a new phone or whatever. He used these cheap phones with prepaid cards. Or he's so mad at me he's found a way to block my number." Trevor showed me the toothpick. "Look done to you?"

"Yeah," I said, very much wanting to leave.

"Can you tell me anything more about this Sullivan guy?" Matt asked. "Where he lives? Where he works?"

"All I know is that he sells a lot of weed to Wharton College kids." Trevor sighed. "That's, like, his main clientele. Jimmy mentioned that once. And he mentioned a couple of times meeting him at the bar called the Cha Cha. You heard of that place? Near the college?"

"Of course," Matt said, clearly lying.

"Okay. Well, sorry to disappoint you, but that's all I know." Trevor held up his Santa mitts apologetically.

"You didn't disappoint us," I said, pulling Matt toward the door now. "We're going to let you get back to your baking. Thanks."

CHAPTER 15

"You hungry?" Matt asked as we pulled away from Trevor's house. "That cake smell made me pretty hungry."

"Umm . . ."

"I am," Matt said. "I want a greasy cheeseburger, or something."

"I thought you were maybe a little hungover?" I said.

"Not enough not to eat. And they say fatty food helps. After that, maybe we can go try to find Sullivan."

Wharton was at least a half hour away, south of Colesbury. And I wasn't sure I was up for stalking a big-time drug dealer today.

"I don't think I have time to go to Wharton," I said. "I have a ton of homework to catch up on. And no, I'm not that hungry. But you should stop if you want something."

Matt pulled over to the first fast-food place he saw, and after we ordered, we drove around for a while, eventually finding a park with his GPS. He wanted to stop and eat somewhere outside.

The place we found was empty except for one lady pushing a toddler on a swing. There were no picnic tables, so we sat on a bench overlooking the playground.

Matt handed me the fries I'd ordered, then unwrapped one of his two enormous bacon cheeseburgers.

"Do you think it's weird that Andrea was hanging out with

Jimmy at his cousin's place?" I asked. "I mean, obviously she wasn't just buying a little pot from him."

"It's not so weird," Matt said. "I *did* know they were hanging out, even if she didn't always say *where*. But their relationship in general—that started with Jimmy's mom. Did I tell you that?"

I shook my head.

"Jimmy's mom was doing work for Andrea's parents. You know she sometimes cleans houses?"

"I guess I'd heard that, yeah."

"Well, Andrea's folks weren't really the type who would usually hire a housecleaner. But her dad's had all of these issues with his knee replacement. In and out of work, and couldn't really help Andrea's mom much around the house. So they hired Jimmy's mom. First just to clean, but they liked her a lot, so sometimes to watch Andrea's little sister, Bella, too. So she was around Andrea's house pretty often, and Andrea said she liked her a lot. They talked about their favorite TV shows, I guess, and Jimmy's mom was really good with Andrea's little sister. So, when Jimmy came around a couple of times to see his mom, I guess he'd go try to see her at Andrea's house sometimes. You know, to avoid running into his mom's crazy boyfriend at her own house."

"Uh-huh," I said.

"So she got to know Jimmy that way. I think at first she talked to him just to be polite to his mom, but eventually it turned into something else. She thought he was funny. That was usually what she'd say about him, when she talked about him."

"Do you think they were ever . . . more than friends?"

Matt lowered his hamburger and stared at the jungle gym in front of us. "No."

"Why do you say no? You seem to think he hurt her in some way. Isn't that more possible if they were into each other?"

His face darkened. "I just don't think she'd ever be with a guy like that."

"A guy like what? *What* was Jimmy? Not good enough for

her?" Maybe what made him so sure was that there was more between himself and Andrea than he was willing to admit. Just like Cecilia had implied. On the other hand, I had no idea why I was sticking up for Jimmy. The guy he'd grown up to be was not the kid who'd once played at our house. Maybe I wished I was wrong about that.

"I didn't say that," Matt said. I could tell by his tone that he mistook my awkward silence for anger. "I just don't think she would've been into him, is all."

"Does Jimmy's mom still work for Andrea's family?" I asked. It seemed to me that would be pretty awkward.

"No," Matt said. "See, some of Mrs. Quinley's jewelry supposedly went missing. They asked Jimmy's mom about it, and I guess it caused a lot of tension."

"Did Andrea think that Jimmy's mom did it?"

Matt shrugged. "I remember her saying that she didn't want to think so, but couldn't think of any other explanation. I think that they didn't fire her, actually. She got upset and quit."

"Was Andrea sad about that?" I asked.

"Yeah. I think she was sad for Jimmy's mom. It's hard to say. It was around that time when she was weird about all sorts of things. Around when she quit basketball."

"Oh," I said.

We were quiet for a little while. Matt finished his hamburgers. I ate a fry or two and tried not to listen to all of his chewing and smacking. Maybe I'd liked him better with an innocent orange in his hands. After the burgers were gone and the wrappers crumpled into our to-go bag, Matt turned his attention back to me.

"Why do you live with your grandmother?" he asked.

I was so startled by the question that I sat for a minute or two without making a sound. My fatigued fry drooped in my hand.

"It's a long story, Matt," I said finally.

It was a story I told no one but Carson, in fact. Telling it felt disloyal. Not to my mom so much as G. Clara. The story showed how screwed up my mom was—which was fair, because she was. But it also felt like it implicated G. Clara somehow, to have such a screwed-up daughter. And that part of it had never felt fair.

"I don't have anywhere to be," he prodded.

I decided it was okay to half tell it, since it had been so long since anyone else had asked.

"Well," I took a breath. "My mother got pregnant with Noah when she was very young. Her first year of college. And then she married my father. And then they had me a couple of years later. But when I was little, she had kind of a breakdown. Drinking, other stuff. She and my dad divorced. G. Clara says they were never a good match, anyway. They were both young, it wasn't anyone's fault . . . That's how she put it."

I hesitated. How much was I willing to divulge about how *I* would put it? I decided to keep it short and stick to the facts.

"Anyway, it started with us just staying there a lot while my mom worked and went back to school. She worked in the daytime and went to school at night. We never saw her. It was really like G. Clara was our mom. So when my mom graduated, she got a job in Virginia."

"Uh-huh," Matt said vaguely, waiting for more.

"Well, she didn't last long. But that's another story. Then she suggested we all go out there with her, but I was in second grade by then, and Noah was in fourth. We had friends here, and it was the middle of the school year, and we didn't want to leave G. Clara." My face felt hot. "I feel like the house was nicer then," I added quickly. "But probably it was just that I was a little kid and didn't care. It was home."

"You talk about your house like it's a dungeon. It's not so bad."

I decided not to tell him about the bathroom mushrooms. Even Carson didn't know about those. "Anyway. My mom didn't have a plan for school for us. The public schools in the district where she'd be living weren't great—not as good as Colesbury, anyway. And G. Clara convinced her that she should let us stay with her until the end of the school year, and make a plan for that, and then we'd talk about it that summer."

"Which didn't happen, obviously."

I bit my lip. "Obviously."

"What *did* happen?"

I sighed. "The story doesn't get any more interesting, Matt. The gist is that G. Clara wanted us to stay with her, and my mother didn't find it hugely difficult to leave us, ultimately."

Matt nodded. He looked away. "Do you see her?" he asked quietly.

"Holidays and summers when she can afford a ticket here, or is up for the drive. But that almost never happens. She's had this one boyfriend for years. They live in Georgia now. He takes care of her when she runs into screwups."

"Are you mad at her?"

I thought about this for a long time. "I don't know. I guess I would be more, if I didn't have G. Clara. She's always made us feel taken care of. Anyway, she's always telling us that my mother's brain doesn't work like other people's. That she would love to get her shit together, but there's something off about her chemistry that prevents her from being able to. 'She loves you kids,' she's always saying. 'She really does.'"

Matt turned to me. "Is she an alcoholic?"

"G. Clara has never put it that way."

"But that's what it sounds like she's trying to say."

"Maybe," I said.

"Sometimes I think Payson is going to be an alcoholic," Matt offered. "Sometimes I think he already is."

Or maybe he's just a jerk, I thought. I wasn't sure how Payson was relevant to this conversation, but it was a relief. I was glad enough to stop talking about my mom.

"Are you worried about him?" I asked.

Matt's dark eyes appeared to be studying me in a way I didn't quite understand. "I'm worried about all of us, sometimes."

I didn't ask for an explanation. I was pretty sure I knew what he meant. I worried about all the people around me, about everyone close—sometimes.

Matt pushed an inch closer to me. His dark eyes were beautiful, but his hamburger breath was gross. Suddenly, his eyes were closed and his lips were in my face. Before I could think about it, I'd turned my head, so his lips mashed my ear.

"Oh!" I said, smacking my arm. "There was a bug on me."

Matt straightened up, looking perplexed. He couldn't tell if I'd dodged him purposefully or cluelessly. I wasn't sure myself.

"I guess we should head home," he said.

CHAPTER 16

Back at home, I sat in front of the computer with my pathetic lunch: a yogurt and a handful of crackers. Carson saw me as soon as I opened Facebook. I'd hoped he would, of course. I needed to talk to him. I felt like I was about to jump out of my skin.

How'd your little sleuthing trip go? he asked.

No way was I going to tell him about the near-miss kiss. Guys like Matt weren't supposed to want to kiss girls like me. I didn't know what to make of it and wasn't ready to discuss it with Carson. I needed Carson to take my mind off of those dark eyes.

Okay. I typed. *Seems no one's seen or heard from Jimmy in months.*

Carson paused for a while before writing back.

Does Matt think he killed her or something?

I'm not sure why I was shocked to see these words on the screen.

He doesn't come straight out and say that, no, I typed back.

Carson: *Interesting.*

Me: *As crazy as Jimmy was, I don't really think that's possible.*

Carson: *I know you knew him as a kid, but did you really know him well enough, recently, to say that for sure?*

Me: *I don't want to go there.*

Carson: *Why doesn't Matt just have you do a tea-leaf reading to tell you where Jimmy is? Better yet, where Andrea is?*

I took an angry bite of cracker before typing: *Shut up.*

Carson: *If you're going to take that tone, I'll just go back to my AP Lit paper.*

I should have known better than to count on Carson to distract or console me. *This is why he doesn't have many friends,* I reminded myself. I finished my yogurt and stared at the screen, wondering if I should keep writing to him.

And then my Inbox dinged. Surprised, I clicked on the mailbox. I didn't get a ton of email these days. I didn't check it every day. My dad wrote me an occasional message, birthday wishes and stuff like that, but mostly it was crap from school.

The message was from an address I didn't recognize, though: a long string of numbers and letters that didn't spell anything. Just like the address on the emails Matt had received.

The message said:

Think twice about what you are doing. And do not trust a word Matt Cotrell says.

I stared at the screen for a moment, then flipped back to Facebook.

Carson? I typed.

Carson: *Yes. Have you come back to apologize?*

Me: *Did you just send me an email?*

Carson: *No. Why would I do that?*

Me: *Are you messing with me?*

Carson: *I don't know what you're talking about.*

I logged off Facebook and went back to the email, hit Reply, and quickly typed, *Who is this?* My heart raced. I couldn't swallow. I thought of the headlights following me last night. I took a few deep breaths, reminding myself that I wasn't alone in the house. I could hear Noah opening the microwave, then tossing something into the sink.

I sat there for an hour, refreshing my email account. But no one replied.

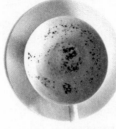

CHAPTER 17
October 13

Matt wasn't in school on Monday.

I was relieved not to have to talk to him. I still hadn't decided whether I'd tell him about the weird email. Who would warn me against Matt? And why? What had he said to me so far that I *ought* to mistrust? Things he said about Andrea? About himself? It seemed I should believe in Matt over some loser who hid behind an anonymous email account. But then, maybe that loser was afraid of Matt? But *why?*

And how many people even knew I was spending time with Matt? Cecilia. Carson. Phoenix. Payson. That girl named Hannah from the party. Trevor. The guy at the party whose name I didn't know.

After school, I met Cecilia at the Clover Café.

Cecilia sipped her tea slowly, even reluctantly. I wondered if she'd grown tired of me and my readings—or if she felt some of my nerd magic had worn off now that we were hanging around with the same people.

"So . . ." she said, cradling her teacup with both hands. "Have you and Matt talked since the party?"

"A little," I admitted.

She nodded. Her forehead was creased; something was troubling her. "I've been thinking about this pretty hard," she finally said. "And there's something I think you should know."

"What's that?"

"Well, what I was saying about Matt and Andrea . . ." Her grip tightened on the cup. "There's more to it than you know about."

"Okay?"

"Last year, see, there was this little party at Phoenix and Payson's place. It was the usual kind of thing. I wasn't there because I was away for a Model UN weekend. But Phoenix texted me a picture that night. Of Matt and Andrea snuggled on her couch, Matt kissing her."

I took a breath. "Like, a real kiss?"

"Well, it was kinda on the nose more than the mouth, from what I remember. I guess they were both a little drunk, from what Phoenix told me. She sent that picture and texted something like, '*What did I tell you?!*' You know, like this moment sort of confirmed this theory she had all along, that when those two let their guard down, they couldn't keep off of each other."

My thoughts raced. "Do you still have the picture?"

"Uh, no. That's the thing. *Right* after it happened, Phoenix asked me to delete the picture. She said she'd mentioned it to Andrea and she was upset about it, so she asked me to delete it as a favor. Phoenix felt bad she'd done it."

"And this was when? Right before Andrea disappeared?"

"Mmmm, no. A couple months before, at least. It was winter still, I remember. And Andrea said that Phoenix had it all wrong. That she and Matt were always like that with each other. Even when they were kids. She was sick of Phoenix and everyone else hinting otherwise."

"Uh-huh," I said, studying Cecilia's fraught expression. "And do you believe that?"

"From what I remember of the picture . . . no."

I didn't know what to say.

Cecilia looked at me. "I wasn't sure if I should tell you. Especially because Phoenix told me to forget about it."

"Have you mentioned it to Phoenix recently? Asked her if it was okay to mention it to me?"

Cecilia paused for a moment. "Nope." With that, she quickly rotated her cup, tapped it, and gave it to me. "I'm sorry. Let's just do the reading, okay?"

I nodded and forced myself to concentrate on the leaves. "I see a curtain," I said, after a moment. "That's promising. Because I think a curtain means a secret."

"Oh." Cecilia sounded disinterested. I wondered if she suddenly felt uncomfortable around me, now that she'd spilled what she'd seen. "One I'm keeping or one being kept from me?"

"You tell me," I said.

Cecilia's gaze snapped back to me. "No. *You* tell *me*. That's how this works, right?"

I bit my lip. "Probably being kept from you. Happy?"

Cecilia seemed more interested now. "Kept from me. By whom? Is it a *big* secret?"

I peered back into the leaves. "It doesn't exactly overwhelm the cup. But the size of the symbol doesn't always indicate the significance of the event."

"Hmm. Okay, what else do you see, then?"

"Well, here's something," I said. "About halfway down the cup, there's a keyhole."

"What's a keyhole mean?"

I had no idea what a keyhole meant. A *key* usually meant money or success; I was sure of that. But a keyhole? I'd have to guess, because I couldn't remember reading about that particular symbol.

"Well . . . I think maybe it means you *know* the source of your problem. You *know* what you're looking for. Maybe you even know what this secret is—if the two symbols are connected. Not that I'm necessarily saying they are. But you have to narrow your focus and really look at it. Like, looking into a keyhole. Does that make sense?"

Cecilia nodded slowly.

"And maybe it has nothing to do with liking Payson," I offered. "Maybe all of this confusion with Payson—how he feels, or doesn't feel, about you—is your way of stopping yourself from looking at or thinking about something more important or more difficult." I held my breath after I said this. It was a wild guess, and I usually try not to make wild guesses. But it *was* a keyhole. The more I stared, the clearer it became.

"I don't know about that," Cecilia said, after considering my words for a moment. "Remember when I told you there was this one party when something happened?"

"Yeah?"

"Well, something happened between Payson and me. That's part of the Payson thing that I've never told you."

"Okay?" I prompted.

Cecilia folded her arms in front of her chest. She seemed to shudder inwardly. "It was at another party, a different one from the one I was just talking about. Payson and Matt were saying they really wished they had some pot." She hesitated. "Andrea was like, 'Hey, I can totally score you some right now. I know a guy and I'll bet he could be here in less than an hour.' So she calls Jimmy Harmon. He didn't even come downstairs into the basement—just met with Andrea upstairs and left. So after they'd put the stuff in a hollowed-out cigar . . . that's how Payson likes it . . . everyone took at least a puff."

I glanced into the teacup as I listened. The curtain seemed more distinct to me now than it had earlier. It seemed now that we should've talked more about it. I'd maybe wasted too much time pretending I knew what a keyhole meant.

"And I can't remember how exactly it happened that Payson and I ended up alone upstairs watching TV," Cecilia continued. "But we ended up fooling around. I mean, just a little. Making out while we watched *My Strange Addiction*. Which is kind of ironic, but whatever. We stopped because we heard Matt screaming at Andrea. So we go down there and there's Andrea, giving something to Phoenix's mom's Persian cats. Matt was all like, 'What the hell, Andrea! Don't waste it!'"

I put down the teacup. I had a feeling I knew what was coming.

"And then Andrea says, 'You guys, it's catnip,' and just collapses on the floor laughing."

"Oooh," I said delicately. "She tricked everyone." I figured that was more polite than saying, *She tricked you all.*

Cecilia winced, careful not to meet my eyes. "Yeah."

"Were people mad?" I asked.

"Payson was. Before we went upstairs, he was going on and on about how stoned he was. So he looked stupid."

"Was Phoenix mad?" I'm not sure why I asked this, but Cecilia didn't seem surprised.

"No. She thought it was funny. She said that Payson went off on Andrea, saying she owed him. He made Andrea promise that she'd get him something else from Jimmy."

"Something else?"

"I don't know the details. But something more exotic than pot, was my impression. Molly, probably. I know Payson wanted to try that. Not that I was planning to join in, if I was invited. I mean, I'm not even into pot."

"When did this all happen, Cecilia?"

She slumped back in her seat. "Around Christmas. I remember that after the cats snuffled up the catnip, one of them went bonkers and tried to climb the Longs' Christmas tree."

I hesitated. "You think Jimmy was in on it?"

"Sure. Why not?"

I tried not to roll my eyes. "Why would he bother to drive out to the Longs' house to help Andrea with a prank he didn't even get to see?"

Cecilia shrugged. "I've heard that guy was kinda nuts. But how should I know?" She stared at me. "Anyway, the reason I'm telling you all of this is because of *Payson.* It was like he needed an excuse to show he liked me. But . . ."

"The pot was fake, so—"

"So, the excuse was, like, imaginary. And the whole thing embarrassed him. But where does that leave me?"

I looked into Cecilia's teacup again. I felt as fake as Andrea's "weed." I'd done about twenty readings for Cecilia about Payson, and never once picked up anything to indicate that they'd already actually sort of *been together*. Forget tea leaves. How insightful was I, even, as a person? I was never sure if my readings were accurate or lucky or something in between, but I liked to think I was at least *perceptive*.

"Um," I said.

The door of the coffee shop jangled, and in walked Matt.

"Hey, you guys," he said. "I was hoping to find you here." He sat with us and tapped his fingertips on the table. Cecilia raised her eyebrows at me.

"Fancy meeting you here, Matt," she said. "You're looking well, for someone who couldn't make it to school."

"Had to skip," he said, looking around the room. Maybe checking for teachers. "Hmm. Maybe I'll get something to drink."

"Not an espresso drink, I hope," I said. "You seem kinda jumpy."

After Matt went to the counter, Cecilia said, "I should probably go."

"You sure?"

"Yeah. I think Matt seems eager to talk to you."

"Maybe he wants to talk to you?"

"No, Marnie." Cecilia picked up her stylish backpack, mint green with dark brown polka dots. "Don't play dumb. I'll say goodbye to him on my way out."

She did, and Matt didn't look surprised. He approached the table with a purplish smoothie in a tall glass.

"Where were you today?" I asked.

"I went to that bar that Trevor mentioned. The Cha Cha, near Wharton College."

"They let you in?"

"It's also like a restaurant sort of place." He spoke quickly but didn't sound defensive. "I had lunch there. I asked everyone I could if they'd seen either Jimmy or Sullivan around."

"And?"

"And they all looked at me like I was nuts."

"And this is a surprise to you?"

Matt ignored the question. "This one guy, I'm pretty sure I saw a reaction on his face when I said the name Sullivan. Anyway, tomorrow I'm gonna go to the Wharton College cafeteria, maybe some of the student lounges or whatever. Maybe I'll have better luck there."

"Uh, maybe. Are you worried about getting caught for cutting?"

"No. I just told my mom I needed a mental health day, and she called the school."

I wondered what would happen if I ever suggested that to G. Clara. She'd probably still make me go to school, then make me walk three miles to a shrink appointment afterward.

"She lets me have them every so often." Matt said. "Especially since . . . Andrea. But look. There's something else I wanted to tell you. I got another one of those emails."

He took out his phone and showed me. Again the address was a random string of numbers and letters. I hadn't memorized the address of the message I'd gotten, but I remembered that it started with the number eight. Like this one.

Matt. Do you know about that night? What do you know about that night? I need to know.

"What night?" I said slowly. "What is she . . . um, or he . . . talking about?"

"I seriously don't know."

"When did you get this?"

"After I dropped you off yesterday."

I glanced at the time of the email. 1:22. I couldn't remember exactly when mine had come in, but it had been when I was eating lunch. I handed the phone back. "Did you write back? Try to get them to respond?"

"Yeah, but it didn't work."

I nodded. "Creepy. You going to tell the police about this one?"

"Eventually. But I'm going to do a few other things first. See if I can find that guy Sullivan. I have a feeling he'd know how to contact Jimmy."

I watched Matt take a long, labored sip of his smoothie. I wondered if he knew how transparent he was. His interest in Jimmy had been replaced by an interest in Sullivan—practically the very instant he'd heard that Andrea said he was cute.

"If Jimmy's really in New Jersey," I pointed out, "I don't think he'd still be getting his marijuana from some guy up here."

Matt shoved his drink aside. "I'm not saying that he does. I'm not an idiot. But I have questions about Jimmy. About Jimmy and Andrea. And did you even *hear* what his cousin said? About Jimmy dealing pills? Doesn't that worry you, when you consider everything I told you about how Andrea was acting before she disappeared?"

"Yes, but . . . haven't the police considered all of this already?"

"But I have different questions than the police had," Matt mumbled.

"Like what? And speaking of the police . . . If you let them know this person is still writing to you, they could probably try again to trace where the emails are coming from."

"They won't care. They'll just say it's a hoaxer again."

"How do you know?" I persisted. "Why not just let them know?"

"*Marnie.*" There was a sudden anger in Matt's voice. Even the lethargic barista looked up. Matt leaned close to me as he lowered his voice. "I'm not talking to the police. Not now."

I just nodded, avoiding the eyes of the chai-sipping middle-aged ladies at the table next to us. The words of that anonymous email came back to me. *Do not trust a word Matt Cotrell says.* I hadn't really taken the message seriously. But I wasn't sure, now, how to take it. Maybe the writer meant *Matt Cotrell is losing it.* And maybe the writer was right.

Matt stood up. "You want a ride home?"

His tone was indifferent. He knew what my answer would be.

"No, thanks."

"Cool." Matt nodded. "Probably won't be in school tomorrow. But I'll let you know what I find out."

"Good luck," I said softly.

AFTER I CAME AROUND the corner approaching G. Clara's house, I stopped for a minute to look at Noah's spray-painted picture on the shed. I wondered what the neighbors must think of it.

It was a messy rectangle with rounded corners, longer in the vertical direction, and split across the middle with a wavy line. It was full of little dots, heavy on the bottom, but thinning out over the top half and around the rectangle. It was all in red—bright against the dingy white of the shed—which I supposed gave it a little bit of a Satanic feel for the more nervous neighbors who might go there.

I had never asked Noah what it was supposed to be, although I'd guessed a pill bottle or a pepper shaker. G. Clara hadn't asked him either, to my knowledge. He'd painted it in the middle of the night, a day or so before his overdose, so he probably didn't even know what he was drawing.

A sharp breeze blew past me. I pulled my jacket tight around my shoulders and felt a certain satisfaction in realizing that it was getting colder. I hated winter, but the quicker it came and went, the quicker I'd feel I was getting this "junior year" thing over with. So far in high school, I'd been keeping close count on "how much time was left" until I could get the hell out of town and stop feeling like the requisite bag lady character in everyone's Colesbury learning experience. Two years down and winter coming on the third year. I was finally on the downhill side of high school.

"Hello?" I called once inside the house. I knew Noah was there, because his car was in the driveway.

"Hey," he grunted from the kitchen.

I went to my room, flung my backpack on the floor, and

closed the door. I had a ton of homework but didn't feel like getting to it just yet.

My tea-leaf-reading book was buried beneath a pile of T-shirts in one of my dresser drawers. I pulled it out and looked in the *K* section of the index in the back. A key meant success—exactly as I'd remembered it. After that was *keyhole.*

Keyhole: A warning, particularly about a seemingly trustworthy person who may in fact have hidden intentions or unpleasant secrets.

Well, then, I'd been a little off in what I'd told Cecilia. Though, of course, the tea-leaf reader had a certain amount of discretion in interpreting symbols. But nonetheless . . . *a seemingly trustworthy person.*

I shuddered. Who had written that email about Matt? I thought then of the foxes—in Matt's teacups and my own dreams. *Jimmy?* Could he be the fox?

Jamming the book back into the dresser, I had a thought I'd never had before.

Maybe, occasionally, some of the pictures I saw in teacups were not for the tea drinkers. Maybe some of them were for me.

But which ones? Cecilia's curtain or Cecilia's keyhole? Payson's doughnuts? Matt's dragon?

CHAPTER 18

The fox was out of sight now. I didn't know how many min-utes—or even hours—had passed since he had gone. Snow fell quietly around me. Time passed. Or did it? How long had I been standing here in the snow, staring in the direction the fox had gone? I missed him now—his canine smile, which I should've recognized, from the start, as friendly. Alone now, I started to feel the cold around me. To feel it for real. My toes and fingers ached. I wondered if the blood was freezing in my capillaries. The thought felt more distinct than anything around me. I tried to lift my foot to take a step toward the faint pawprints still left in the snow.

Was the fox taking me home? Or somewhere else? Maybe it didn't matter—because to walk toward him meant I'd have a destination, which was better than letting my blood slow to a standstill and freeze like a red raspberry Popsicle.

I pushed my feet forward, following the prints into the endless white.

CHAPTER 19
October 15

"Marnie!"

I jumped up from my pre-calc homework, pulling off my earbuds.

"What?" I demanded.

Noah was in my doorway. He'd probably heard me singing along to Florence and the Machine, but it had likely embarrassed him as much as it did me.

"There's someone here for you," he said.

"Someone?"

Noah was already headed back down the hallway. "He's on the front steps."

I knew who it was.

"Hey, Marnie," Matt said when I got to the door. "Can I come in? I want to show you something."

I tried to remember just how messy the kitchen was. Had the breakfast dishes made it into the dishwasher yet?

"I guess," I said reluctantly. "Your mom let you have another mental health day?"

Matt ignored my question and shoved his phone into my hands. "I got another email. It's getting kind of crazy."

It was from an address similar to the one from before—a string of numbers and letters—but this one started with a three, not an eight. So it was a different address, though I guessed created by the same person.

Are you stupid???

I can't take this anymore.

The body is probably behind the tracks. But didn't you already know that???

"Jesus," I said. I gave him back his phone. My hand felt clammy.

"Told you. Crazy."

"Matt, I think you need to tell the police about this. They'll want to know someone is harassing you about a *body*. That's cruel. And tracks? What tracks? What's the closest train to Colesbury? New Haven?"

Matt just shook his head. He looked tired. Purplish circles ringed his eyes. I led him into the kitchen.

"They're messing with you," I said. "They're cruel. Whoever they are. And you can't let them keep doing that. They'll do it until you take the bait."

I offered Matt one of our kitchen chairs.

"You hungry?" I asked.

"No," Matt said. He kept staring at his phone. At least it kept him from taking in our broken cabinet and our crusty linoleum. Or our ancient cookie jar shaped like a fat lady, with one of her eyes and half her nose ghoulishly chipped away. "I need to know if this is real."

"I'd think the police would want to know that as much as you."

He looked up sharply. "Can you cool it on the police for just a few minutes?"

"Who else is gonna help you, if someone is stalking you and giving you shit like this?"

Matt took a breath and put down his phone. "Was kind of hoping you would."

"*Me?*"

"Give me a reading, Marnie," he said softly.

"Matt," I said. I thought about how to say what I wanted to tell him without offending him. "I think these last emails have really upset you."

Matt stared at me. "Yeah?"

"And I don't think a teacup can tell you anything that's going to help you with that. Like, why don't you start with the basic questions instead? For example, who would be able to get ahold of our email addresses?"

"*Our* email addresses?" Matt repeated, frowning.

"I mean . . ." I hesitated. "Your email address."

"I already explained that, remember?"

He wouldn't stop staring at me, his dark eyes sad but determined. Yes, maybe the whole Andrea thing had made him a little bit crazy. And it occurred to me that I could hardly blame him for that. What if Carson disappeared one day? What if he'd tried to call me that same day, and I hadn't answered? I would probably do even crazier things than ask a two-bit high school fortune-teller for help.

"Marnie," Matt whispered. "Something happens when you look into a teacup. I'm pretty sure."

I turned away. "What happens is I look for pictures."

"I've hardly ever been able to make out the pictures you say you see," Matt said. "Sometimes, I think you're full of shit with that part."

I was startled by his bluntness; it felt like a slap in the face. "Then why—"

"I don't think it has anything to do with the tea leaves. I think something happens to *you*. Cecilia and I were talking about it at the party, when you were outside. Something happens to you, and it seems like you *know* things."

"I *know* things," I echoed dumbly, though my heart was beginning to race. I was supposed to be the "diviner," and Matt and Cecilia the "seekers." And yet they'd both picked up on something I hadn't been willing to acknowledge myself.

"Yes," Matt said. "You do."

If I gave in and did a reading for him, maybe I could avoid finishing this conversation. I picked up G. Clara's teakettle.

"Let's get this over with, then," I said, filling the kettle under the tap and then setting it on the back burner. "What's the point of this reading going to be? Deciding whether you should trust this mysterious email writer? Trying to figure out who, specifically, it is?"

Matt shrugged, putting his phone back in his pocket. "We'll just see what comes up."

"I'm doing this reading for you on one condition," I told him.

"Which is?"

"You forward me those emails."

"Why?" Matt asked.

"I want to study them a little closer," I lied. "Don't you think it will help me to . . . *know* things?"

Matt considered this.

"And as a show of good faith," I added. "Do you want the reading or not? I never ask for anything in return. You can do this small thing, right?"

To my surprise, Matt shrugged and took out his phone. "What's the address?"

I gave it to him.

"Doing it now," he said, tapping it. "And done." He showed me his phone. "There's my Sent file, see?"

I nodded. He gave me a "so there" kind of smile, and we both turned to the teakettle, which wasn't yet boiling. I took cups out of the overhead cabinet in one quick and careful motion. The quicker I did it, the less chance moths would fly out. Less chance a panicked daddy longlegs would dance into view.

While I rinsed the cups, Matt said, "I like this kitchen. It's cozy. You can imagine people sitting around the table with their coffee on a Saturday. Like, a few generations, around this table."

"I guess," I said. "Carson says hanging out at my house makes him feel closer to the earth."

"That guy's an asshat," Matt said.

I turned off the faucet. "He's also my best friend."

"Then he shouldn't say that stuff to you."

"He's allowed," I said. "Because his house used to be the same way."

Carson's family owned the biggest house on Maple Street— a giant Victorian with a little tower in the front. It was even creepier than ours before his family moved in and remodeled the place at great cost. He always said he missed the way it was when he first saw it.

I could hear the kettle begin to rumble against the heat of the electric burner. Good. Soon the water would boil, and we'd have something else to talk about.

After I'd poured the tea and we'd let it sit for a couple of minutes, I rustled around in the packages on the counter, looking for something to serve with it that wasn't stale. Behind me, Matt gulped from his cup.

"Done," he said, earlier than I expected, and flipped his cup over.

As I sat down, I thought I heard a noise in the dining room.

"Noah?" I said. I stepped into the dining room, but there was no one there.

"Did you hear that, Matt?" I said.

Matt shook his head. "I think you were hearing me turn my cup."

I nodded as I sat at the table with him. He tapped his cup three times.

"Why do we do that, anyway?" he asked. "Tap the teacup?"

"Two reasons," I said. "To let any last loose leaves fall out or fall into place. The more superstitious reason is that it's like knocking on a door. Like, 'Spirit of the cup, can I come in?'"

Matt glanced at his cup skeptically.

"Never mind," I said, grabbing the cup from his hand. "Just give me the stupid cup. *You* asked."

I looked at the leaves. "Umm . . . I see birds."

"And what do birds mean?"

"Depends. Like, a hawk is danger. A parrot is gossip. A stork is probably a baby on the way."

"Get that stork one out of your head, Marnie Wells. What kind of birds do you see?"

I took a deep breath. When I wasn't really concentrating, most tea leaves looked like birds to me. So I closed my eyes for a moment. When I opened them, I focused on a big clumped mass of leaves at the bottom of the cup.

"Great big blob at the bottom," I told Matt. "Maybe a big,

dark cloud, I don't know. But around the sides, some more delicate images. I'm going to focus on those, for now."

"Okay. Go for it."

Finally, an image came into focus.

"I see a horse," I said.

"A horse," Matt repeated. "What does that usually mean?"

"Usually it means strength, but . . ." I held the cup closer to me face. "This maybe isn't a real horse. I think it's like a merry-go-round horse."

"How do you tell the difference?"

"Because it's got a pole sticking out of its back . . . see?"

I pointed into the cup, showing Matt where I meant.

"Huh," Matt said. "A merry-go-round."

We were both quiet for a moment.

"A carnival?" I said. "Maybe what I'm supposed to be telling you is that this thing with the messages you've been getting is, like, a carnival. A fun house or a house of mirrors. Someone messing with your mind."

Matt gave me a bored look. "You're going to read any symbol that way. Because that's all *you* want to think about it."

I stared at the merry-go-round horse again, determined to come up with some other interpretation, just to prove him wrong.

"You ever go to Forest Wonderland when you were a kid?" I asked, blurting out the first thing that came to my head.

Forest Wonderland was an amusement park in the next-door town of Mixville. It had closed down when I was about ten, but parts of it were still standing, the land basically abandoned. Apparently no one had bought the property or wanted to turn it into anything else. I'd heard that its rickety old roller coaster was still there. It was called the Mindbender, and it was legendary back when the park was open—not for how fun it was, but for how dangerous it seemed due to its age. I remembered G. Clara calling it the Spinebender, because it was just a matter of time before it collapsed and everyone on it broke their necks.

Forest Wonderland was also the first place I'd ever been on a merry-go-round.

So maybe this interpretation of the leaves was more about me than Matt. I glanced at Matt to see his reaction. He'd pulled his hands into fists and buried them in his lap. He seemed to be avoiding my gaze.

"Did you ever?" I said. "You know, it has a little trolley for kids, around the back of the park. The tracks went into the woods a little bit."

"Once," he answered. "I went once. Not as a little kid. Recently."

"It's pretty creepy now," I said. "That's what I hear, anyway."

"I know," Matt said. "We went there on Halloween last year, right after I got my license. Andrea and me and a few other kids. It was Andrea's idea."

"Why?" I asked.

"Just a scary place to go." Matt paused. "But the rumor is that drug dealers hang out there."

That sounded like a Colesbury urban legend to me: drug dealers skulking around an abandoned fun park. "But what would drug dealers do there, exactly? Sell to the ghosts of carnies past? Dare each other to climb the old haunted roller coaster? Sell each other dime bags at the old ring-toss booth?"

Matt stood up and stuck his hands in his pockets. "I don't know, Marnie. It's a place to go where you won't be *seen*, anyway. And if Andrea . . ." He didn't finish the thought.

He started to pace around our kitchen.

"You need a bathroom or something?" I asked.

"No, no," he muttered, opening our fridge.

"You hungry?" I said, surprised. I'm not exactly an etiquette expert, but I would never open someone else's fridge. "Is there something you're not telling me?"

"No. I just have a feeling you're right." Matt's voice was low now. "It's a place she knew. Maybe she went there again for some reason, and something happened. Or maybe she went with Jimmy. Or that Sullivan guy."

"And that mystery emailer is writing to you for what reason, Matt?"

He was quiet. And in the quiet, I thought I heard a floor-board creak in the living room. Matt didn't seem to notice.

"I'm going there," he said. "I'm going there right now."

"Where?" I asked.

I already knew the answer.

"Forest Wonderland."

"What do you think—?" I stopped, hearing the tremor in my voice. I tried again, attempting to steady it. "What do you think you're gonna find there?"

"Don't you believe in the power of your own reading, Marnie?"

I sucked in a breath. I realized that I *did*. More than ever. Which made the idea of going to Forest Wonderland ourselves more scary than ridiculous. Even though I'd been trying to play it differently.

"Show the police the note," I said softly. "Tell them you think it means there's something near the trolley at Forest Wonderland. Tell them you think that's what the tracks thing is in the note."

"Based on what, Marnie?" Matt stood up and put on his jacket. "Based on tea leaves? Yeah. Let's waltz into the police department and tell them that. Are you going with me or not?"

I stood up, wishing I could physically stop Matt.

I picked up the teacup and stared into it, turning it every which way, hoping I could see something else besides a carousel horse. But there wasn't much aside from that dark, thick mass of leaves.

"You can't take it back," Matt said. "I know that's what you saw. So are you coming with me, or no?"

"What're you gonna do, man?" I practically shouted. "Bring a shovel and start digging?"

When I said that, Matt turned white. I gulped. I'd forgotten for a moment that this was his best friend we were talking about.

"Matt," I said, trying not to plead now. "Listen. I know how hard—"

"I'll call you later," Matt said.

"Wait," I called. "I'm going with you."

CHAPTER 20

All of the Forest Wonderland parking lots were blocked off with cement barriers, but it was possible to get pretty far down the main driveway. The chain blocking the main entrance was broken. Matt parked a few yards from the front ticket kiosk and we went in together.

The first game booths and refreshment stands were boarded up. A couple of them had been spray-painted with names in multicolored letters. The graffiti was big and brash, far more ostentatious than my brother's minimalistic efforts. By comparison, Noah's vandalism looked desperate. Or not like vandalism at all.

"Wow." I sighed. "Just being here kinda makes me want to eat a big piece of greasy fried dough."

"Never had it," Matt said, walking fast by the Mindbender.

"I pity you," I said, genuinely meaning it.

"So you came here as a kid?" Matt asked.

"Yeah. My grandmother took us here a few times when I was little. I think I was five or six, the first time."

"I think by then—I mean, by the time we were that age—it was already pretty sketch," Matt pointed out.

"*Sketch* doesn't bother my grandmother," I said. "Have you seen her house?"

I stopped to stare up at the roller coaster. The wood was gray-brown. There were some loose pieces hanging down, with a jagged appearance. For a moment, those seemed closer to me than the other parts of the coaster. *Broken old bones.*

I shook off the thought, figuring the words had come to me because of G. Clara's old "Spinebender" joke.

Matt turned around and waited for me to catch up, looking impatient.

"People wouldn't notice about your house so much if you didn't talk about it all the time," he said.

"But you're saying that they *do* notice?" I asked, with a sinking feeling. Why did I ask questions to which I didn't really want to know the answer?

Matt sighed, walking faster. "You're missing the point. Nobody gives a shit, really. Except you."

"Let's not talk about it, then," I snapped.

We walked toward the middle of the park. I assumed Matt knew that the trolley was along the wooded part at the very back.

"Was it fun?" Matt asked.

"What?"

"Riding the trolley. When you were little."

"Of course it was. I was five or six. At that age you don't care if things are dirty or corny or whatever. If you're too little to have heard of Disney World or Six Flags, a place like this is awesome."

We were approaching a dirt circle in the pavement.

"What do you think that is?" Matt asked.

"Clearly that's where the drug dealers worship their devil," I said. "Don't you see that faint pentagram inscribed there?"

Matt slowed his pace. *"What?"*

"Kidding," I said. "I think it's where the carousel used to be."

Matt turned red.

"Sorry," I said, although I wasn't really. I was still a little annoyed at him for calling Carson an asshat. It was probably kind of true, but he was *my* asshat, so I should be the only one allowed to point it out.

After that, we didn't speak again till we reached the trolley tracks.

"I can just see the young Marnie here," Matt said, "chomping on pink cotton candy, waiting for her big trolley ride."

Matt put his hand on my shoulder. I felt a jolt travel up my arm as I remembered how he'd looked at me in the park the other day. That day I'd been distracted by his hamburger breath. Now I wasn't. I could hear us both breathing into the cold autumn air.

"I actually hate cotton candy," I said. "It feels like you're eating a sweaty old clown's wig."

I didn't know why I said that. Matt let go of my shoulder, now staring into the trees beyond the pond and trolley tracks. We stood there in silence.

I THOUGHT OF THE time Jimmy came here with Noah and G. Clara and me. Not the first time we came, but sometime after that. I know that G. Clara generally thought Jimmy was a pain in the ass, but she always let him do stuff with us because in her words, "He at least *tries* to be good." I remembered Jimmy and Noah begging to go on the Mindbender even though all of us were still too small.

And I remembered Jimmy and me sitting on a picnic table under the pavilion. We'd both gotten hot dogs, but Noah had wanted pizza. G. Clara had parked us together at the closest table she could find to the pizza stand, and told us, as she always did if she had to leave us alone for a moment, "If anyone grabs you, scream and stick your fingers in their eyes, or kick them between the legs."

Jimmy found these instructions hilarious, and laughed with his mouth full of hot dog and bun.

"I can see your food," I informed him, before taking a dainty bite of my own hot dog.

Jimmy turned to me. He looked like he was considering apologizing. Instead, he grinned and said, "Are you trying to tell me you can see my wiener?"

He opened his mouth as wide as he could, and said, "Aaaahhh! Oh no! You can see my wiener, can't you? Aaaaahh!"

I tried not to giggle but did in spite of myself. And then Jimmy laughed so hard at his own joke that he tipped right off the end of the bench and his hot dog fell under the table. The bun stayed put but the hot dog kept rolling, finally coming to rest at the foot of a teenage girl at the table next to ours. Jimmy's face fell. I tore my hot dog in half and gave him the smaller part. He took it in silent surprise.

When G. Clara and Noah returned, I said, "One of the hot dogs fell off the table. Can we get another one?"

"How did it fall off the table?" G. Clara asked.

"I don't know," I said.

G. Clara sighed. "Let me have a minute to eat my pizza," she said. "And I'll go get another one."

Funny that G. Clara thought that Jimmy "tried to be good." I was probably too little to notice that about him. It had never seemed to me that he tried terribly hard. I had, truth be told, sort of liked that about him.

"BEHIND THE TRACKS," MATT murmured, bringing me back to the present. "Are you coming with me?"

"I guess so," I said.

Matt led me around the side of the tracks, past the trolley's little bridge, and into the thick trees behind it.

"'Behind the tracks,'" he repeated. "There's a lot of 'behind the tracks' here. These woods probably span out at least a mile or two."

"Probably," I said, hoping this meant Matt was considering abandoning this search mission.

No luck. He kicked the newly fallen leaves as he went. *Shush-shush-shush.* Normally I liked the sound of leaves underfoot, but something about Matt's movements made it feel more frantic than anything. He took long strides on those varsity-basketball legs, leaving me to scurry behind him, growing winded. Soon I was several paces behind him.

The trees were sparser farther in, as were the leaves. Matt

could go faster. I stopped to catch my breath. Something about this spot—not a clearing, exactly, but a spare spot where maybe a walking path had once been—felt familiar.

"You coming?" Matt was calling behind him.

He already seemed so far away. I looked around. The fox. The fox dream. It was in a spot like this one.

"Marnie," Matt called.

Woods look like woods. Any spot in any woods would look vaguely like this one, right? How much variation is there in New England woods, really? Probably my brain *wanted* to see my dream here, for its own sick and twisted reasons. Brains are like that.

I looked up. Far above my head, an arching tree branch met the branches of the tree beside it, tangling in a formation that looked like a birdcage. A chill ran up my back. I forced my gaze back down to the ground, trying to ignore the sensation.

Just as I began to put one foot in front of another, something under a maple tree caught my eye. It was silvery and mashed into the ground near a raised tree root. I bent down to work it out from the moist dirt. It took only a moment to get it free.

I stared down at the thin silver bracelet. It had a broken clasp and a round charm the size of a nickel. Wiping dirt away from its surface, I saw an engraving of two fish jumping in opposite directions, tail to nose, to form a sort of circular symbol together. Beneath the lower fish was the word *Pisces* in tiny letters. This was a zodiac bracelet just like Phoenix's.

With my heart hammering, I shoved it in my jacket pocket.

I ran to catch up halfway with Matt, calling his name.

He didn't answer—he was too far away. I kept running toward him.

"Matt!"

"Yeah?" he said, finally turning around.

I froze, stopping just short of catching up with him. The bracelet was cold against my hand in my pocket. I realized that I couldn't bear to show it to him. Not yet.

"When was Andrea's birthday?" I asked, trying to keep my voice steady.

I didn't know all of my astrology signs. But since Noah's birthday was February 27, I knew Pisces birthdays were around then.

Matt gazed at me, his brow furrowed just slightly. I clutched the bracelet hard inside my pocket.

"March third," Matt said. "Why?"

My pulse raced, but I tried to keep my face from showing any reaction. *This was Andrea's bracelet.*

"I was just wondering . . . who was older. You or her?"

"My birthday's in January. So I'm a little older. Not enough to matter, of course." He kept walking.

I tightened my fingers around the bracelet so much that it hurt. He could not see it. He *could not* see it. "I think we should get out of here."

"Why?"

"We're not going to find anything, and you're only going to upset yourself."

He shrugged. "If you don't want to be here, you don't have to stay." A twig snapped as he stopped and turned around again. "Are you scared? Is that what you're saying?"

"No. Not at all."

"Could've fooled me. Suddenly you seem kinda jittery. Look, I don't mind if you go home. I don't mind doing this on my own."

"How am I supposed to get home?" I hated whining, but I was willing to try anything to get Matt out of here. What if he *did* find something? Something much worse than a bracelet?

"Can you call your brother?" he asked. "Or your grand-mother?"

I stared at him.

He sighed and walked toward me. "How about I give you my keys? You can wait in the car."

"In that creepy old parking lot?" I said. My voice was growing shrill. "I have a very, very bad feeling about this place."

"Good!" Matt began kicking the leaves furiously again. "Then that means we're getting somewhere."

"No, Matt . . ." My voice dropped to almost a whisper, and I knew he couldn't hear me anymore. "It doesn't." I turned and ran toward the parking lot.

I took out my phone before I was even out of the trees.

"Carson," I said softly, when he answered. "I need you to pick me up. And I need you to take me to the Colesbury police station."

CARSON DIDN'T COME INSIDE the station with me. I told him he didn't need to, and that it probably wouldn't be a good idea for him to be involved. I wasn't entirely surprised when he stopped arguing and just left me at the front steps of the station. He probably had too much homework to make an issue of it.

As soon as I started talking to the cop at the front desk about Andrea's and Matt's emails, he brought me to Officer O'Reilly.

I recognized him, a paunchy, middle-aged white guy, always in uniform. He was what they called the "Youth Officer." He came to the school for assemblies about school bus safety and "Don't Do Drugs" sort of stuff. Or if somebody tried to punch a teacher or whatever. Kids sometimes called him Officer Oily. I'm not sure why. My best guess was because he smelled so pungently of aftershave.

He seemed to know all about Matt and his first email from "Andrea" over the summer.

"You're saying he's been getting more?" Officer O'Reilly said gruffly. "And why hasn't he come to us himself, then?"

"He says you wouldn't do anything."

"We asked him to let us know if he got any more."

I shrugged. "I didn't know that." Then I pulled out my phone and showed Officer O'Reilly the one that mentioned the body and the tracks. He didn't seem surprised.

"If you kids bait this person, they're gonna escalate things," he said as I shoved my phone back in my pocket. "Make it even more upsetting."

"Well, it worked. And now Matt's wandering around the

woods behind Forest Wonderland, looking to find God knows what behind the trolley tracks."

"Why Forest Wonderland? How did you make the jump from tracks to *those* tracks?"

"Umm . . ." I knew this was where I had to be extra careful. "Because Andrea used to hang out there. Sometimes. With friends. More than anywhere else that had . . . tracks."

Officer O'Reilly considered this, rubbing his scratchy chin. "I see."

"I'm worried about Matt there by himself," I said. "Do you think you could go get him?"

The officer regarded me with kind but pitying eyes. *Oh, the naïve, sheltered children of Colesbury,* he was probably thinking. He probably thought that a few dozen times a day.

"Marnie," he said. "Now, help me understand why you're worried about him? I understand that the Wonderland isn't the *safest* place to hang out, but . . . maybe we ought to contact his parents and have them either call his cell phone to check on him, or pick him up?"

"I'm not worried about his safety, exactly," I explained.

"Then what are you worried about?"

"I'm worried that he'll find something," I whispered. I felt the bracelet with my fingertips. I knew that I should give it to him, that it might convince him of the seriousness of what I was saying. But my thumb and forefinger tightened around it, unwilling to part with it, unwilling, for some reason, to entrust it to Officer O'Reilly.

"Speak up, Marnie," he was saying.

I was about to repeat myself—*I'm afraid that he'll find something*—but then I realized I was taking the wrong approach. Nothing about what I was feeling could be explained in terms that Officer O'Reilly would understand. He wasn't trained to respond to hysterical teenagers freaking out over hoax emails, or acting on wild hunches. There *were*, however, certain circumstances for which he would feel responsible.

"Please," I said. "I'm worried he'll do something."

"Something?"

"I'm worried he'll hurt himself," I said. I hated myself for having to lie, but I was panicking. I was afraid it was already too late. "The emails he's been getting . . . they've been making him feel responsible. Depressed. I'm worried about him alone there in those woods."

Officer O'Reilly straightened up in his chair. Now he was listening. "Does he have anything with him that he could use to hurt himself? A weapon? Drugs?"

"I don't know," I said softly. "I just know someone needs to do something."

CHAPTER 21

I sat in the back of the cruiser while Officer O'Reilly and Officer Marksman—a nice older lady with tight, dark curls and a noisy little piece of gum in her mouth—chatted softly in the front. Mostly they talked about antioxidants as we drove.

"I'm pretty sure blueberries are as good as it gets."

"Dark chocolate. I eat a ton of dark chocolate."

"Are you eating a really dark one, though? That's the thing. Most people don't eat a high-enough percentage one. Percentage of cocoa, I mean."

I stared out the window and tried not to let their conversation give me a stomachache. Outside it was starting to drizzle a little. Finally we reached the Forest Wonderland driveway. Officer O'Reilly parked just behind Matt's VW.

"You're going to stay here with Officer Marksman," he said to me, and then got out.

"Oh," I said. Now I realized why she had come along: to babysit me and make sure I stayed put.

He disappeared behind the front kiosks, heading in the direction of the trolley tracks.

Officer Marksman and I sat quietly for several minutes, until she finally turned around and said to me, "This Matt your boyfriend, honey?"

"No," I said.

"Oh. Just a friend?"

"Yeah. We haven't been friends long." I realized this didn't sound quite right, and added, "Just this school year. We have some of the same friends, though."

Officer Marksman nodded and turned to face the front windshield again. She sighed, and blew her nose. Then she asked into the rearview mirror, "You got a favorite subject in school?"

Did I have a favorite subject? *Divination? Devilry?*

It was getting darker now. Would Officer O'Reilly have trouble finding Matt? How deep into the woods had he gone? Or could he have circled back to the area where I'd found the bracelet?

The pavement outside of the car was starting to spot with rain.

"Uh, French, I guess."

"French? That's interesting. Are you good at languages?"

"I try to be. I want to get a job that will have a lot of travel. I just don't know what kind of job yet. When I get to college and have more options, I want to study another language. Arabic, maybe."

I'd surprised myself by saying this, because I hadn't told anyone else about this possibility besides Carson. I was reluctant to tell G. Clara how deeply I wished—planned—to travel far, *far* away.

"Arabic," Officer Marksman repeated, then scrunched up her eyebrows. "Where are you going to go with that?"

"Somewhere," I said absently. *Somewhere not much like here.* More spots on the ground. My eyes focused on a constellation of them. They seemed to form a circle. A fully formed circle. According to *Cosmos in a Cup,* a circle meant the end of a cycle and the start of another: no going back. Why hadn't I thought of that when I'd told Payson Long his teacup had a doughnut in it? *No going back* at least had an ominous respectability to it.

I shut my eyes.

"What about Chinese?" Officer Marksman was saying. "Have you thought of studying Chinese? I bet there's a lot of demand for that, these days."

"What?" I murmured. When I opened my eyes, the circle was gone as quickly as it had appeared—now that the rain was falling harder, filling in all of the spaces between the spots that had formed it.

"I was saying . . ." Officer Marksman trailed off, staring through the front windshield.

I saw what she was looking at. There was movement in the main thoroughfare of the park. Two figures were coming toward us: Officer O'Reilly and Matt. As they came closer I could see that Matt wasn't really walking willingly. Officer O'Reilly was holding him against his shoulder, pulling him along.

Matt was shambling, resisting. Like he was confused about the direction he was supposed to be heading. He kept pulling away from O'Reilly and trying to walk back to where they'd come from. And he was screaming, *"Andrea! Andrea! Andrea!"*

Matt's eyes, usually so sleepy, were open wider than I'd ever seen them. Painfully and grotesquely wide. I had to look away for a moment.

"Jesus," I heard Officer Marksman whisper.

Matt collapsed, and his screams stopped sounding like a name or even a word.

"Stay here, honey," said Marksman sharply, and opened her car door.

As she rose, O'Reilly said, "Call Dispatch. Have Brian send Forensics and backup from the Mixville PD. Stay with the girl till they get here. Do you have your water bottle?"

Marksman slipped back into the car and didn't say a word to me, grabbing a Nalgene bottle from the cup holder. After she handed it to O'Reilly, she slammed the door. We both watched as O'Reilly led Matt to a patch of dry grass beneath a maple tree and had him put his head between his knees.

When Matt finally lifted his head, O'Reilly handed him the bottle of water.

Matt pushed the water away, spilling it onto the grass. His screaming had faded to gasps, and I felt guilty for my sigh of relief. Because I knew what the word *forensics* meant. I knew it from all of G. Clara's cop and CSI shows. I knew that Matt had seen something horrifying in those woods.

CHAPTER 22

Officer Marksman drove me home as soon as Officer O'Reilly's backup arrived. She told G. Clara—standing stunned on the doorstep in the rain—that a friend of mine had found some skeletal remains while hanging out in the woods in Mixville, and that I should stay home and avoid talking to anyone about what had just happened.

"We'll probably know a lot more by tomorrow," she said. "Another officer will come and talk to you, I'm sure."

G. Clara served Noah and me spaghetti with jarred sauce and didn't say another word about it. None of us ate much, and Noah and I both retreated to our rooms after we put our dishes in the dishwasher.

If the police were trying to keep the whole thing a secret, they didn't do a very good job. When I opened up my computer, there was a message from Carson, all caps:

DID YOU HEAR ABOUT THE BONES? DID YOU KNOW WHEN YOU HAD ME DROP YOU OFF?

I wrote back: *No. Not then. Where did you hear about this?*

Carson: *Everyone's talking about it. On FB and elsewhere. I think Sid Pulnik's dad heard it on the dispatch, or something. Bones they think could be Andrea's.*

All I could think to write back was, *Yeah.*

Carson: *Matt found them?*

Me: *I think so.*

Carson: *Jesus. Isn't that a little suspect?*

Me: *You don't know the whole story. He was getting these weird notes. And the one he got today told him to look there.*

I didn't want to write anymore. If Carson were here with me, I might feel less alone. But typing back and forth only made me feel more so. I wondered where Matt was now and how he was feeling. Was he still at the police station?

Carson: *You there?*

Me: *Have to go. Feeling sick. Going to lie down.*

I shut my laptop and picked up my jacket, which I'd thrown on the bed earlier. I fished out the Pisces bracelet.

My heart thudded hard as I stared at it. I should've given this to the police. But something had stopped me. A sense that it was mine for now. That I was supposed to have it. I opened the lower cabinet of my desk, the one that held a bunch of mildewed old puppets I couldn't bear to throw away. Several of them had been birthday gifts from my mother when I was small. I picked up my favorite pink pig puppet and shoved the bracelet inside it.

Then I crawled onto my bed. I stared into the darkness for a long time. And then things got a bit fuzzy. The dark turned to white.

Snow.

Again in the snow. I was tired from walking so far in the heavy snow—now deeper than a foot. So much snow I couldn't see anything around me. When I tried to look up and open my eyes, the sharp sleet blinded me. So I kept my eyes closed. Scared. Where could I go with my eyes closed?

I looked down, since that was easier than looking up or ahead. And there, in the snow, was the same blood spot I'd seen beneath the fox so long ago. He'd led me in a circle and we were back where we had started.

I heard a scream, and it scared me.

I heard it again, and realized it was not the sound of a person. It was a barking sort of scream. A fox's bark.

I forced myself to move in the direction of the fox's plea.
I hear you, I whispered, pushing my legs through the cold.
Please don't make me go in that circle again. I hear you.

"MARNIE?"

"Mmm?"

"Do you hear me?"

"Yes. I said I hear you."

"Then open the door, please," G. Clara said.

I picked up my phone and looked at the time. It was just past 10 P.M. I'd slept a couple of hours.

"Come on in," I said.

When G. Clara opened the door, she was still wearing her teacher clothes: long denim skirt and cheerful purple sweater set, both rumpled from apparently falling asleep on the couch. "Did you hear the knocking at the door?"

"Huh?"

G. Clara ruffled the back of my hair to wake me up. "Someone's here for you. Your friend. Matt."

I jumped off my bed.

"I'm surprised his parents let him go out tonight," G. Clara whispered. "Especially at this hour. Now, when did you start spending time with this fellow?"

"It's a recent thing," I said, trying to slide past G. Clara and through my bedroom doorway.

"Do you think his family knows he's out like this tonight? Do you think maybe he ought to be with his family?"

"I'll find out," I said. "If you'll let me go downstairs."

G. Clara took me gently by the arm. "Marnie," she said sharply.

"Yeah?"

"You have to be careful with that kid."

"Aren't I always careful?"

G. Clara leaned against my doorframe with her arms wrapped loosely across her middle. Her head rested against the dark wood of the doorframe as if she was too tired to hold it up.

"Usually. But this might require a different kind of careful than you're used to. That's all."

"I get that," I said.

She smiled weakly, then pulled her hair out of her clip. It fell to her shoulders, a cascade of white. I remembered how beautiful I thought her gray hair was when I was little—how I thought she looked like a fairy.

"Do you think my hair will all turn so white so early, like yours?" I asked.

"Your mother's hasn't," G. Clara said. "But then, your mother didn't have a daughter like mine."

"What?"

"I'm saying your mother turned my hair white."

"Maybe I'd have turned hers white, too, if she'd given me a chance."

"I doubt that," G. Clara said. "You ought to get downstairs now. I'm not sure what you can do for the poor kid, but some company would probably help."

Matt was sitting on our old velour sofa, staring at the television. When I saw that one of G. Clara's forensics shows was on, I quickly steered him to the front door.

"We're going out for a little air," I called to G. Clara.

It wasn't until we were down the front steps that I realized I'd forgotten my jacket. It had stopped raining, but the air was chilly and damp.

When we reached the front lawn, we stood a couple of feet from each other in silence. I knew I should be the first to speak but couldn't think what to say.

"You were in that police car?" Matt asked hoarsely. "When Oily pulled me out of the park?"

"Yeah," I admitted.

"I'm glad," Matt said.

"Glad?"

"I don't need to pretend, I mean. I don't need to pretend I'm fine."

"Who would expect that?"

"I don't know. Maybe that was the wrong thing to say. You're the only one I could come to who doesn't need to hear the story."

"I'm so sorry, Matt."

I couldn't see his eyes very well in the dark.

"Yeah," he whispered, after a while.

I led him to the single concrete step under the door of our toolshed. "Do your parents know you're here?"

Matt shook his head. "I told them I really wanted to be with my friends right now. But I think they'd assume that meant Payson and Phoenix."

I nodded and motioned for him to sit down on the step.

"Aren't you cold out here?" Matt asked. "Do you want to go inside for a jacket?"

"I'm okay," I said.

Matt turned on his phone. "Everybody's been texting me, but I haven't answered yet. I don't feel like it right now."

"You will when you're ready. You're probably in shock."

"Am I?" Matt said vaguely. "Phoenix says, 'Can't stop crying. Call me. Please.'" He spoke in a monotone.

I didn't know what to say.

"And Payson: 'What the fuck happened? I don't want to believe the rumors. Call if you can.' And then Cecilia: 'So sorry, Matt.' Everyone thinks she's clueless, but turns out she's the only one with the sense not to demand a phone call."

"They're all probably as shocked as you," I offered. "You're the only one who has more information than they do."

"Information," he muttered, and I felt like an idiot.

Instead of turning off his phone, he aimed the light toward the side of the shed, illuminating Noah's spray-paint art. "I meant to ask you about this. Was someone mad at your grandma or something?"

"No. My brother did it," I admitted. I got the feeling Matt was desperate to talk about anything other than what he'd been through. "Right before his overdose. He said that he saw it in a dream, or something like that."

"What does that mean?"

I let out a sad little laugh. "You know what? I don't ask him a lot of questions. I just wish he'd repaint the shed."

"You could do it. I could help you."

"No, G. Clara wants him to do it. When he's ready."

"Oh. That makes sense, I guess."

Matt shut off his phone. We sat silently for a couple of minutes. I was starting to notice the cold a little more now. I was struggling to keep my teeth from chattering, and I wanted to tell him I needed to go inside soon, at least for another layer of clothing. But it seemed a terrible time to leave someone alone in the dark. While I considered this, I heard Matt sniffle once, and then let out a low wail. It frightened me before I realized he was crying.

I reached out in the dark and touched his foot. This felt like a "careful" thing to do. I wasn't sure if G. Clara would agree, but all I could do was try.

I don't know how long he cried. My toes and fingers were frozen by the time he was able to sit up straight.

"You should come inside," I said, shivering.

"Your grandmother will make me go home," Matt said, his voice hoarse. "And I don't want to go home yet."

"She won't, though," I assured him. "She's probably dozed off, anyway."

He unzipped his jacket and thrust it into my arms.

"Don't," I said. "You need it."

"We'll take turns with it." Before I could protest, he draped it over me. His hands remained on my shoulders, and he leaned close to my face until his cheek—wet and clammy from his crying—touched mine. It was a strange sensation, to feel another person's tears on my skin. Before I could recover from it, his lips were on mine. While we kissed, a chilly feeling crept up my chest. I wasn't sure if it was a sort of thrill or a sort of dread. Maybe a little of each.

What was happening? Why were we doing this? Why was I letting it happen?

It wouldn't be happening if he hadn't found Andrea today. Did I want it to happen at all?

Think twice about what you are doing. And do not trust a word Matt Cotrell says.

Matt's hands fell from me, as if he sensed my hesitation. Or maybe he had some himself.

"I don't know if this is going to make you feel any better," I said.

"I wasn't thinking of it that way," he murmured.

"I just mean—"

"You're right. I'm sorry. I actually wasn't thinking at all. I haven't had a clear thought since Forest Wonderland." He turned away.

"I feel like this night is going to last forever. And not in a good way. Not in a magical way. The opposite of magic."

I hesitated. I considered what Matt might need instead of a kiss.

"Do you want to tell me what you saw there?" I asked finally. I really didn't want to hear what he saw. But maybe he needed to tell someone. Someone besides Officer O'Reilly.

"Two bones," Matt whispered. I expected him to say more, but he didn't.

He shivered. I stood up and dropped his jacket back over his shoulders. He sat still. He didn't protest, and didn't even seem to notice. His phone lit up briefly.

"My mother's left another voice message," he mumbled. He turned it toward the shed, staring once more at the painting.

"You really can come in if you want," I said.

Matt shook his head. "I should get back home."

CHAPTER 23

October 16

I woke up early and dragged myself to the living room. G. Clara was sitting on the couch, watching TV while she drank her coffee and ate her usual wheat toast with apricot preserves.

"When did that kid go home?" she asked, eyes on the screen. "I checked when I got up to go to bed, and he was gone."

"He was here about an hour," I said.

"He seem okay to you?" G. Clara wanted to know.

"Not really," I admitted. "But well enough to get home, I thought."

G. Clara nodded. The show had cut to a commercial for pot pies. A baseball-capped little boy was bleating, "What's for dinner, Mom?"

"Make it yourself, you little shit," G. Clara mumbled, then took a bite of toast.

After the commercials, a big blue "Channel 14" graphic flew on the screen to the sound of the familiar, frantic stringed theme music of the local news. The next shot was of a pretty lady with perfect makeup and hair. She had on an ugly orange blouse and a grave expression.

"At the top of this hour," she said, "more information coming out about that body that was found at the site of the former Forest Wonderland in Mixville."

G. Clara glanced at me warily but kept the TV on.

"Investigators believe it was the body of young man from Colesbury," the anchorwoman continued.

G. Clara's hands twitched, knocking half of her toast to the floor. Surely she was thinking the same thing as me.

Don't you mean young woman?

"We're going to begin our coverage with Cheryl Stimson, who has been at the scene since the earliest hours of this morning. Thank you for joining us, Cheryl."

"Hello, Alison. Yes, grim news from Mixville this morning, although not the news we were expecting. Some skeletal remains were found yesterday afternoon, and we're told there was reason to believe that it was Andrea Quinley, the Colesbury girl who disappeared early last spring. Police worked through the late hours of the night to gather all of the remains that were found in the woods of Mixville. Some were partially buried, but some were scattered by animals. It's an ongoing investigation, but police believe the body to be that of James Harmon, a nineteen-year-old male, also from Colesbury."

G. Clara gasped and grabbed my arm. I put my hand over hers.

"His family *has* been notified," said the reporter, "and they're working with police this morning. Because of the state of the body, a DNA test will be needed to confirm the identity, but all parties here do believe this is a correct identification, based on some evidence at the scene."

The news moved on to a story about a traffic accident. G. Clara dug in the couch cushions for the remote and turned off the television.

"Jimmy. Oh my God," she whispered. "That boy. Oh, my God. I wonder what he got himself into? Drug overdose?"

All I could do was shake my head.

"Where's your brother?" G. Clara demanded.

"Still sleeping," I said.

"I'll tell him," she said. "You go have some breakfast."

I cleaned up the overturned apricot toast and brought it to the kitchen. I took the apricot jam out of the fridge to prepare another piece of wheat toast for G. Clara. If she felt anything like I did, she probably wouldn't feel like eating after the news. But it seemed like a nice gesture. I hesitated before opening the bread box, remembering that this was one of Jimmy's favorite hiding places. Those pranks, when he'd steal and relocate our old toys and stuff. For a second, I had a half-crazy hope that I'd find an old stuffed animal of mine in there. I pulled the box open to find a third of a loaf of wheat bread and an old package of hot dog buns.

THE LAST TIME JIMMY hid one of my things, I must have been about eight. My mother had won me a stuffed monkey in a Denny's—from one of those machines where the claw comes down and grabs the toys. It was one of the last things she'd given to me. The monkey had unevenly sewn nostrils and was wearing a musty-smelling yellow dress.

"That thing probably lived in that Denny's for years before you adopted it," G. Clara would say. "It smells like a dishrag."

I didn't care. It was a gift from my mother. I named her Bonnie and slept with her for several months. One day, a year or so later, when Jimmy was over playing video games with Noah, I opened the microwave and there was Bonnie, her long monkey arms folded, a frilly toothpick sticking out of her mouth like a cigarette. And I burst into tears.

It was cold, but I ran outside. I ran to the shed. It wasn't any warmer, but I knew I could be alone there. I hid behind the rakes and the lawn mower. Eventually, I heard Noah and Jimmy outside, looking for me.

"Don't worry about it," Noah was saying. "She probably just went to her little friend Amy's house."

"Why don't you check there," I heard Jimmy say.

And then their voices fell silent. A couple minutes later, the shed door squeaked open.

Jimmy crept in. I could tell he saw me right away.

"You shouldn't have done that!" was all I could manage.

Jimmy poked Bonnie through the bars of the lawn mower, handing her to me.

"It was from my mother," I said through my tears.

"Yeah. Noah just told me."

"You wouldn'ta hid it if you knew?" I asked. I realized, while I was saying it, that I wasn't actually upset that he'd hid Bonnie. More upsetting was that he'd probably found her under a couch or something. That I'd stopped sleeping with her long ago and failed to notice.

"I don't know," Jimmy admitted. "I probably still would've. But I probably would've felt bad about it."

I sniffled. Jimmy reached through the lawn mower to wipe my cheeks with his dirty sweatshirt sleeve.

"Don't cry," he said, reaching out the other sleeve for my other cheek. "She's not lost."

"It doesn't matter," I whispered, turning my face away. "That's not why I was crying."

"Oh," he said. And then after a moment, "Then come back in."

"In a few minutes."

"It's too cold out here."

"Maybe for you," I said. "But not for me."

"Okay," he said, "Sorry. Sorry, I didn't know the monkey was, like, your special thing or whatever."

Now I closed the bread box and fumbled with the wheat bread. I put a piece in the toaster and watched the toaster coils turn red.

AT SCHOOL THAT DAY, I was careful to keep to myself and avoid everyone. When I got home, Noah was sitting on the couch in the silence of the living room—staring at the television that was usually on when he was in that spot. In his hands he held an unpopped bag of microwave popcorn.

"Noah?" I said softly.

"Yeah?" His voice and eyes were exhausted.

"Are you all right?"

He sighed but didn't reply.

"Did you go to school?" I asked, because it was any easy question.

"I went to one of my classes but I left. I didn't feel like sitting through the second class."

"I wish I could've skipped out on school today."

"Was everyone talking about Jimmy?"

I hesitated. A lot of the kids didn't remember Jimmy. He hadn't attended Colesbury High for a couple of years. The kids weren't talking so much about Jimmy's body being found. They were talking more about the fact that the body found wasn't Andrea's.

"Some kids," I offered. "Were you planning on making that popcorn?"

Noah looked down at the bag. "I thought I was hungry, but then realized I wasn't."

He set the bag on the couch and rubbed his eyes.

"Are *you* all right?" he asked.

I sank into G. Clara's tag-sale rocking chair. "Umm. Well, I'm really shocked. Like you are, I'm sure. But Noah, I didn't really *know* him, so it's maybe not the same for me as it is for you."

Noah sucked in his lips, looking like he was deciding whether or not to say something. After a moment, he murmured, "I didn't know him anymore, either. I hadn't known him for a long time."

I nodded. "But you *did* know him. You can't *un*know someone you knew when you were a kid."

He stared into his lap before lifting his gaze to meet mine. "But I'm not the one who knew where his body was," he said. "I'm not the one who saw it in a teacup."

I froze.

"Marnie," Noah said quietly, but didn't add anything.

"You were listening. Yesterday."

"Yes," he whispered.

"You shouldn't have been."

"No. I'm sorry. But I was."

"*Why* were you listening, Noah?"

"It's the first time you ever did one of those readings at home. At least, the first time when I was home, too."

"So?"

"And that kid seemed so . . . desperate. I was . . . suspicious."

I didn't reply. I didn't want to say anything about Matt right now.

"I wonder," Noah said slowly. "If you're good enough with those tea leaves to find Jimmy's body, I wonder if you could figure out what happened to him."

My stomach clenched. I felt sick. I began to rock in the chair. "The leaves didn't tell me where the body was. The email to Matt did, basically."

Noah shook his head. "I heard most of your reading. The email gave a clue. Your leaves told you what it meant."

"But we thought it was Andrea Quinley. And the leaves didn't tell us it was Jimmy."

"I think you're missing the point here, Marnie. The leaves obviously told you *something*. Something pretty significant."

I stopped rocking.

"Yes," I admitted, my voice unsteady. "They did."

"There's a reason he's come to us now," Noah said, standing. He crossed the room and stared at the greeting cards on the mantelpiece. G. Clara had put them there last Christmas, and no one had bothered to take them down. "There has to be."

"Come to us?" I repeated.

Noah paced back to the couch but didn't sit down. "He'd call me, you know. Last year. Jimmy would call me sometimes, even though we weren't supposed to be friends anymore."

"Call you for what?" I asked.

"Just, when he needed someone to talk to, I guess. He never suggested we hang out or anything. He'd just be like, 'Hey, what's up?' But you know what would bother me? You know why I usually wouldn't call back, like if he left a text or whatever? He'd call me when he was out of his mind on—I don't know. *Something*. I was never sure what. I never asked."

"Did you ever buy pot from him, Noah?" I asked. I'd been wondering.

"Once," Noah admitted. "But just once. It felt weird. It didn't feel like I should be encouraging him. I was supposed to be one of the people who had higher hopes for him than that."

"And did you?"

"Not really, no. But buying pot from him felt like I was coming right out and saying it."

"And you think that by the time he died, he was doing a lot more serious stuff than pot?"

Noah shrugged. "The way some of those phone calls were, I'd say yes."

"What does that mean?"

"Just that he wasn't making sense half the time. I was, like, leave your drug-addled gibberish on someone else's voice mail, man."

"You said that to him?"

"No. I just thought it. But the last time he did it, he left like four or five crazy messages on there over the course of about two hours. I was asleep the whole time, so I never picked up."

"Crazy how?" I asked.

Noah considered this question for a moment. He rolled his eyes back slightly as if trying to access the information in a specific part of his brain.

And then he collapsed on the couch, buried his face in his hands, and let out a sob.

"Noah . . . ?" I said, as gently as I could.

"I should've called him back," he said, palming tears out of his eyes. "I should've known he didn't have anyone else. Even if we weren't friends. I owed it to him to tell him to snap the fuck out of it, if no one else was willing."

"He had other people. He had his cousin."

Noah squinted at me. "I don't know what you heard about his cousin, but Jimmy told me that guy would throw him under the bus if his girlfriend told him to. And if his cousin was so great, why was it always *me* he called whenever his brain wasn't right? You should've heard him, the last time he called me."

"What did he say?"

"He said something like, 'Noah, I think you've gotta come get me. I don't think Santa Claus is coming, so I think you're gonna have to.' And something about how he's tired and he's going to need to rest. Like, 'If I could just get to my bed, just for tonight, I could figure out what I'm gonna do next.'"

"Santa Claus?" I repeated.

"He was fucked up. The next message was a bunch of weird insults. He was all like, 'Those snakes, those ungrateful douches, those meatloaves, those creepers!'"

"Meatloaves? Is that a thing? To call someone a meatloaf?"

Noah just shook his head. His chin began to quiver, but he took a deep breath and spoke again. "And then he kept saying he was trapped."

I waited for him to continue, feeling a cold sensation creeping up my arms.

"He was saying stuff like, 'I'm trapped in a sparkle-storm. I'm trapped in a fluffer-nutter. I'm trapped in a wedding cake. I'm trapped in a tightie whitie.' He said about twenty crazy things like that. And then the last call, like twenty minutes later, he was just kind of whimpering. 'C'mon, man. Are you there?'"

I stared at Noah. "*Were* you there? Did you turn your phone off because he was calling?"

"I *told* you. I was sleeping. He left them in the middle of the night, and I didn't get the rest of the messages until the next morning. I texted him asking if he was okay."

"And?"

"He texted back something like, 'Yeah, I'm okay. Might leave town again soon.' As if nothing had happened, or he didn't remember. And that was the last I ever heard from him." Noah's face seemed to crumple again.

"Jimmy was a mess, Noah," I said. "Just like you said. You can't beat yourself up about it. Listen, did you know about this Sullivan person he was associating with?"

Noah wiped his nose with his sleeve and frowned at me. "Sullivan? You mean Perry Sullivan? How do you know about him?"

"So you *do* know about him?"

My brother shrugged. "Sure. He's everyone's favorite weed dealer at Wharton College. And a lot of that pot ends up here in Colesbury. But he won't deal directly to high school kids. What Jimmy did was buy from him, and then jack up the price for the service. Who mentioned Sullivan to you?"

"Uh . . . Matt and I heard about him, and Matt's been trying to track him down and talk to him."

"Talk to him? About what?"

"About Andrea Quinley, actually. And Jimmy."

Noah made a face. "Why would Sullivan know about Andrea Quinley?"

"Because he was friends with Jimmy. I think Andrea even met Sullivan at least once. Based on what Jimmy's cousin told us."

"You've been talking to Jimmy's cousin?" Noah was staring at me now, hard. His eyes had cleared.

"Once," I admitted.

"Marnie . . ." Noah grabbed the hair on top of his head and gave it a hard yank. "Have you asked yourself yet why this person who emailed Matt . . . why they emailed *him*? Why would they tell *him* where Jimmy is? Doesn't that strike you as odd? Well, not just odd. *Scary?*"

"Well, yes." I didn't meet his gaze, which was increasingly fierce and accusing. It was starting to feel like I should tell someone about the emails *I* had received—but Noah probably wasn't the right person at the moment.

"Marnie, are you listening to what I'm saying?" he asked. "Why did Matt come to *you?*"

"I think because I was the closest he could get to information about Jimmy."

"And why did he want information about Jimmy?" Noah demanded.

I wasn't even sure anymore. "He wouldn't come right out and say it . . . but he thought Jimmy was in some way connected to Andrea's disappearance."

Noah considered this for a moment. His lips formed a stiff, tense line. "And does he still think that *now?*"

"I don't know. I haven't talked to him since they figured out the body was Jimmy. He wasn't in school today."

We were both silent, the words *the body was Jimmy* hanging in the air like a foul and overpowering odor. In that moment, I felt the cold and damp of our house grip me tighter. I tried to think of something to say that would make this room feel warmer, something to distract us from those words I'd just spoken. But it was pointless to try.

Then I heard the squeak and groan of the front door. Footsteps and a sigh—and there was G. Clara in the doorway of the living room.

"Hey you two," she said. "How're we all holding up?"

"Okay," I said, exhaling.

"Speak for yourself," Noah mumbled, rising from the couch. "I'll be upstairs."

G. Clara threw down her tote bag full of school papers and sat on the couch. "How's he doing, you think?"

I wondered for a moment if she was asking if Jimmy's death was going to set Noah off again and potentially cause some more "incidents."

"He's wondering if there's something he could've done."

G. Clara nodded.

"I'm going to go for a walk, okay?"

I grabbed my jacket as G. Clara turned and gazed up the stairs.

Once I was out of the house, I turned in the direction of Matt's house. I was thinking of all of Noah's questions.

Have you asked yourself yet why this person who emailed Matt . . . why they emailed him? Why would they tell him where Jimmy is? Doesn't that strike you as . . . Scary?

I'd handled Matt with kid gloves last night because I believed he now knew for certain he'd lost his best friend. I'd woken up this morning to discover that wasn't true. And now I had some questions for him.

CHAPTER 24

I couldn't tell if Matt was happy to find me on his doorstep.

"Hey, Marnie," he said, rubbing his head. All of the devastation that had been in his face last night seemed to have disappeared, and the usual sleepiness of his eyes had returned. His mouth was slack, unsmiling.

"You walked all the way here?" he asked.

"Why not?" I shrugged. "I had a lot to think about. Can I come in?"

"Um, okay." Matt bit his lip, thinking. Then he opened the door for me. "But there's someone else here, just so you know."

"Someone else?" I repeated, stepping inside. His house was so warm, and smelled like clean laundry.

"Phoenix Long," Matt said. "She wanted to talk."

Matt seemed to be waiting for my reaction. If I had a car, or if I hadn't just walked over two miles, I might have offered to come back later.

"Great minds think alike," I said. "I want to talk, too."

Matt took a deep breath and held the door for me. Phoenix was in the kitchen, perched on a stool, clutching a crumpled paper towel in both hands. She jumped slightly when she saw me, then sniffled and wiped her nose. Her hair and lip gloss both looked perfect and shiny, but there was something different about her today. It took me a moment to notice what it was. She wasn't wearing eye makeup. So there was nothing smudged even though she was crying. She looked even prettier this way, I thought. And she looked a lot more like her brother.

"Oh. Hi, Marnie." Phoenix shoved her paper towel into her pocket. "How are you doing?"

"I'm okay." I felt my eyes being drawn to Phoenix's wrist. I stared down at her zodiac bracelet. "How are you?"

"Umm . . . well . . . you know, not great. I . . ." Phoenix sniffled again.

I kept looking from Phoenix's face to her bracelet. It had a lobsterlike image on it. It took me a moment to remember what sign that might be. A Scorpio.

"I'm sorry about Jimmy Harmon," she was saying. "I know he was a friend of your family, when you were kids."

"Oh." I looked up at her. "How'd you know that?"

Phoenix got up off her stool. "Matt told me."

"Oh," I said. The three of us stood there awkwardly for a moment. I tapped the countertop lightly.

"I'm gonna go now," Phoenix announced, hurrying from the kitchen. "Not because you came, Marnie. It's just . . . I'm supposed to help with dinner tonight. Wednesday's my night."

After we heard the front door close, Matt turned to me. "You want a drink or something?"

I shook my head. "She's really upset."

"I don't want to downplay Jimmy's death at all. But she's upset about what it means for *Andrea.* You know they're searching the whole park now, right? And the woods behind it?" His voice tightened. "Phoenix is worried they're gonna find Andrea, too."

I stared at him. "Why would she think that?" I asked.

"Well . . . a few reasons. She wanted to see the emails. I think she was really hoping something would stand out and show her that they were from Andrea. Convince her that she's alive."

"She didn't know about the emails before?"

Matt shook his head. "Anyway. She saw them now, and she isn't convinced."

"Huh." I hesitated. "Well, I can't blame her."

Matt sat on a stool and met my eyes. "She also wanted to know how I made the jump from the emails to Forest Wonderland."

"And what did you say?"

"I did a quick save so I wouldn't have to tell her about your tea. I told her the same thing we told the police. That Andrea would talk about hanging out there."

I thought about this for a moment. "I would think that would work better on the police than on Phoenix, though. Because Phoenix knows it's not really true."

Matt shrugged. "She seemed to believe it. In fact, she said part of the reason she was so afraid they were going to find Andrea was because Andrea told her they *did* hang out there sometimes. Her and Jimmy.

"Which was news to me." He looked down at the floor. "Phoenix's theory is that they got ahold of some kind of bad shit and both OD'd or something, or that they ran into someone who Jimmy had gotten in trouble with and killed them both, or something like that."

I hadn't considered any of these things. It had never crossed my mind that Andrea could have died *with* Jimmy.

"If something like that happened, they'd find her right there with him," I said, mostly to myself. "They'd have found her by now."

Matt nodded. "That's what I was trying to tell her. She just keeps saying, 'I *want* to believe she's still alive. I just can't quite do it.'" He seemed to be avoiding eye contact now. He got off his stool and asked, "You want to hang out in my room?" Without waiting for an answer, he turned and started up the stairs.

I followed him.

"If Andrea had told Phoenix that she'd sometimes hang out with Jimmy at Forest Wonderland, did she tell that to the police *before*?" I asked. "When they were first investigating Andrea's disappearance?"

Matt opened the door to his room. It was slightly messier than the other rooms in the house, with sweatpants on the floor and movie posters on the walls.

"I didn't ask her that. She was so broken up, it didn't seem like a great idea to make her second-guess anything she'd told or not told before. I feel like we've all had too many what-ifs about Andrea. I mean, *I* have, anyway."

He sat on his bed and I sat on the floor. I noticed a pink-and-purple My Little Pony baseball cap on the plush blue carpet. I picked it up and put it on. Matt slipped off the bed and sat next to me. Then he reached out and touched the hat.

"Looks good on you," he said. "You should keep it."

I was about to ask what was with him and the pink and sparkly stuff. But I realized instantly that I didn't really care. What I cared about was his hand moving gently from the side of my head down to my chin and then to the back of my hair.

"Do you think I'm a nice person?" he whispered.

"Umm," I said, my heart thumping. "Sure?"

And then, as suddenly as the night before, we were kissing. But unlike the last time, we kept going. A few seconds later, we were both on the carpet. The hat fell off my head. His hands were tangled in my hair.

I let go of him.

"What?" Matt asked.

"Umm . . . I kind of had a question."

"Yeah?"

"Did you ever do this with Andrea?"

Matt sat up, staring at me. "This?"

"Because I heard that you did," I said quickly.

"Who . . . ?" Matt's eyes were wide.

"Cecilia." I scrambled into a kneeling position. "She said that there were pictures of you guys together. Or a picture, anyway. Pictures Phoenix had everybody erase, or something."

Matt's mouth was open, but nothing came out for a moment. "But Cecilia didn't get those pictures," he said. "Or . . . wait. Did she?"

"A picture of you and Andrea together. Like, kissing."

"Oh." Matt stared past me, looking confused. "That. But that wasn't anything."

I considered saying *never mind* and letting him off the hook. But then, he was clearly deciding whether or not to clarify something. And it bothered me.

"So, were you guys ever more than friends?"

Matt shook his head but still looked distracted. "No. I told you that already."

As he said it, my phone vibrated in my pocket. I pulled it out and looked at the number. Noah. I was reluctant to interrupt this conversation, but Noah *never* called me.

"Noah?" I said as I picked up the call.

"Have you been reading the *Connecticut Courier* updates on Jimmy?" he demanded.

"What? No. What are you—?"

"They filed a new story a couple of hours ago, and I just read it. His landlord on Birch Street said the last time he saw Jimmy was January sixteenth. *January sixteenth!*" Noah's voice was about to break.

"Calm down, okay?" I stood up and moved toward the door of Matt's room. "What's the big deal about January sixteenth?"

"That's the same date as the messages he left. He really was calling me for help. Oh, God."

My pulse quickened. "Noah, do you want me to come home? Should we talk about this at home?"

"I should have answered." Noah was whispering now. "I'm no better than the rest of them."

"The rest of who?" I asked. But by the time I'd said it, Noah had hung up.

I glanced up at Matt.

"Who was that?" he asked softly.

"My brother." I shook my head, still clutching the phone, too anxious and distracted to focus. "I think I'd better go home and check on him."

Matt stood up and touched my elbow. "But you just got here."

"I know, but . . . these are weird circumstances."

Matt paused, looking at his feet.

"What happened on January sixteenth?" he asked.

I paused, weighing what to tell him. I didn't know exactly what was going on, but I was pretty sure it would be disloyal to Noah to tell Matt about Jimmy's phone calls. "I guess that an article just came out on the *Connecticut Courier* online, and . . . and . . ."

Wordlessly, Matt took out his own phone and started tapping away.

"Here it is," he said, and then read silently for a minute. "So this guy says in the article, 'It was a memorable weekend for me. My sister was visiting. She asked me if my new tenant usually kept such late hours. I told her he hadn't been staying long enough for me to know his habits yet. When a couple more nights passed without him coming back, she scolded me for not getting this guy's background before letting him move into my house. But the way I figured it, I'd gotten the first and last month's rent out of the deal, and the deposit. If he wanted to abandon ship after paying all of that, it was his business.'"

"That's the landlord they're quoting there?" I asked.

"Yeah."

"January sixteenth," Matt repeated, and looked up at me. "Your brother was freaked out about the date, right? Why?"

"I'm not, um, totally clear on that." I went to the kitchen and pulled my jacket on. "I think the whole thing is a shock to him still."

"Uh-huh," Matt said. He had followed me into the kitchen.

"And, yeah. I should go home. I should see how he's doing. That call was weird."

"Uh-huh," Matt repeated, staring at his phone.

This was when he normally would offer to drive me home.

Think twice about what you are doing. And do not trust a word Matt Cotrell says.

"Text me later, okay?" I said.

A grunt was Matt's only response.

🖉

I SPEED-WALKED ABOUT HALFWAY home, eager to get back to Noah. I tried his cell phone two more times, then G. Clara's landline. He didn't pick up either one.

Eventually, I started feeling tired and slowed my pace a little.

I played over in my head what had just happened with Matt. Had I wanted it to happen? I must have, on some level. But I was afraid that that "level" was some immature part of me that was still in ninth grade, pining for the attention of some cool older guy. Here it was happening under very shady circumstances, and still I couldn't help myself. Like that part of me couldn't resist watching this old fantasy finally play out in reality. No matter how many times I'd told myself I was over this sort of thing. No matter what Matt's motivations, and no matter what the cost.

Not smart.

I thought of the dragon in Matt's tea leaves.

Self-delusion.

Maybe I was the deluded one.

Why would Matt be interested in me, for real?

Was my connection to Jimmy useful anymore? Now that Jimmy was dead? Was there something else Matt wanted from me? Or was he just half out of his mind right now, after what had happened at Forest Wonderland?

Yesterday's rain had left some puddles in the potholes. Streaks of mud and dirt swirled over one spot in the sidewalk where a car must have splashed into a deep puddle. My eyes only grazed the mud as I walked over it. But something made me stop a moment later.

It's not the tea leaves. It's you.

Matt's words from yesterday.

But what should I believe? Could I trust *anything* that came out of Matt's mouth? Did he really know me, or did he just know how to play me?

I didn't want to turn around. But I knew there was a picture on the sidewalk behind me. Mud, tea leaves; the medium might not matter if what Matt was saying were true. And what if I got home and wondered what it had been?

I turned around slowly and stared at the sidewalk.

The splash had formed two roundish splotches of mud across two squares of sidewalk—one on the top, one on the bottom—joined where they narrowed. Seen as a whole, they could have formed an eight. Or it could be an hourglass. Especially since there were pebbles cast across it, giving it a speckled appearance.

Hourglass: Time might be running out for you to finish a particular project or endeavor. Alternatively: Imminent peril.

The hourglass was one of the first symbols I'd ever learned from my book. I remembered committing it to memory and hoping to see it in someone's cup—before I'd even started doing the readings. There was just something juicy about that particular symbol. I imagined myself saying it darkly to an unsuspecting seeker: *I'm afraid peril might be imminent.*

This wasn't the first symbol that I'd recently seen outside of any teacup. There were the raindrops on the pavement at Forest Wonderland. The tree branches in the woods with Matt. The fox in my dreams. Suddenly the idea of imminent peril didn't seem so delicious or exciting.

I gazed at the pebbles. Maybe their appearance was more snowy than sandy, more snow globe than hourglass. It was hard to say.

I turned from the mud and started back home again.

It's not the tea leaves. It's you.

CHAPTER 25

No one was home when I got there.

I turned on my laptop to check for news about Jimmy and the police investigation. I wanted to read the whole article that Matt had excerpted aloud. I did a search for the local news website and found that they had updated the story just within the last half hour.

MITZIE MARTIN TO FEATURE STORY ON POSSIBLE QUINLEY-HARMON CONNECTION

Oh boy. The late-night *Martin Report*. Andrea's disappearance had become national news when the *Martin Report* had first picked it up. Old Mitzie had briefly put Colesbury on the map, turning our home town into a circus of cameras and bright lights and sound trucks. Now it looked as if she might do it again.

Before I could read the article, my email dinged. I opened it.

THINK TWICE ABOUT WHAT YOU ARE DOING. AND DO NOT TRUST A WORD MATT COTRELL SAYS.

My heart raced. Same email as before, this time in all caps. I checked the address. Another string of numbers and letters, similar but different.

There was a tap on my bedroom door.

I jumped and whirled around.

"G. Clara! You scared me."

"Are you okay?"

"Uhh . . ." With a shaking hand, I closed my email. I was glad G. Clara was home. "Yeah."

"Where's your brother?" she asked. "When I went out to get a pizza, I was worried that you weren't back, and now I come back, and you're here and he's gone."

"He was gone when I got here," I said. "He's not answering his phone."

"I know." She forced a smile to hide her worry. "Let's start this pizza and hope he joins us. Should I make a salad to go with it? I was thinking you kids should eat more greens."

"I'll make it," I offered. We went downstairs.

CHAPTER 26

We have Police Chief Robert Swindon here to tell us a little about this shocking new development in the Andrea Quinley case. For those of you just tuning in, a classmate of the deceased has apparently been receiving anonymous emails from someone claiming to be Andrea. The content of those emails has led local police to a body—the body of a young man with whom Andrea had some association, although the nature of their relationship is unclear. His name was Jimmy Harmon, and he was nineteen years old. Chief Swindon, do I have all of that correct?

Um, yes, Ms. Martin. The FBI has been brought onto this case, and they are working together with both Colesbury Police and Mixville Police Departments. Colesbury, of course, was home to Jimmy Harmon and Andrea Quinley. Mixville is where the body was found.

I assume that Mr. Harmon's death is being treated as a homicide, Mr. Swindon?

Yes. It is. For now. But as it's an ongoing investigation, I can't comment any further.

Have you or the department or the FBI traced the emails that this young man received—this friend of Andrea's?

I can't comment on that, Ms. Martin.

I COULDN'T SLEEP AFTER watching Mitzie Martin. Noah still hadn't come home. G. Clara's cop shows and lawyer shows burbled on downstairs.

I picked up my phone and looked at the time. Only ten thirty. I texted Cecilia. Are you up?

Cecilia wrote back right away. Yup. What's up? I'm sorry about Jimmy H. I know u weren't friends but still.

Can you talk?

A few seconds after I sent it, my phone started playing its frog-ribbit ringtone, and I picked up.

"What's up?" Cecilia asked.

"I wanted to ask you a random question," I whispered, even though the door was closed and I knew G. Clara couldn't hear me. "Does the day January sixteenth mean anything to you? I mean, January sixteenth of this past year? Can you think of anything special or out of the ordinary that was happening on that day?"

"No, not off the top of my head. Why?"

"I mean, anything with Andrea or Matt?"

Cecilia yawned. "Andrea wasn't gone by then, right?"

"No. Andrea didn't disappear until early March."

"Oh. You're right," said Cecilia. "Sorry. I'm a little tired. So, January sixteenth. That's around midyear exam time, right?"

"Right," I said. "But it was on a weekend. Would that have been a weekend you guys all got together?"

"We get together *lots* of weekends. That was so long ago, I don't remember."

"Can you maybe look back at your text messages, or something?"

"Uh . . . I guess. But I doubt I'd find anything. Everything from last year kind of runs together until Andrea disappeared. I mean, *that* was memorable."

"Could it have been the weekend Andrea did that catnip trick?" I asked.

Cecilia thought for a moment. "No. That was right before Christmas. Remember? I told you that the cat attacked the Christmas tree after Andrea gave him the catnip."

"Oh. Right. It's just that everybody's acting a little weird about something that happened on that date."

"Who's everybody?" Cecilia wanted to know.

"Well, Matt in particular."

"Let me check my phone a sec," Cecilia said. "Can you hold on?"

"Okay."

I opened my blinds and peered out into the yard. Our porch light illuminated Noah's shed art just enough to make it visible in the dark.

"Umm, Marnie?" Cecilia sounded uneasy.

"What is it?"

"January sixteenth was the weekend of that picture. From Phoenix. That I erased."

"How do you know, though, if you erased it?"

"Cuz there are all these other messages from around then, about the Model UN meeting I was at that weekend."

"Oh. Okay."

"I can't remember if I told you. Phoenix wasn't the only one who took pictures of Matt and Andrea. Because she was like, 'And you may as well erase any pictures my brother sent you, too.' She knew he'd texted them to a few people. She thought he'd included me, but he hadn't."

"That's weird. So Payson thought the same thing? That Andrea and Matt were hooking up?"

"Um, well, I'm not sure. He doesn't really care about that kind of gossipy stuff."

"Did *he* still have a crush on Andrea? You mentioned he asked her out once."

"A long time ago," Cecilia protested. "I don't think it meant much. It was homecoming freshman year and he didn't want to go by himself, or whatever." She hesitated. "I can ask him if you want, actually. I wasn't sure if I should tell you this, but he and I have been spending a little more time together."

"Since when?"

"Just the last couple of days. Called me out of the blue yesterday." Cecilia said. "Then he wanted to hang out."

I was silent for a moment. I wasn't sure how to react, since I still didn't think Payson would be so great for Cecilia. Not to mention his timing seemed a little strange.

"And so you did?" I asked.

"Yeah. At my house. He even stayed for dinner. He pretty much invited himself over. It was kind of weird, actually."

"Well . . . congratulations, I guess?"

"I guess," Cecilia repeated. But she sounded small and far away—and not particularly happy. I wondered if there was something about Payson she wasn't saying. Something that was making her have second thoughts. "Good night."

"Good night," I said.

CHAPTER 27

I could see him through the snow. He was several yards away, holding his face upward toward the sky. He snapped at the snow-flakes, as if trying to chew them like food. Their lack of substance appeared to annoy him, and he chomped harder, his jaws snapping so loudly that I took a frightened step backward and fell.

The fox snarled at my clumsiness, staring at me for a moment before biting upward again. His yellow eyes pleaded with me now.

He wasn't trying to eat the snow. He was trying to get me to look up. I tipped my head back. But the snow had turned to sleet. It stung my eyes. I couldn't see. Still, I kept squinting and blinking.

The fox snapped his jaws again, and then screamed.

I WAS SHAKING WHEN I woke up.

After my heart stopped pounding, I thought of Noah and wondered if he was home. I picked up my phone to check the time. It was 1 A.M. Cecilia had written to me just after eleven.

Tried to see if Phoenix's old text could be recovered, but it's gone gone gone. Call me, I want to talk to you about it.

"Great, Cecilia," I muttered. I wasn't sure why she'd think I'd want to look at an old picture of Matt kissing Andrea under these more serious circumstances, but it was nice of her to try.

I crawled out of bed and tiptoed down the hall—toward the light coming from the crack beneath Noah's door.

I tapped on the door. No answer. I tapped again, then slowly opened it.

Noah was lying on his bed, eyes closed, but with his earbuds in. It seemed to me he was listening to something—not asleep. I touched him on the hand, and he jumped.

"What!" he yelped, tearing out the earbuds.

"Where did you go?" I asked. "G. Clara was worried about you at dinner."

"I talked to her when I came in. She was still up watching TV. I was at the police station. Telling them what I told you."

"Oh," I said. "And what did they think?"

"They didn't say what they thought. They just thanked me for the information."

I nodded. "Did you have any pizza? G. Clara was worried about you not eating."

"I had some. I sat there in the living room and ate two pieces in front of her. Just to make her happy."

"That was big of you," I said.

"In fact, I think I'm gonna have another piece right now," Noah said, getting off his bed. "You want one?"

"Maybe," I said, and followed him down to the kitchen.

Noah slid three pieces of pizza into the oven, and we sat in silence for a moment—until a scratching noise came from behind the oven. A mouse, surely. Neither of us moved in response. We're used to mice.

"Give me a reading, will you, Marnie?" Noah said.

"What?"

"A tea-leaf reading. About my old friend Jimmy."

I shook my head. "I don't think a tea-leaf reading is going to—"

"I haven't even said *what* I'm going to ask the leaves. You're going to say no before I tell you that?"

I still felt clammy from the nightmare. "Okay," I said, resigning myself to this conversation. "What do you want to ask the leaves?"

Noah spread his fingers out on the kitchen table and stared

down at them. "Ask them if he died the night he called me. January sixteenth."

I shook my head. "I'm not going to do a reading on that."

"How about just a reading, then? No specific question. Just a reading. Humor me."

"Right now?"

"Yes."

I sighed. I didn't want to do it. But I had missed Noah since he'd gone silent so many months ago. If this were a way to draw him back into the world, it was worth indulging him. Besides, if I could do it for Matt, I could do it for my brother.

"Okay," I said.

"Good. Now let me finish my dinner in peace."

AFTER HE'D EATEN HIS pizza and downed his tea, Noah opened a packaged chocolate pudding and sprinkled wheat germ into it.

"That's nasty," I said. But I was smiling.

"The nutrition's gotta come from somewhere," Noah said.

"There are bananas and apples in the basket on the counter," I reminded him. "Come on, let's do this. I'm tired. Turn the cup over and rotate it three times counterclockwise."

He added banana slices to his pudding while I examined the teacup.

The clearest symbol was at the very bottom.

"I see a window," I told him.

Noah pulled the cup toward himself, so we were both holding it. "Where?"

"See there? That little rectangle, with a few tiny leaves splitting it in half?"

"I never would've seen that as a window."

"What would you have seen it as?"

Noah stared at it for a moment. "An open book."

"So which should we call it?"

"That depends. What does a window mean?"

I hesitated. "It can mean a new perspective on things. Or . . . psychic ability."

Noah let go of the cup, releasing it to me again. "Let's go with that, then."

"Okay," I said. "Let's."

"Aren't *you* supposed to be the one interpreting the symbols?" Noah asked.

"Maybe," I said. "But maybe *you* have a window, in a sense, on what happened to Jimmy. Maybe just, like, a connection that comes from you two knowing each other when you were so young. A connection that's real, but impossible to explain."

Noah picked up the pudding cup and began scraping out tiny spoonfuls. "When did you become such a good bullshit artist?"

"Are you saying that's not true?"

"What else do you see, besides the window?"

"I see lettuce a little closer to the edge. That means sleeplessness."

"Brilliant. It's two A.M. How did you memorize all of these symbols' meanings, anyway?"

"Flash cards," I said.

"Seriously?"

"Yup. Over the summer. I'd read G. Clara's tea-leaf-reading book a few times by then, but I wanted to know most of the symbols for doing readings. Of course, you're supposed to allow yourself to do your own interpreting to some extent. But it's good to have a solid base of traditional symbols in your head."

"Why the hell does lettuce stand for sleeplessness?"

"I have no idea," I admitted. "But when I was doing the flash cards, I remember picturing in my head someone using lettuce as a sleep mask, as a kind of mnemonic."

"Well, that doesn't sound nerdy at all, does it?" Noah muttered.

I ignored him and stared into his cup. "I see . . . threads. Threads show a connection between things. Like, specifically, between the past and the future."

"A connection between the past and future? Really going out on a limb there, Marnie."

I shot him a look. "Why did you ask for this reading if you're going to be like that?"

I pointed out the formation—running from the bottom of the cup to about halfway up. "I'm telling you what I see."

"Okay, okay," Noah said, taking the cup from me and setting it on the table. "Let's go back to the window. Obviously you brought that up for a reason."

"Yes. Because that's what I saw."

"I take it that G. Clara has recently given you her little talking-to?"

"What? The 'I don't want any great-grandchildren for at least another decade' talking-to?"

Noah shook his head. "No, not that. About . . . well, I just assumed that she talked to you around the same time she talked to me. When I was in . . ."

"Rehab?" I prompted.

"It wasn't rehab, Marnie. I wasn't addicted to anything. It was, like, psychiatric. Maybe G. Clara didn't want to tell you that. They kept me a long time because they thought I'd tried to kill myself."

Did you? DID you? I wanted to scream.

"I didn't, okay?" he said, clearly reading my expression. "And G. Clara knew it, too. I explained what happened and she understood. But there's no way either of us could get *them* to understand."

"Who is them?" I asked.

"The shrinks at the hospital."

"Oh," I said. "So what was it that happened? That G. Clara understood?"

"That I took the pills I took to make the *sights* and *sounds* stop. To numb them. Not to make my *life* stop."

"What sights and sounds?" I whispered.

"Like the one I painted on the shed," Noah said.

"What is it supposed to be a picture of?" I asked.

Noah stared at me. "You're joking, right?"

"No."

"You need to see something, Marnie. Let's go look at it."

Something deep inside me clenched. "It's dark."

"I'll get a flashlight."

A FEW MINUTES LATER, against my protests, we were outside. I was shivering. Noah was shining a heavy-duty flashlight at the spray paint. A vertical rectangle, split in the middle. My heart began to thud hard.

"It's a window," I said.

"Yeah," said Noah. "I thought that's why you said it."

I couldn't tear my eyes away from the graffiti. I could never put my finger on why I found it so disturbing. "You were thinking of a window right before you OD'd?"

"It wasn't so much the window as what I saw through it. Snow."

I stared at the red speckles scattered over the picture, heavily over the bottom, less so over the top. I thought of the speckles of dirt I'd seen on the sidewalk, in that hourglass image.

"Why red?" I breathed.

"Red and green were the only colors I happened to have lying around. I just grabbed red. It wasn't like a project that I'd *planned*. It didn't involve a trip to the hardware store or whatever."

"Don't take this the wrong way," I said. "But a window with snow through it . . . that doesn't sound like that bad of a thought. Like—OD bad, anyway."

Noah was quiet. He circled the light around the image a few times before speaking.

"It wasn't the snow itself, but what I knew was *behind* it. Under it. I couldn't see past the snow but I knew that once it settled, it was going to be something bad. Like once it stopped snowing, a face would appear just beyond it, staring at me through the window. Of someone evil. Or someone dead."

I held my breath, waiting for Noah to go on. I thought of the fox in my dream, snapping at the blizzard.

"So I wanted it to keep snowing and snowing and snowing. I drew it here so if I looked out my window—I mean, my real window—this is what I'd see. My snow. The snow that's never going to stop."

I looked from the shed to Noah's bedroom window. They were directly across from each other, except for Noah's room being on the second floor.

"The first time I looked out at it I felt like I could hear Jimmy, saying those same things as when he called. 'I'm trapped in a fluffer nutter! I'm trapped in a tightie whitie! I'm trapped in a wedding cake!'"

"Snow," I said softly.

"Yeah, snow." Noah paused. "And then one night I couldn't stand to hear him anymore. I had to make it stop." Noah waved the flashlight back and forth over the snow and the window, as if scribbling over it with light.

"I didn't mean for it to turn into an emergency. To do that to G. Clara. But I wasn't really thinking. I only wanted it to stop."

"Did you tell her the truth?" I asked.

He was quiet for a moment.

"I didn't tell G. Clara the *specifics* of the visions. She didn't ask. But she *understood.* And she told me not to go into it in detail with the doctors and nurses. Because they might not understand. They might call it schizophrenia, or something. Just like they so often don't understand with Mom, she said."

The zigzagging light against the shed was making me dizzy. "Don't understand *what,* Noah?"

"The way we are. G. Clara, Mom, me . . . you."

I'd stopped shivering. I was unable to move. "And how are we?"

Noah turned to me, his eyes tired. "We see things."

"Everyone see things—"

"Marnie." Noah shook his head. "I heard you give that reading to that Matt kid. I know you know what I mean."

"I mostly only see things in teacups," I protested.

"Mostly?" Noah repeated.

I didn't say anything.

"G. Clara says you need to find a way to compartmentalize it. Maybe you're lucky. Maybe you've already found that. You focus your energy on tea leaves, so it doesn't leak into other parts of your life."

"How do you do that?" I wasn't ready to talk about the images that appeared outside of teacups—in raindrops on pavement, in mud on the sidewalk, in branches overhead at Forest Wonderland.

"You tell me, Marnie. You're the one who seems to have found a way to do that. You're the one who seems more like G. Clara, and I'm the one who seems like Mom."

"How am I like G. Clara?" I asked.

"G. Clara focuses her energy on objects. You know all of that tag-sale shit she brings home?"

"Yeah?"

"She kind of lets those things talk to her. And then she puts them on a shelf and forgets about them. Somehow she doesn't let all the crazy shit in."

I blinked, struggling to process all of this. "And Mom?"

"She's never been able to focus it, or control it. And that's why she drinks, G. Clara says."

"How come G. Clara hasn't told me any of this?"

Noah shut off the flashlight. "But she has," he whispered. "Just not in so many words. How many times has she said Mom's brain isn't like other people's?"

"I always thought that was a really awkward way of saying she's an alcoholic."

We stood silently in the dark for a moment.

"If you really didn't know any of this, how come you took up tea-leaf reading?"

I hesitated. "For fun."

"For real, Marnie?"

"For fun," I repeated.

I didn't want to tell Noah the real reason. I had become tired of being just anyone in Colesbury. Tea-leaf reading was something no one else did, and no one else was likely to try. It was something of my own. A way to survive the perfectionism of this town without being perfect. If I couldn't be perfect or athletic or Yale-bound, I could at least be weird, and I could at least learn to like it. And I'd found *Cosmos in a Cup* on G. Clara's shelf at exactly the right moment. Just when I'd gotten so tired of everything that I'd thought I might go crazy.

"Flash cards for fun?" Noah said skeptically.

"Let's put it this way. Ever heard the expression 'Let your freak flag fly'?"

"Sure. So you knew you were a freak. You *did* know we have this thing. And you were corralling it on your own terms."

"Did I say that?" I cried.

Noah ignored me. "The weird feelings? The visions? Feeling like a freak? That started for me when I was around fourteen or fifteen. G. Clara says that's how it was for Mom, too. She told me that she wasn't sure it was going to happen to you, too . . . but clearly . . ."

"Clearly nothing," I snapped.

"You're supposed to think of it as a gift," Noah said. Even in the dark, I could see his grim smile.

"A real gift all right, what Mom's got," I muttered.

Noah didn't reply.

"A gift that drove you to swallow a whole bunch of pills," I added. "What kind of pills were those, anyway?"

He sighed. "Pain pills. Oxycodone, mostly."

I started at the familiarity of the name. I don't know much about pills, but I was pretty sure Oxycodone was something Jimmy's cousin had mentioned.

"Did you get them from Jimmy?" I demanded.

"Of *course* not. I hadn't seen Jimmy in months, by then. In fact, I was pretty sure he was dead."

"Pretty sure? What are you talking about?"

"I saw it. I felt it. Haven't you been listening to what I've been saying? It was *that* feeling that I was trying to get rid of. That . . . *window*."

"Did you get the pills from Sullivan?" I asked Noah.

"Sullivan? Hell no. Sullivan doesn't deal that shit. Sullivan is *very* careful. That's why he'd never sell to a high school kid himself. That's why he'd only do it through people like Jimmy."

"Where'd you get it, then?"

"The medicine cabinet. Remember when G. Clara fell on her wrist two years ago, and then had to have that surgery? They gave her a ton of those pills, and she barely took any of them."

"Oh," I said.

"But you know, it makes me wonder. After the thing about Jimmy's landlord . . . I wonder when was the last time *Sullivan* saw Jimmy."

"Any chance you could talk to him about it?" I asked.

"Sure. Sullivan changes his cell phone number every so often. But I know where he hangs out, near the college."

"Why don't we go talk to him?" I suggested.

"We?" Noah repeated.

"Please?" I said.

"Why do you want to involve yourself in this?"

I thought about this question for a moment. I stared forward, thinking about the spray-painted drawing that stood before us in the dark. Taking the flashlight from Noah, I turned it on and illuminated the drawing. I thought about my fox dreams. And my memories of Jimmy. The times he'd tried to be good, and the times he hadn't. I thought about the sidewalk again.

"I see the snow, too," I said. "I don't think you're looking through that window alone."

AFTER NOAH HAD GONE to bed, I stayed up and looked up some old online weather reports from earlier in the year. There had been two big snowstorms last winter, but I couldn't remember when exactly they had been.

The reports confirmed one of them had been the weekend of January sixteenth.

I knew I didn't need to tell Noah about this. He already knew.

CHAPTER 28

October 17

Noah picked me up right after school. The plan was to drive to the place where Sullivan usually hung out—a Laundromat-and-diner strip mall near the outskirts of the Wharton College campus.

"Did you tell your friend Matt you were doing this?" Noah asked as he drove.

"Of course not," I said. "You and I agreed I wouldn't."

"Just checking."

"What?" I demanded. "You don't even know him."

"Yeah. And do *you?*"

I stared out the window instead of responding. Noah was right. I didn't know Matt all that well. There *was* something off about the whole situation. Something Matt wasn't telling me. Admitting this to Noah would make me look naïve, however, and I didn't want him to change his mind about allowing me to tag along while he talked to Sullivan.

"He's not, like, your *boyfriend*, is he?" Noah said, stopping for a red light.

"No," I murmured, keeping my gaze fixed out the car window. I imagined Noah could see our kissing session in my reddening face.

Do you think I'm a nice person? Matt had asked.

Thinking about it now, it was a strange thing to ask before kissing someone. Wasn't it? And yet I'd kissed him back. What was wrong with me?

"No," I said, speaking louder now.

"Good," was all Noah said as the light turned green.

THE DINER WAS A long, narrow, claustrophobic sort of place. Its walls were painted dark yellow and seemed almost to be collapsing inward from the weight of all their framed pictures of chickens and eggs. All of the counter seats were occupied by old men, but most of the tables were empty.

"Hey, Noah," someone called from the back.

Approaching us was a scrawny guy, bespectacled, with brown stubble on his face that looked like it was grown with great effort.

"Hi, Sullivan," Noah replied, surprising me.

This was Sullivan, the famous big-time pot dealer?

Sullivan led us to his table, where he was apparently nursing his own pot of coffee.

"Should I have Sally bring you two some cups? Noah, are you going to introduce me to your friend?"

"This is my sister," Noah said. "Marnie."

"Your sister?" Sullivan frowned. "*Little* sister?"

"Relax." Noah rolled his eyes. "We're not here to talk about a transaction."

The familiarity with which Noah talked to Sullivan made me think he'd downplayed his previous experience with him.

"We wanted to talk to you a little about Jimmy Harmon. You've heard what happened, right?"

"Yeah." Sullivan shook his head and made a little clicking-sucking noise with his mouth. "Tragic. Was he a good friend of yours? I'm sorry, man."

"A good friend? No. But we knew each other when we were kids. Marnie and me both. So it is a shock, yeah."

Sullivan refilled his coffee cup. "So . . . what did you want to talk about?"

"Well . . . first of all . . . when was the last time you saw him?"

Sullivan eyed Noah—and then me—over his coffee cup as he drank. "Last time? I don't know. A long time ago. Let's see . . . last winter, maybe? Maybe even before that? He and I stopped . . . uh, associating regularly . . . oh, like a year ago."

"And why was that?" Noah asked.

"Because he was getting into some risky business that I didn't like. Didn't want to be connected to."

Noah nodded. "The Molly and the other shit."

"Yeah. I told him he should quit messing around with that other shit. That's opiates, man. I told him a couple of times—there are different laws about that. They can twist that to slap you with some real jail time, I bet."

"Who was he getting it from?" Noah asked.

"I don't know. Someone in New Haven, I guess. I think he said something like that. I didn't ask a lot of questions. I told him I didn't want anything to do with it."

"How long had he been doing it, you think? When he talked to you about it?"

Sullivan shook his head. "No idea. I think not that long. He said he had one good, consistent client in Colesbury who was willing to pay quite a lot for the service. Said if he could get a few more like that, he'd be all set."

"Did he say who it was?" I asked.

Sullivan's lip curled up as glanced at me. I had the feeling he preferred to speak only to Noah.

"No," he said. "But he had a nickname for him. Called him 'Chuckles.' But he never gave a real name or any details. You know, discretion was actually one of Jimmy's finer qualities."

"Really?" Noah said.

"Well . . . I *thought* so. But maybe . . . maybe he screwed up and made somebody mad. Maybe this Chuckles person. Or maybe whoever was supplying him with the pills. I don't know. He didn't tell me everything. We weren't pals."

"Right," Noah murmured. "But do you remember when the last time you saw him was? January?"

"Umm . . . I think it was even before that. And then some-time in the spring I get some weird text saying he was living with some new girlfriend in New Jersey, and *sayonara!* I was like, whatever, guy. Thanks for sharing."

"Did you ever meet his friend Andrea?" I asked.

Noah glared at me.

"Once," Sullivan said. "The girl who disappeared, you mean? Yeah. Once. Like a year ago. I was kind of pissed at him for bringing a stranger along. He knew I don't like to associate with minors. But . . . now, what the hell was a girl like that doing with *Jimmy?* Trying to get a rise out of her parents, or what?"

Noah and I glanced at each other, but neither of us replied.

"Anyway, I don't know if you want to hear any of my theories about poor old Jimmy. But I think maybe he got in over his head way too quick. Whoever was giving him that stuff to sell— maybe he got in with some bad dudes and he offended them somehow."

"But why Forest Wonderland?" Noah asked.

Sullivan shrugged. "Who knows? Maybe he agreed to meet someone there? Look. You really weren't planning on buying something today? Or making an arrangement for later in the week?"

"Well . . . no. I just wanted to talk about Jimmy."

Sullivan nodded. "I get it. I'm sorry you lost your friend."

"Thanks," Noah said. He stood up and motioned for me to do the same.

WHEN WE GOT HOME, G. Clara's car was in the driveway. Noah kept his car running.

"I'm going to drop you," he said.

"You're not going to come in?"

"I don't feel like being home right now."

"And you think I do?"

He drummed his fingers on the wheel, avoiding my eyes. "I'll be back in a little while. I need some time to think. I have a few ideas about who 'Chuckles' might be."

"Oh. Anyone I would know?"

Noah ignored the question. "See you later, Marnie. Tell G. Clara I won't be long."

I knew there was no point in pushing him. "Fine," I grumbled.

After I'd slammed the door, Noah backed out and waved. Before going inside, I stood in front of the shed drawing for a little while. The red against the white didn't seem Satanic to me anymore, or even creepy. It seemed sad and desolate and pleading. Red against fatigued white. Blood on dirty snow.

I turned from it and went inside.

I found G. Clara upstairs, furiously scrubbing the bathroom mirror.

Squeaky-squeaky-squeaky-SQUEEEAAAK went her paper towel against the glass.

"G. Clara?" I said softly, unsure if she'd seen me in the doorway.

"I didn't notice how *filthy* this thing had become," she said, still scrubbing. "There could be someone else's reflection in this mirror and I wouldn't even notice at this point."

This is often how it goes with G. Clara. She notices one dirty thing in a room and cleans it until it's gleaming—but rarely notices that everything around it is just as dirty. Beneath the mirror, the sink was streaked with toothpaste scum and dotted with speckles from Noah's last shave. And the counter was littered with hairy combs and half-empty soap and lotion bottles.

"I'm sorry I haven't cleaned up in here in a while," I said.

Squeak. Squeak. Squeak.

"It wasn't a criticism, honey. We all use this bathroom. I just noticed it."

"Right," I said, and then tapped my fingertips on the countertop. "So . . . when were you going to tell me about the family . . . 'gift'?"

"Gift?" she repeated.

Squeak. Squeak. Squeaky-squeak.

"You know, the psychic thing?"

G. Clara stopped scrubbing and stared at me in the mirror. "Oh."

I stared back. "So . . . Noah wasn't kidding."

"No, certainly not." G. Clara dropped her crumpled paper towel in the sink. "I wondered, at times, if you *needed* to be told. There was no sign of it in you until you took up that tea thing you do, and you took that on with such ease, I wondered . . . well, I thought I'd see where it went."

"Even though Noah . . . Noah can't handle his visions."

"Was that the word he used? Visions?" G. Clara asked.

"Uh . . . I think so."

G. Clara whirled away from the mirror to face me directly, her gray eyes suddenly fierce. "He'll *learn* to handle it. And you're not Noah."

I turned away, feeling suddenly small. I gazed at Noah's shaving specks in the sink. "What am I?"

"That depends." G. Clara reached out and nudged me on the shoulder, gently. "How accurate are you finding your tea readings?"

"Sometimes not at all. Sometimes scary."

Then it all came out in a rush: I told G. Clara about the carousel horse I saw in Matt's teacup, and how that led us to Forest Wonderland.

G. Clara thought about this for a minute.

"Come here," she said finally, and led me out of the bathroom.

In my bedroom, she reached across my desk and picked up the oversized mug that held my pens and paperclips. On its side was a picture of an eggplant.

"Remember where you got this?"

"From you."

She nodded, eyeing the image. "I found it at a tag sale. They had about a dozen mugs lined up, but this one jumped out at me. It talked to me."

Then she put the mug into my hands.

"Of course I don't mean *talked* in a literal way. It had a certain energy, a certain warmth. Like it had seen happy times, and been present for happy conversations, or good news. And it wanted more. So I brought it home and drank out of it for a while, to make sure I was feeling it right. And then I gave it to you."

"For good luck or something?"

"Good luck?" G. Clara repeated. "Probably not. *Something*, yes."

"I'm not sure that clarifies anything."

"I didn't say it would. Like I said, the talk isn't literal. It's a feeling."

I deposited the mug back on the desk. "That's charming."

"Well, then. I'll give you another example that's not so charming. You know that hutch with the dishes in the dining room?"

"Yeah?"

She sighed. "Every time I open it, it screams at me. Not like a bloodcurdling scream. Like a nagging, dissatisfied scream. Luckily I only use those dishes on Thanksgiving or Christmas."

I turned toward her. "Why do you keep it here, then?"

"Because it was my grandmother's. And I figure I'm supposed to be hearing that scream, for whatever reason."

"Maybe the hutch just wants to be dusted more."

G. Clara smiled. "Maybe. But if that's what it wants, it should talk to me nicer. Wouldn't you agree?"

I had to smile, too. But it faded as I sat on my bed. My eyes wandered to the quilt folded up at its foot. It was white, with a blue border and big yellow daisies appliquéd into it. G. Clara used to actually sew sometimes, before Noah and I moved in with her. It was more yellow than white I saw now, dingy and stained from when I used to drag it outside for doll picnics.

"And for you . . . it's just *objects* that do this to you?"

G. Clara sat on the bed opposite me. "It used to be more than that. But over time I learned to control it, to apply it only to objects. I put it there and I let the objects speak to me, so that part of my brain gets heard on a daily basis. So it doesn't get in my way at other times."

"And that works?"

"Well, not all the time. But see, I put it in old music boxes and cookie tins and jelly jars because I can. And because there has always been someone to take care of, and I needed to focus on that. You kids, and before that, your mother."

I traced one of the daisies with my finger. "But what about before that?"

G. Clara hesitated. "That was so long ago, Marnie. Now, are you finding it hard? Is it getting out of control for you?"

"I didn't know there was anything I needed to control. Until I started reading tea leaves."

G. Clara nodded. "I'd wondered if it had skipped you somehow. Until you started doing those readings."

"It spills out into other things," I admitted. "Lately."

"Other things?"

"I see my tea symbols, but not in teacups. In trees. In mud splashes."

"That can't really be helped," G. Clara said. Her forehead was creased. "When there's something very powerful happening . . . it won't allow itself to be contained."

I couldn't think of what to say. I could see her concern for me etched on her face. I realized that I wanted to show something to G. Clara. I opened the cabinet of my desk, found my pig puppet, and pulled out the Pisces bracelet.

Thrusting it into G. Clara's hand, I said, "How do you feel when you hold this?"

G. Clara stretched it in her fingertips, examining it carefully. "Whose is it? Not yours?"

"I don't know," I said softly.

"Isn't . . ." G. Clara paused. "Isn't this like the bracelet Phoenix Long wears?"

"Like hers, but not hers," I said. "Hers is Scorpio. This is Pisces."

"Oh." G. Clara slipped the bracelet onto her wrist, then pulled it off. "It's very pretty. But . . ."

"But what?"

"But where does it come from?" G. Clara asked, lifting her eyes to me.

"I found it," I admitted.

"Where?"

"On the ground," I said vaguely.

"It's pretty, but it's cold. Really cold." G. Clara paused for a moment, and then said softly, "Too cold, and then too late."

I held my breath and waited for her to say more.

Instead, she tossed the bracelet on the quilt between us. "I don't like having to hold it. It's too heavy and too cold. Holding it is like . . . a burden."

"A burden?" I repeated, picking up the bracelet and trying its weight for myself.

I tried to put the bracelet back in G. Clara's hand, but she pulled away so quickly that I jumped as well.

"Marnie, where did you find this?" G. Clara demanded.

"What are you not telling me, G. Clara?" I shot back.

"I asked you a question," G. Clara said, twisting her hands together and staring at me. "You're the one who's not answering. Whose is it? Where did you get it?"

"Life or death?" I asked quietly. "Did you feel life or death when you held it?"

G. Clara stood up. "It doesn't work that way. Whose bracelet is it, honey?" Her voice was strained—as if she was struggling to keep from yelling. "Where did you find it?"

"Just say one. Life or death. Just, if you *had* to—"

"Answer my question, Marnie!"

"No." I stood up and moved close, my face inches from her own. "Just *say*. Life or death? I know about us now, and you can't protect me forever. Just *say*!"

"Death," G. Clara said. "All right? Happy now? Death. Now tell me whose it is."

"I think it's Andrea Quinley's," I said.

G. Clara nodded, unsurprised. As if that was the answer she'd been waiting for the whole time. Her shoulders sagged.

"It's yours now," she said. She wasn't looking at me any-more. I followed her gaze to the bracelet, then my pillows, then the window above my bed. She turned away from me and started to leave the room. But at the doorway, she spoke with her back to me.

"Do you think it sparkles?" she asked.

"What? The bracelet?"

G. Clara sighed. "Of course you do. You think everything in this town sparkles. Everything but you."

"What are you talking about?"

"I don't think I can explain. And I have more cleaning I'd like to do," she said, and went quietly down the hall.

CHAPTER 29

Above our heads, the tree branches come together to form a thatched white structure. Domed, like a birdcage. Are we trapped in a giant white birdcage? Have we been in one this whole time? Is that why we walk in circles?

I keep staring up. The fox is still screaming. I see that the cage is not so giant. We are not inside it, but next to it. And it is not really a cage, but a beautiful little structure. Beautiful and white like a wedding cake. Or at least it would be beautiful if the fox's blood had not stained the snow right beside it.

The fox is still barking, and I am still saying I hear you.

I hear you.

Because I recognize that little white dome. It is not a cage or a wedding cake.

I really hear you now.

CHAPTER 30

October 18

When I woke up, my chest was tight and there was one word volleying in my head, making it throb.

I said it out loud.

"Gazebo."

The word felt powerful on my lips, groaning at the beginning (*gah!*) and then playful (*zee!*) and then ending with a determined thud (*bo*).

I yanked up my shades and immediately knew I'd slept late. The midmorning sun was shining through the bright yellow leaves of the tree in the front yard, and both Noah's and G. Clara's cars were gone.

It was Saturday. And because of that one word in my head, I knew what I had to do today. I had a feeling I knew what was happening in the snow—in Noah's and mine. I had a feeling I knew what that fox was trying to tell me.

I TEXTED MATT, AND he didn't text back right away. I wondered if he planned to ignore me until Monday, when we'd see each other in school.

G. Clara was probably off hitting the last few tag sales of the season. I texted Noah, who said he was having coffee with a friend and wouldn't be home for an hour or two. Reluctantly, I set off on the long walk to Matt's house again.

Along the way, I held the Pisces bracelet inside my pocket.

I thought about G. Clara's reaction to it. It didn't feel cold to me, but I didn't have the same tag-sale magic that G. Clara did. Funny that she seemed almost afraid of the bracelet, but that she didn't ask me not to hold it or keep it myself.

It's a burden.

It's yours now.

She'd said those words with sadness. Was she sad that she couldn't take that burden from me? I wasn't sure.

The most reasonable way to deal with the bracelet itself was to give it to the police. But something inside had kept me from doing that. I didn't want to give Mitzie Martin another reason to make this town go crazy over Andrea. Wasn't *Andrea* the one everyone was hoping to find in Forest Wonderland, after all? Everyone was treating Jimmy's body like a "clue" in the great Andrea Quinley mystery. This piece of evidence would push everyone even further in that direction.

But someone needed to care about Jimmy.

AT MATT'S HOUSE, A slim woman with cropped gray hair answered the doorbell. She looked startled to see me.

"Hello," I said, as she peered at me with her sculpted eyebrows raised. "I'm a friend of Matt's. Is he home?"

"I don't believe we've ever met," the woman said curtly. "I'm Matt's mom. And you are?"

"Marnie," I said.

"Marnie," Mrs. Cotrell repeated, then frowned in exaggerated confusion. "One moment."

I stayed in the doorway while she disappeared into the house.

"Matt. Matt, honey?" Her voice grew muffled. "Do we wish to visit with a Marnie? She doesn't have a car. I think she walked here."

She sniffed loudly enough for me to hear it, as if walking were some crazy peon activity. Imagine a sixteen-year-old without a car!

Do we wish to visit with a Marnie?

Who talks like that in real life?

I forced myself to take a deep breath. I was going to try not to dislike Matt's mom. After all, her son had been getting threatening emails and had subsequently stumbled over some human remains in the woods. She was being protective.

"Oh. Uh, okay," I heard Matt say. "Yeah."

It took Matt a couple of minutes to get to the door. When he did, he had a terrier on a leash. Then he pulled the door shut in his mom's face.

"Bye!" he said to her through the window. "He needs a walk."

Then he turned to me. "There's nowhere in the house we can have any privacy."

I hesitated. "What do we need privacy for?"

Matt ignored the question and led the little dog to the end of the long downhill driveway. I followed him.

"After this, could we drive somewhere?" I said, eager to get out of the cold.

"I can't," Matt said.

"Why?"

Matt glanced toward his house. "Stuff's happening. My mom's nervous. Doesn't want me to go out anymore. My parents were mad when I didn't respond to their texts right away, when I was at your house the night of . . . Forest Wonderland."

"But what does 'stuff's happening' mean?"

Matt stepped closer to me. "Those emails . . ."

"Yeah?" I prompted. "Did you get more of them?"

"No, but . . . they're getting the FBI involved. Oily told my parents last night. Since they led to the discovery of a dead body, of course the police are taking them more seriously now. They think that if the FBI can trace the emails, they'll be able to do it pretty quickly."

"Oh." That did sound pretty dramatic. Now I understood Mrs. Cotrell's jittery distraction.

"She wants me to stay close to home till we get some kind of word on that. She'd probably be mad if she knew I was telling you."

"Close to home," I murmured, noticing one of the blinds of a front window shifting open, then jiggling back into place. "How close?"

"Like I came out with the dog so she'd at least let me leave the yard."

"Okay."

I looked down at the terrier.

"You guys kept the dog?" I asked. "The lost dog?"

"My dad made us put up a Craigslist notice and an alert at the pound, but yeah. Unless someone shows up saying they lost him, he's staying with us."

"That's awesome," I said. "Nice of your parents. Considering next year you won't be around to walk him."

Matt let the little dog pull him down the walk.

"I guess it was a dog after all," he called to me as I followed behind them.

"What?" I said.

"In that first teacup. A dog. Not a dragon."

I watched Matt turn a corner onto the sidewalk. Remembering that dragon now emboldened me to ask Matt what I'd come here to ask him.

I jogged to catch up with him. "Matt. What happened with Jimmy and Andrea at the Longs' house?"

Matt stared down at the dog, who was peeing on some hedges. "Jimmy and Andrea?"

"Something happened to them. Or to one of them, at least. Outside."

"Outside?" Matt repeated. "No."

"Inside, then. Whatever. But at Phoenix and Payson's house, either way."

Matt headed a few steps down the sidewalk, tugging the dog now.

"I don't know what Cecilia told you. But she doesn't know anything, because she wasn't even there that night."

Cecilia. Of course, he thought I'd learned something from

Cecilia. Which saved me from having to admit that I was asking these questions because I'd had a dream about a gazebo.

"What happened to Jimmy at the Longs' house that night, Matt?" The anger in my own voice surprised me—but maybe not as much as it did Matt, whose mouth fell open.

I lowered my voice to a whisper. "Tell me, Matt. Don't you want to be the one to tell me?"

He wrapped the leash around his wrist so tight that it looked painful. Then he looked up at me.

"Nothing much happened," he said. "All I know is that Jimmy was there."

"*Why* was he there?" I asked.

"Well, Andrea brought him. Mostly just to hang out. But there was this idea that Jimmy owed Payson something. Because of the whole catnip thing."

"Happy pills? Some Molly? What?"

Matt stared down at the dog. "I don't know much about what happened. Because I left."

"You didn't leave right away. You were there long enough for Phoenix to take a picture of you and Andrea kissing."

"Kissing? We were just fooling around. Like always." He smiled briefly, his voice faraway. "Phoenix is so dumb about that stuff."

"But you *did* hang out for a while after Andrea and Jimmy got there. Right?"

"Well, yeah. But Jimmy started to annoy me. So I left."

I considered this information for a moment. And then I considered Matt's reaction yesterday, when I asked about the photo Phoenix had taken.

"And Payson never told you anything about that night? About doing the Molly, or whatever it was? About whether he liked it or not? Or if Andrea did some, too?"

"No. No, he never talked about it. Not exactly. Except . . ."

Matt wouldn't look at me. I knew this meant something.

"Tell me," I said.

"Except when he asked me to erase the pictures he'd sent me from his phone. From that night, after I left."

Pictures. We couldn't be talking about pictures of Matt and Andrea kissing because they were pictures from after when Matt had left. If Matt was telling the truth.

"What were they pictures of?" I asked.

Matt shrugged. "Just dumb stuff. One was of Jimmy crawling around on the floor without a shirt. Andrea was holding him on a leash. The other, he was eating out of a cat food bowl. But he looked game. I mean, he was smiling. Who the fuck knows what he was on?"

I thought about this—along with what Cecilia had told me, about Phoenix asking her to delete the picture of Andrea and Matt kissing *and* any extra pictures from her brother.

"And the pictures were from Payson?" I asked.

"Yeah. He texted them, and asked, 'Which one goes on Snapchat?'"

"And did you answer?"

"No. The whole thing just annoyed me. That Andrea brought Jimmy over. That Payson thought he needed to be the tough guy doing the hard drugs. That he needed to get his little revenge for that catnip thing—"

"And did Payson end up putting the pictures of Jimmy on Snapchat?"

Matt shook his head. "No. At least, I don't think so. A couple of days later, he asked me to erase them. He didn't want to be associated with Jimmy. He said that he thought Andrea was asking for trouble, hanging out with him. Suggested I do something about it. I mean . . . we all thought as much before that. But it felt like there was something about that night that made Payson more serious about it."

I held Matt's gaze. "Right. Like, give me some drugs, and then after that, get the fuck away from me and my friends. Kind of a fast change of attitude, don't you think?"

Matt rolled his eyes, which infuriated me—wasn't he the

thickheaded one here? "I didn't say Payson was a great person," he muttered. "Or a smart one. I'm just telling you how it was."

"How come you didn't tell me this before?" I tried not to sound as upset as I was.

"Do you think Andrea knew about these pictures?"

Matt looked back down at the dog. "She never mentioned them. But I assume Payson sent them to her, too."

"Well, do you think she felt bad about it later?" I demanded.

Matt shook his head again. "I don't know how bad she needed to feel about it if Payson deleted the pictures. I mean, the pictures weren't even that bad."

Matt allowed the dog to get closer to me. The dog sniffed my foot. Matt was smiling slightly. I couldn't tell if the smile was for his dog's cuteness or for the ridiculousness of what he was saying.

"You know what your problem is?" he said after a moment. "You think we're all assholes. You came into this having already made that judgment. I could see it on your face the whole time you were at Payson's house."

"I've never said anything like that," I shot back. "You came to *me*, remember?"

He looked up. But the sharpness was gone. "I came to you about Andrea," he said.

"After that night, she said she was hanging out with Jimmy sometimes, still. But she didn't talk about him *as* much after that. I mean, I told you how depressed she was."

Depressed. Now that he said it again, the word didn't sound quite right to me.

"You want to think she was depressed because of something Jimmy did," I said softly.

"I don't *want* to think it. Why would I want to think that?"

The dragon in the leaves. Self-delusion.

I didn't say anything.

"What are you saying, Marnie?" Matt was yelling now. His dog looked at him, and then me, and yipped.

"What are you SAYING?"

"What's this little guy's name, anyway?" I asked, backing away, trying to think of a way to leave this place.

But Matt's mother was already running down the front steps in her socks, stumbling slightly over the pebbles on the front walk. When she reached him, she grabbed his arm. "Matt. Come in now, honey."

Matt didn't respond. He also didn't pull away from her.

Mrs. Cotrell spoke through her teeth. "I need you to come in."

"Can Marnie come in, too?" Matt asked.

She looked startled to hear my name, and then looked at me as if I'd just appeared.

"Oh." She dropped Matt's arm. "Marnie, I hope we can visit another time. Matt and I are going to need to talk now. It's a private matter."

"But Mom, she lives kinda far—"

"Matt," Mrs. Cotrell said sharply. "Come *in* now."

Matt sighed deeply and gave the dog's leash a hard tug as his mother nudged him up the steps.

"Matt," I said quickly, remembering that I had another question for him. "Does the nickname 'Chuckles' mean anything to you? Does anyone ever call Payson 'Chuckles'?"

Matt was at the top of the stairs now, but turned to squint at me. "No. Andrea called her dad that sometimes, though. Charles. Chuck. Chuckles. Why?"

Before I could answer, Mrs. Cotrell had shoved Matt inside and slammed the door closed. *Thunk.*

I stared at the closed blinds, wondering if both Matt and his mother were watching me from their living room. Then I turned and headed back toward the main road.

I WAS TIRED OF walking, but I didn't have a choice. I zipped my jacket up to my neck.

At the corner, I stood motionless for a moment, trying to take everything in. Mr. Quinley. *Chuckles?* Could that really be true?

And why was Mrs. Cotrell so nervous? She probably heard us fighting in the front yard, but that didn't seem like enough. It seemed something else had spooked her.

I thought about everything Matt had told me about Andrea's dad. That Andrea had felt he no longer noticed anything she did. And that he'd had knee surgery a few months before that. Wasn't that a very painful surgery? One whose recovery often involved strong painkillers?

And I thought again about the dragon in the leaves of Matt's teacup, the first time I'd read for him.

Self-delusion.

Was that symbol meant for me or for him? He was the one who told himself that the pictures of Jimmy didn't mean anything. But surely they'd meant *something*, because they were taken on the last weekend anyone had seen Jimmy around here. January sixteenth.

But maybe I was looking at the self-delusion thing all wrong.

I was the one who'd opened myself to this guy, who'd even kissed this guy, not realizing what kind of information he might be keeping from me.

I reached my hand into my jacket pocket and touched the smooth metal of the bracelet. Pretty but cold. *A burden.* I gripped the metal tightly as I walked past Colesbury Veterinary Hospital, a few more houses, and then the post office.

"Marnie!" someone called from a car.

I looked up, and looked around. I was at the Stop and Shop now—halfway home.

"Marnie!"

It was a female voice that I didn't recognize until a gray SUV pulled up next to me. Cecilia was hanging out the window.

"You need a ride somewhere?" she asked. "We're headed in the direction of your house."

Only then did I see that Payson was driving.

"Get in, Marnie," Cecilia said. There was an insistence in her voice that I didn't quite understand. Payson was pulled over in a sort of busy, awkward spot. I got in quickly.

"Thanks," I said.

FOR A WHILE, AS we drove down Colesbury's main highway, I thought about what Matt had told me, about Payson's pictures. Cecilia and Payson's silence was unsettling me, but I let it go. I'd be home soon. I couldn't wait to see what Noah thought of the whole Chuckles thing.

As we approached a red light, I stared at the window. There was a smudge there—it looked like someone had been scribbling in the mist with a dirty finger. The smudge extended down the glass, thick at the top and then coming to a point. Two little dabs were visible below the point.

"You just got a text," Cecilia said to Payson, picking up his phone from the cup holder between them. "You want me to read it to you?"

"Sure," Payson said, staring ahead at the light.

It was long. We were the only people sitting in the intersection.

"Payson?" Cecilia's voice was suddenly a whisper. I could see in the rearview she had turned white. I held my breath.

"It's from your mom," Cecilia added.

Payson turned to her. "Yeah?"

"She says . . ." Cecilia gripped the phone. "Um. 'Three police officers here for you. Have questions. Sent out cruisers looking for you. If they find you, go with them but don't answer questions. Do not talk to them. Dad calling lawyer. Wait for us. Love you.'"

We all sat still.

Cecilia cleared her throat. "'Do not talk to them' is in all caps."

As she said this, my gaze caught on the window smudge again. My heart seized. What *was* it? A knife dripping something?

Before I could form another thought, my whole body was being thrown forward, snapping back against my seatbelt. There was a screech of tires. Cecilia was gasping. We tore through the red light at full speed.

"Payson!" Cecilia screamed. "What're you *doing*?"

His lips were pressed into a tight line. Gunning the engine, he made the first right. I was flung to one side, my head nearly knocking into the window.

"Stop!" Cecilia was screaming. "This is a neighborhood! What do you want to do, run over some little kids?"

The car came to a screeching stop.

Payson whipped around and stared at her. "No. No, I don't." He carefully maneuvered the car around the street's cul-de-sac and then pulled back onto the main road—this time in the opposite direction—toward the Whitfield River area.

"I just want to kill myself," he murmured, and then slammed his foot on the gas again.

MY HEART RACED. PAYSON drove silently.

"Stop it, Payson! Stop!" Cecilia was screaming. "Are you afraid of the police? Did you do something? What did you do? And now you're going to kill yourself? Or kill all of us?"

Cecilia's questions sounded muffled to me. The smudge on the window seemed to brighten and snap. Maybe we were going so fast that the light through the trees made it flicker in bright flashes. Maybe my brain was playing tricks on me. Maybe I didn't want to see that Payson had lost control.

It wasn't a knife. It was an icicle. With an innocent drop of water melting off it. It reminded me of G. Clara's words when she'd held the bracelet.

"So cold," I murmured over Cecilia's screams. "Pretty, but cold. It was too cold, and then too late."

Payson slammed on the brakes. My head collided with Cecilia's headrest. When I straightened, I caught Payson's stare in the rearview mirror.

"What did Matt tell you?" he demanded. "What did Andrea tell him? Because that's the only way he could know *anything*."

"Matt didn't . . ." I said softly. *"What?"*

"I told you not to believe a word."

Before I could consider a reply, Cecilia's door was open and she'd hopped out of the car—and out of cold panic, I was tumbling out after her.

Payson sped away.

I WASN'T SURE HOW much time had passed. I could still hear the roar of Payson's engine, off in the distance.

"Jesus H. Christ," Cecilia finally gasped. "My heart won't stop. Marnie. Do you have your phone? I think mine's in his car seat. What just happened? We should call the police, right?"

"I think he's going to crash his car," I said when I caught my breath.

"Well, obviously. Give me your phone." Cecilia grabbed my arm. "I'll call 911. Hello? Yes. I'm standing on Whitfield Road with my friend. Our other friend is speeding in his car. The police are looking for him, I think. His name is Payson Long. What? Speeding. We're pretty sure he's thinking of crashing his car. Yeah. Like, killing himself. He's acting crazy. Yeah. That's what I said. Whitfield Road. What? Uh . . . longish hair, reddish brown. Tall, athletic. He's white, yes. What? Hello?"

Cecilia let her hand drop, with my phone still in it. "Your phone just died, but I think they got the point."

She handed me my phone.

"Oh, my God. What the *fuck* was that?" she wailed. She collapsed beneath a tree and clutched the top of her head with her hands.

"Something was off with Payson even before he got that text. That was why I was so glad I saw you. I was feeling weird, being alone with him. I'm sorry . . ."

"Don't be sorry. What was off? What did he say?"

"He was repeating himself. He kept saying he didn't want to go home and 'Have to deal with Phoenix.' Whatever that meant. Then I spotted you."

I nodded. I felt sick. Cecilia had kept the clearer head during that ride. But it was what I'd said about it being "cold" that had made Payson finally stop the car long enough for us to get out.

As if she'd read my mind, Cecilia asked, "So, what was it you were saying, in the car, about it being cold?"

It took so much energy for me to try to breathe again—I wasn't sure I could explain.

"I was so nervous I was just saying whatever. I don't know, exactly."

"And what he was saying about Matt." Cecilia picked up a leaf and began tearing it to bits. "He told you something about Matt?"

"No." I clasped my hands together, trying to stop them from shaking. "He must be talking about . . . Payson sent me emails, I think. Anonymous emails."

"To you? Why? What did they say? Did he confess something?"

"No. They just said I shouldn't trust Matt."

Cecilia froze. "Oh, my God. Payson. Matt. Do you think they *both* killed Andrea?"

"Why do you keep talking about someone killing Andrea?" I asked. "When *Jimmy* is the one whose body they found?"

The color drained from Cecilia's face.

"Jimmy," she said.

"Yeah, *Jimmy*."

Cecilia spoke quickly. "I meant to tell you. That's why I was trying to access that old picture on my phone that night. Because I was thinking about it, about how there were a couple of people in the background. They were sitting behind Matt and Andrea in that picture of them kissing. That part of the picture had been fuzzy, and I hadn't thought about it much at the time, but—"

"But Jimmy was one of those people?" I suggested.

"Yeah," Cecilia said.

"You think maybe that's why Phoenix wanted it erased? Not

because Andrea was sensitive about her and Matt, but because *Jimmy* was in it?"

Cecilia swallowed. "I didn't want to think so," she said.

"Payson had Matt erase some other pictures with Jimmy in them, too," I said.

Before she could reply, we heard tires screeching in the distance, and then a crash.

CHAPTER 31

It took Cecilia and me an hour to get back to downtown Coles-bury. The sound of the crash and the sirens had been from the opposite direction, we were pretty sure.

"I should be getting home," she said as we approached the Clover Café. "But I don't want to yet."

I knew what she meant. I felt like Cecilia and I had just sur-vived something together that neither of us likely would have on our own. There was a certain safety in her company. And once we both got home, we'd plug in our phones (or in Cecilia's case, her computer, since her phone was probably gone for good) and get lost in bad news.

"Can I buy you something to drink?" Cecilia asked.

"As long as you don't make me look at any tea leaves," I said.

"Of course I won't," Cecilia said. "We'll just stop for a minute." She went to the girl at the counter—who for some reason seemed as anxious and distracted as I felt—and bought us each a hot cocoa to warm our hands. We sat on one of the café couches for a quick rest.

"Can I ask you a question?" I said to Cecilia, one eye on the register girl, who kept pacing.

"Sure."

I gazed at Cecilia over my cup, trying to stay calm. "The night of the party at the Longs' house: Did Payson by any chance leave soon after I did? In his car?" I had thought that I'd been followed by a random creep, but now that I knew Payson was writing the emails, I wondered if he'd been at the wheel.

"No." Cecilia sipped her hot cocoa. "Why would he? He was too drunk to even get up. Phoenix would never let him . . . wait. Payson didn't leave, but Phoenix did."

"For what?"

"Snacks. She said there was no good food in the house. Yeah. I guess she came back with some of that cheesy popcorn, and some other stuff . . ."

She paused, her eyes following a bearded young man who'd rushed in. He ran straight for the register girl. "Sorry I'm late," he apologized, out of breath. "My phone died and traffic's all tied up on Route Ten. Some kid crashed his car."

Cecilia and I stared at each other, but neither of us made a sound. All of a sudden, Cecilia hopped up and approached the guy. "Was there an ambulance? Was it bad?"

"Yeah, there was an ambulance," he muttered. "They rushed him off. Looked to me like just one person was in the car, but I was kind of too far away to see everything—"

"How badly was the kid hurt?" Cecilia interrupted sharply.

The bearded guy blinked. "I'm not sure. He wasn't dead, though. So, that's good, right?"

With shaking hands, Cecilia placed her cup on the counter and turned to me. "I want to go home," she said.

AFTER CECILIA BOLTED, I walked home, sipping my cold cocoa and focusing on my feet. I didn't want to see any shapes in the clouds or the trees. I wanted to see the path home. I wanted to see a way to the end. As I turned the corner onto our street, I felt a twisting feeling in my stomach—worried, oddly, that G. Clara would not be home. But then I saw her car and Noah's, and the sensation faded.

"G. Clara?" I called. Noah was in the living room, tapping on his laptop with the TV on.

"Marnie," G. Clara called. I joined her in the kitchen and was

surprised to see she was baking banana bread. "Thank good-
ness. I was getting a little worried."

I hugged her. "Was the oven asking to be turned on?"

"Very funny. No. I had a bad feeling, even before I heard all
of those sirens. Started cooking to keep me busy. We had these
old bananas."

I hesitated. I was about to tell her about Payson. But then I
decided she didn't need to know right now. And I doubted I
could find out much in the next couple of hours.

I went into the kitchen to tell Noah he could probably stop
looking for his "Chuckles."

OFFICERS O'REILLY AND MARKSMAN came by about an
hour later. Since Cecilia and I had placed an emergency call
from my cell phone, the police wanted to hear exactly what had
happened in the car, specifically what Payson had said. I told
them as much as I could remember—leaving out the part about
the icicle in his windshield—and showed them the emails he'd
written me.

After they'd gone, G. Clara declared that we were going to
have a cozy and relaxing family dinner. And we did.

It was delicious but weird. G. Clara baked a whole chicken.
We pretended to be a normal family for a little while: Noah,
the young guy with the hearty appetite; G. Clara, the homey
grandma happily pushing more roast chicken onto his plate;
me, the dutiful girl trying to smile but refusing seconds. Nobody
mentioned windows or dark visions or talking hutches, even
though we all knew now. I wondered if this was how it would
always be. That we wouldn't talk much about it, in the same way
we didn't talk much about my mother.

G. Clara filled the silences more than usual, though. Over
dessert, she summarized for us the television movie she'd
watched on the previous night, in which a serial rapist was
nabbed through DNA evidence collected from a cigarette butt
he'd dropped while a detective was trailing him.

"It was based on a true story," she informed us.

"Isn't everything, really?" Noah mumbled.

"No," G. Clara said. "Not everything is."

UPSTAIRS IN MY ROOM, flopped on my bed and alone with my phone, I saw that Carson had called (three times) and Cecilia had texted me.

Payson is alive but in bad shape. In surgery.

I called her. "You okay?"

"I've been better." Her voice was scratchy.

"Where are you?"

"Home now. But I went to the emergency room. I talked to Phoenix a little. Just a couple minutes. She wasn't really up for talking, for obvious reasons."

"Did you tell her what happened in the car with Payson?"

Cecilia paused. "Not really. It's a bad scene at the hospital. There are police officers waiting to talk to him after surgery or whenever he's, like, with it enough to answer questions. If that happens. And of course his family wants them to leave, but . . . they're not gonna. I'm not a hundred percent sure what they think he did, but something about some emails? I guess related to the kind of emails he was sending *you?*"

I rolled over on my back, staring up at the ceiling. "They think he wrote Matt the email saying where Jimmy's body was," I murmured. "They traced it to him. When will Payson be out of surgery?"

A long silence. "I don't know. Look, I'll call you later if I hear anything else, okay?"

"Thanks," I said.

I tossed the phone on the bed and stared across the room at my backpack.

Homework. I'd forgotten it existed. Should I try to pretend it was possible to get some done?

No. Not possible.

Connect with Carson and tell him what was going on?

But that would require too much explaining that I wasn't yet ready to do.

Go to sleep?

Maybe. But I was afraid of meeting that fox in my dreams.

"Marnie?"

It took me a moment to realize that G. Clara was calling me.

"Marnie!" Her voice was urgent. I tore out of my room and down the stairs. I was picturing her clutching her chest and falling to the ground. *"Noah!"*

Noah was at my heels.

When we reached the living room, though, G. Clara was standing up next to the couch, looking quite awake and quite well.

"Look!" she said, waving at the television.

A young woman reporter was standing near the brightly illuminated steps of a familiar-looking building. The Colesbury Police Station.

"That's correct, Jonathan," she was saying. "We are told that Andrea Quinley is indeed en route to Connecticut, flying with police escorts. Again, she was found in Gainesville, Florida. Apparently a credible tip came in when someone she was living with actually saw her picture and her story on Mitzie Martin's report two nights ago. In fact, this person, a young man, we're being told, actually led Gainesville authorities to the apartment where Andrea was staying. Of course, the Quinley family is eagerly awaiting her arrival."

"What the *hell*?" Noah whispered.

"Shh!" I said.

"Authorities have set up a private, undisclosed location where they'll be meeting her. At this early stage, they are reluctant to say how Miss Quinley ended up in Florida, whether she was taken against her will or under what circumstances. But a spokesperson for the Quinley family says they are 'overjoyed that their daughter has been found safe, and grateful for the support they've received these long months since her disappearance, but ask for privacy at this very sensitive time.'

"So, Jonathan, a happy conclusion for the Quinley family, and for all of those Colesbury folks who were so eager to find her. Of course, we hope to bring you more as this story progresses through the night."

"Mitzie Martin saves the day," Noah said. "Words nobody ever expected to hear."

G. Clara clicked off the TV. "Gainesville, Florida?" She wrinkled her nose. "I wonder how she ended up *there*?"

"You were wrong about the bracelet," I said. "She's not dead."

G. Clara looked at me with genuine surprise. "I didn't say she was dead."

"What're you talking about?" Noah asked, looking from me to G. Clara.

"I said life or death and you said—"

"But I didn't say Andrea was dead," G. Clara interrupted.

"Did I miss a bet or something?" Noah asked.

"Shut up," I said. "Never mind. I'm going to bed."

As I stomped up the stairs, Noah called after me. "What? Are you mad that she's alive? Am I missing something?"

NOAH'S WORDS BOTHERED ME as I dressed for bed. To prove them wrong, I picked up my phone and quickly typed a text to Matt: I'm happy about Andrea. Happy for you. But very sorry about Payson.

He wrote back right away. Feels like a dream. Both things. Good and bad dream together. I'm sorry things got weird. Today.

I wrote back. Weird. Was that what today was?

Alone in my room, I could identify now what had distressed me downstairs. I typed it: Jimmy's still dead.

A few seconds after I wrote it, my phone started playing my frog-ribbit ringtone. Matt was trying to call. I let it go to voice mail.

A few minutes later he tried again.

I decided I'd answer if he called three times.

About ten minutes later, the phone started to ribbit again.

"You're up late," I answered.

"What do you expect? I don't think I'll sleep till I see her."
I was silent.

"But I wasn't calling to talk about that," Matt said. "I was
calling to see if you were still mad at me. I mean, are you? Mad
at me?"

There was something off about his tone, something giddy
about the question. A middle-school-dance sort of question. All
of the grit and disillusionment he'd developed in the wake of
Andrea's disappearance were dashed in a single evening. He
could be a golden boy again.

"I'm not mad at you," I said. "I feel sorry for you."

Matt paused. "Why's that?"

"Because you've got your head in the sand."

"How's that, Marnie?"

"All of your friends have secrets from you and you're afraid
to say anything."

I waited for him to reply. He didn't.

"Hello?"

"I said things to *you*, didn't I?"

"That's different. Doesn't it disturb you that Payson was
writing you those emails? That Payson *and* Phoenix wanted any
proof of Jimmy being at their house that weekend erased? Don't
you want to know why? Don't you want to know *everything*?"

Matt let out a long sigh. "What do you mean, *everything*?"

"What each and every one of your friends is hiding, and why,"
I practically shouted. "Why Payson wrote you those emails,
why he crashed his car, why Andrea ran away, why Phoenix is
losing her mind?" I thought about the Pisces bracelet, by itself
in the pocket of my jacket, still hanging in the front hall of
the house. I'd forgotten to take it out when I'd arrived home.
"Don't you *care*?"

"Care? What the fuck are you saying?" Matt had raised his
voice, now, too.

It's a burden. But it didn't have to be. I could tell Matt what

I knew, and he could put that in his Andrea-love pipe and smoke it. Or I could give the bracelet to the police and be done with it. Still, I couldn't. My eyes wandered to the eggplant mug G. Clara had given me, stuffed with pencils and pens. Maybe the bracelet was "talking" to me, too. The way it made me feel, that I needed to keep it secret—to make it my responsibility—for a little bit longer.

In that moment, I knew why. Because this town didn't care about Jimmy. Not really. Maybe I hadn't much, either. But I felt I needed to make it up to him somehow. And I didn't trust anyone else with the bracelet just yet.

Just *watch* this town forget all about Jimmy now that Andrea had come back.

"Prove it," I said to Matt, even though I was half-talking to all of Colesbury.

Matt was quiet for a moment. "How am I supposed to prove it, Marnie?"

"I'm not sure," I mumbled, and then said goodbye.

I turned off the lights and crept under the covers. Then I reached for my phone. Call me after you get to see Andrea, I texted to Matt.

CHAPTER 32

October 24

It had been a week since Andrea had come home.

Matt had gone and visited her a couple of times. He'd convinced her to come to his house on Friday night—for pizza and a couple of movies. Tonight would also be the first night I would see him since she'd returned.

The last of the reporters who'd surrounded Andrea's house on the first couple of days had packed up and left. Still, Matt had told me that Andrea's parents had agreed to let her out to go to his house on the condition that she would stay there and wouldn't go anywhere else.

There might be backlash.

The national media had lost interest as soon as they'd realized this wasn't going to be an Elizabeth Smart or Jaycee Dugard sort of story. And around town, there was a growing sense of annoyance. Bitter talk, dismissive judgments. All the worry, and for what? Andrea was a run-of-the-mill teenage runaway, a spoiled brat who hadn't had the decency to call her own family to let them know she was alive. Her parents were worried someone might do something to Andrea *now*, since she'd made everyone believe that something horrible had happened to her *then*.

On some level, I understood the anger, even though I knew that they couldn't possibly suspect the entire truth. But part of the truth was undeniable: Andrea Quinley had not been taken against her will.

The older guy with whom she'd been living in Florida claimed she said she was twenty before they started shacking up together. They'd met at a bar and she had said she was a student. It wasn't until a friend saw her picture and story on the most recent Mitzie Martin broadcast that he realized he'd been duped. He'd called the police himself. Investigators had apparently believed him, because they hadn't arrested him.

"I'm not sure this is a good idea," Carson said as he pulled out of my driveway. It was well after dark.

I put on my seat belt. "Look, if it doesn't go well, I'll text you and you'll come get me. It's not like anything's gonna happen with his mom and Andrea there."

Carson turned onto the road and picked up speed. "You still haven't told me exactly what the story is between you and Matt."

I stared out the window. "Does there need to be a story?"

"Are you two going out now, or something?" Carson asked.

I hesitated. "Do he and I seem like a good pair to you?"

"You're kidding, right?" Carson's voice was flat. "*No.* Not at all. But that doesn't answer my question. Are you guys together, or what?"

"There was a second, a week or so ago, when it seemed like we could be."

"A second?"

"Yeah. A kind of stupid second. But it's over now."

We stopped at a red light. Carson turned to me. His face looked even paler than usual in the cold glow of the streetlamps. I thought of how the other kids used to call him "Barnabas" in middle school, because with his funny black hair he looked like a character in some vampire movie that was popular back then. He used to pretend he liked it, but I knew it drove him crazy.

"So why are you going over to his house, then?" he asked me.

"I think he was using me before. So now it's only fair I'm using him."

The light turned green. Carson turned toward the road. "For what, though?" he asked as we lurched forward.

"To get to Andrea," I admitted.

I SHIVERED AS I stood on the corner, three houses down from Matt's place. He was supposed to text me when he was outside his back door and ready to let me in. His dad was away on business, and he wanted to make sure his mom was either asleep or engrossed in the television when I came through—and that the coast was clear all the way to the basement, where he and Andrea were hanging out.

I walked down the sidewalk and around the corner, figuring if I kept moving I'd not only keep warm but appear to be confident of where I was going—if any of Matt's neighbors happened to look out the window.

The night air was freezing.

Just as I was starting to consider calling Carson to come back for me, my phone dinged.

Okay. Here at the door. Sorry took so long. Andrea doesn't know you're coming, btw.

I ignored the urge to text *Why not?* as I ran back toward Matt's house. I crept around the side lawn and met him at the back-porch door.

He mouthed *hi* as he let me in. I didn't say anything. The basement door was only a few steps from where we were standing. He held the door for me and I started down the stairs. I stopped two steps down to slip off my shoes. Then I waited for Matt to pass me on the stairs.

"Hey, Andrea," he said softly as he reached the bottom step. "Do you know Marnie? She stopped by to say hi."

Andrea, who was sitting on a big black leather recliner, turned from the television to stare at me. She looked mostly the same as she had before she disappeared. She had darker hair now—growing out at the roots. But she still had the same blue-eyed baby-doll face. I don't know why I had expected that to be different.

"Marnie and I have been hanging out a lot in the past few weeks," Matt offered, as if this explained my obviously awkward presence.

"Uh-huh," Andrea said, pulling her knees to her chest. "Should we go back to the beginning?"

I stiffened.

"Of what?" Matt asked.

"The movie," she said. She turned to me. She reached for some popcorn in a giant bowl by her feet. "You seen *Moonrise Kingdom* before?"

"Yes . . . a long time ago," I said. I glanced at the enormous television affixed to the wall, paused at an image of Bill Murray shirtless in pajama bottoms. This could have been any normal night in Colesbury, a group of kids gathering to watch a random movie.

"I think my mom made Matt promise he wouldn't make me watch anything heavy or something," Andrea said in the silence. "Am I right, Matt?"

"No . . . uh . . . she . . . I . . . didn't."

Andrea looked at him skeptically, then looked back at me. "You can sit down, you know. You guys are making me nervous."

Neither of us made a move. With a smile, Andrea stood.

We were all silent for a moment.

"Why did he have you come here?" she asked softly, turning her eyes back to the frozen television screen.

Matt and I glanced at each other.

"Because I wanted to show you something," I said.

"*What?*" Matt said. "You didn't—"

"Something I found," I interrupted, my eyes on Andrea. "Something I think is yours."

Andrea turned and stared at me.

"How much have the police asked you about Jimmy Harmon?" I asked.

"Marnie," Matt murmured.

"No, it's okay." Andrea folded her arms. "Quite a bit."

"Really?" I asked. "Because Matt here was so worried that Jimmy had done something to you. Given you some crazy drugs to kill yourself with or who knows what?"

"*Marnie,*" Matt said again, this time more of a warning.

"Marnie what?" I snapped.

"I know your family was nice to him," Andrea said quietly. "I know he liked you guys."

"That was a long time ago. I'm talking about more recent things. Like what happened with you and Jimmy at Forest Wonderland?"

"With me and Jimmy?"

"Why were you there?"

"Why was *I* there?"

"I know you were there."

Andrea said nothing.

"You *were* there," I said. "With Jimmy. At Forest Wonderland."

Andrea glanced at Matt, as if looking for assistance. Then she smiled and sighed.

"You have no idea what you're talking about. I was never there with Jimmy."

My heart raced as I reached into my pocket and pulled out the Pisces bracelet. Slipping it onto my own wrist, I said, "But you left this there. In the cold."

Andrea's throat made a little squeak. Her jaw fell open. I watched her try to close her mouth. Her eyes were vacant. She raised her hand—to reach for the bracelet or to hit me, I wasn't sure. By the time her hand reached me, it seemed the impulse had left her, whichever it was. She touched me on the forearm, above the bracelet, and then let her hand fall to her side.

"What is that?" Matt demanded. "Where did you get it?"

I didn't reply. Instead, I watched Andrea as she covered her face with her hands.

Matt shifted on his feet, stepped closer to her. "Andrea? What's wrong? What's going on?"

Andrea slid her hands down her face until her eyes were

visible, her dull stare turned in my direction again. My heart was pounding so hard I thought it might bruise my rib cage.

"It wasn't far from where they found Jimmy's body," I said, slipping the bracelet off my wrist and back into my pocket. "I found it the day I went to Forest Wonderland with Matt."

Matt whirled toward me. "*What?* Why didn't you give it to the police, then?"

"I don't know, or I didn't know at the time," I admitted. "But once Andrea came home, I knew I wanted to ask her about it myself." I hesitated. "For Jimmy."

Andrea didn't say a word. Her breath was coming fast; I could hear it. Her fists clenched at her sides.

"Andrea?" Matt said, his eyes widening with alarm. He reached for her.

Andrea yanked away from him, then kicked the popcorn bowl across the carpet.

"I didn't mean for that to happen to him," she whispered sharply. "I didn't ever want him to die."

I fought to keep perfectly still. "What happened, then?"

"We thought he maybe froze to death," Andrea said. "Or it was from hitting his head. I'm not sure which. Maybe both. Like, he had a concussion and he couldn't get up, and then he froze to death. Phoenix and I had different theories."

"What the *fuck*?" Matt demanded, pacing now.

"How do you think Jimmy got a concussion?" I asked her.

Andrea shook her head.

"Funny," she said. "If there's anyone Jimmy could've picked for me to tell this story to, I think it would be you. We were all drunk. Payson taking his stupid pictures, whatever. It was Payson who kept asking about Jimmy's other stash. And I was like, 'Do you *really* need be trying that, Payson?' And Jimmy gets a big smile on his face and says, 'Well, a lot of people *do* like these things. Your *dad* seems to like them.'"

I nodded. "Your dad was buying from Jimmy."

"Yeah. But I didn't know it. Not till then. Dumbass announcing that to me in front of my friends? He tried to leave then, said he had to walk home, so I got up and I hit him. I hit him hard. Right in the face, and he deserved it. I ran, and he chased me up the stairs . . . and I pushed him and he fell back down. I think he hit his head. But after that, he left for real."

"You knew he had to walk home."

"Well. Kind of. I kind of forgot. I sort of passed out after that. Didn't think about it until the morning, when Phoenix woke me up, saying she found him in the yard."

"So he didn't make it very far."

"No."

"Why didn't you call the police?" Matt demanded.

"I wanted to, at first. But there were a few problems with that."

"What?" I said.

"It wasn't like he'd just gotten wasted and froze to death. I'd bruised his face and pushed him down the stairs. He had injuries. Of a certain kind. We weren't sure the police would believe it was an accident."

"But Jimmy was a fuck-up," I pointed out. "Probably the police would've believed you, if you told them the truth."

"Phoenix wasn't sure," Andrea said. "Phoenix didn't think he froze to death. She thinks it was a head injury that did it. And if they could prove that . . ."

"Why would Phoenix think that?"

"She said that after I passed out, she looked out the window and saw Jimmy still in the yard. Stumbling around and around the gazebo, trying to work his phone, throwing up."

I considered this statement for a moment before its full weight settled on me. *The phone call to Noah.* And the whole time, Phoenix had seen him struggling in the snow.

"Why didn't she help him?" I asked.

Andrea stared at me and shook her head. "I don't know."

"Are you *kidding* me, Andrea?" Matt said.

Andrea ignored Matt's question. "It was Phoenix's idea to put Jimmy's body in my truck and bring him to Forest Wonderland."

The word *body* hit me like a slap. I couldn't speak for a moment.

"Did Payson help you guys?" Matt demanded.

"No. He was passed out all morning. He was up by the time we got home. We told him we'd gone out for coffee and doughnuts. He was all like, 'Why didn't you bring me any?' He didn't remember enough about what happened with Jimmy to even think to ask about him at all."

"At first," I said, feeling sick. *Doughnuts* had some significance after all.

"At first, yeah. But once Phoenix started making a thing about the pictures we took, he started to wonder what was up. And he knows Phoenix better than anyone. He knows she's . . . cold."

"Not *that* cold," Matt insisted. "Jesus."

Andrea's eyes were empty, her tone of voice dull. "You sure of that, Matt? You know Phoenix so well?"

"You and Phoenix brought his body to Forest Wonderland?" I said. "Why there?"

"Because drug dealers hang out there. So, I dunno. It was Phoenix's idea."

"And you thought this was a better idea than calling the police?" Matt demanded.

"Phoenix thought they would be able to charge me with murder, since I'd assaulted him right before he died. Since I might have caused his concussion."

"What did *you* think?" I demanded.

Andrea smiled stiffly. "Phoenix never makes mistakes. Phoenix is perfect." She turned to Matt. "Right?"

Matt's face went pale.

"I mean, Phoenix couldn't stand for everyone to know how imperfect her conscience is," Andrea continued. "Or to let people know it might even be something deeper than that. Worse than that. That she *watched* him stumbling around in the snow and didn't care. That she watched and waited, like she does, and just went to bed."

"What does that mean?" I whispered, my voice shaking.

"That she's a monster," Andrea said.

"But *you're* not!" Matt cried. "You're not . . ." He shook his head, unable to speak.

"Maybe I am now. Maybe she turned me into one. Because there's no going back once you've done what we did. Allow someone to die. Hide the body. By then it's too late. Afterward, I'd come home from practice—" Her voice caught for an instant, and she blinked several times. "There Jimmy's mom would be, giving my little sister milk and cookies. And my parents still treating me like some kind of baby doll. I wanted to kill myself."

I thought of Jimmy's mom, of her eager eyes, a couple of weeks ago in her kitchen, when she thought maybe I knew where Jimmy was.

"And then?" I prodded.

"I chopped off my hair and dyed it. I drove my truck to the river, and Phoenix picked me up there. I made the plan about a week before. Up till the last minute, I was thinking maybe I'd bring myself to jump into the river instead of disappearing. But of course Phoenix got there before I could work up the nerve. Probably I never could've done it. And so I had Phoenix drive me to the train station in New Haven. She did it willingly. She knew I'd probably tell if I stayed. And it was pretty easy to disappear into New York."

Matt backed away from her. "Why didn't you tell me this?"

"Would you have believed me?" she said, her voice rising. "That I got pretty far on the money I made pawning my mom's tennis bracelet and emerald earrings. That I learned it's easy to get a little money and a little food and a place to stay if you're willing to degrade yourself a little. That I wanted to be degraded, kind of? Because . . ."

"Because of what you let happen to Jimmy," I finished.

Andrea shrugged, letting her dull gaze meet mine. "By then, Phoenix was sending out those text messages from Jimmy's phone. Saying he was in New Jersey or whatever. Phoenix knew people didn't really care enough about Jimmy to keep asking questions. And the longer you wait, the colder the trail gets, I guess."

"Except for the police," I said. "What've you told the police? Since getting home?"

"Not much," Andrea mumbled. "I'm just a runaway, and Jimmy's just a fuck-up who probably OD'd."

"What're you waiting for?" Matt demanded.

Andrea stared back at him. "I was waiting for the right person to ask me to tell the truth."

"I asked you things!" he cried.

"Not the right things!" she screamed.

She stepped over to the popcorn bowl and gave it a hard kick. The popcorn scattered across the carpet again. Several of the spilled pieces formed what was almost a circle.

"Got to go to the police now," I mumbled, staring at the popcorn. "Can't go back now."

No one disagreed.

CHAPTER 33

The fox was finally asleep now—curled up in the snow. His fur was still mangy and crusted with blood, but his eyes were closed and his mouth relaxed. I wished I could warm him somehow— throw a blanket over him or carry him home. But I didn't know the way home from this cold and snowy place. He would have to rest here.

CHAPTER 34

November 3

I didn't hear from Matt in the aftermath. Andrea drove to the police station that night and confessed. Phoenix was arrested the following morning.

For the next week, once again, Colesbury was a whirlwind of rumors and news stories and speculation. Would Phoenix and Andrea be tried as minors? What would they be charged with? Assault—maybe even manslaughter? Additional charges for covering up a death and hindering a police investigation? Their parents hired fancy lawyers, so nobody was sure how serious the consequences would be.

Matt stayed out of school. Cecilia said she'd heard his mom was telling everyone he was sick.

"Sick of having everyone staring at him, I'll bet," Cecilia told me. "I know the feeling. I wish *my* mom would let me stay home."

We were hanging out at my house, for a change. Cecilia said she was tired of the Clover Café. She never asked me for readings anymore.

"Have you gone to see Payson yet?" I asked.

Cecilia pulled off her fringed black boots and stretched out on the couch.

"No. But I heard they're sending him home in a few days. Maybe I'll wait till then. I talked to him on the phone again yesterday, at least. He sounded okay, considering. He's going to need a lot of therapy for his leg, he said."

"G. Clara said she heard in the teacher's lounge that Payson isn't going to face any serious charges."

"I think that's right. Both Andrea and Phoenix have said that he was passed out the night Jimmy died. And was still sleeping when they left for Forest Wonderland."

I nodded. Cecilia had told me this before, but she seemed to want to tell it again. Like she needed for me to know that she hadn't been crushing on a total monster.

"He admitted this time that he did notice the girls were acting weird that morning. But he says he didn't have any idea how serious it could be until he heard Andrea saying something while she was drunk once. To Phoenix. About a 'body behind the tracks.' And then a month or two later he found Jimmy's phone in Phoenix's room. That's probably when he started harassing Matt. To find out exactly how much he knew. He assumed Andrea might have told her story to Matt before she disappeared. He was too afraid to ask his own sister."

"Right," I murmured. I couldn't say I couldn't relate. "You think he'll *ever* come back to school?"

"Pretty likely he'll have a tutor for a while." Cecilia thought for a moment, and then snorted. "He and Matt ought to share one. Homeschooling for the damned."

Cecilia rested her head on one of G. Clara's quilted throw pillows. I decided this was not the time to ask if she still liked Payson.

There was a knock on our front door.

"I wouldn't answer it," Cecilia said. "There are a lot of middle school kids roaming around lately, selling chocolates and wrapping paper."

I peeked out the window and was surprised to see Matt on the steps. He was wearing his Hello Kitty T-shirt again—the one he'd worn the first day I did a reading for him. The hole in its shoulder was much bigger now, like it had gotten stretched out in the wash.

When I let him in, Cecilia quickly pulled herself up to a sitting position.

"Hey there," he said, and then ran his hand down the stones of the hearth.

"You can sit down," I offered.

I sat on the sofa, and he sat gingerly next to me—as if expecting to set off a whoopee cushion. We were all quiet for a moment.

Cecilia stood up and pulled on her boots. "I should let you guys talk."

"No, Cecilia," I protested. "You don't have to go."

But within seconds, she was at the door.

"Text me later," she called.

When she was gone, I avoided Matt's gaze and stared at G. Clara's gross braided rug. After a moment, I noticed Matt was staring at it, too. Normally it would've embarrassed me—him looking so hard at something so dirty in my house. But today I felt numb to that sort of embarrassment.

"Do you want to go somewhere?" he asked. "The Clover Café or something?"

"No. I'm happy here."

I'm happy here.

Were these words true? True enough.

I wondered if the words came off as a rejection. I almost rushed to clarify them, but then didn't.

"Have you been able to see Andrea at all?" I asked instead.

Matt shook his head. "I don't want to. Or maybe I do. It's hard to explain. I think we'll always be friends . . . at least on some level. We'll always have a connection, you know? Just like there was always something between you and your brother and Jimmy. Always some connection."

I nodded and decided not to deny it.

"Something like that, I guess," I murmured.

"Do you hate me, Marnie?" Matt asked suddenly.

I wondered if he'd always known, deep down, that something

terrible had happened to Jimmy that snowy night. I doubted it. While that was probably true of Payson, it probably wasn't true of Matt. But Matt knew there was more to what his friends were telling him, something darker. And he was afraid. So he'd needed someone—or something—to help him face it.

"No," I said. That was the truth, too. "I don't hate you."

I wasn't sure if "don't hate" equaled "like." But I didn't feel I needed to figure this out right away. Both he and I had more significant things to think about, for now.

I looked down again at G. Clara's rug. I tried to ignore the dinginess of its white braids for a moment and focus on what was left of its color. Squinting at it, what I saw most was not its dirtiness, but its spiral shape. A snail. Now, what did a snail symbol stand for? I was out of practice. Deliberately. I'd taken a break from teacups. And I'd tried my best not to read anything else.

"You sure you won't let me go buy you a coffee or a juice or something?" Matt got up and flicked gently at my sleeve.

Of course. A snail meant patience. What was I supposed to have patience for? Matt? Colesbury? My life here in this house?

"My grandmother's going to be home soon," I said. "And there's something I need to do with her."

It was a vague and weak excuse, but Matt understood. He stepped toward the door.

"See you tomorrow?"

"Yeah," I said.

I watched him walk to his car. Its hood didn't have its usual sheen, and its front windshield had a half sun of clean showing through the window's grime. The events of the past few weeks had probably distracted him from car hygiene.

I didn't wave as he drove away. Waving felt like something you do when someone is leaving forever, or at least for a long time. And yes—we *would* see each other tomorrow.

G. CLARA PULLED INTO the driveway as I was opening the front door to go back inside. I waited for her on the steps.

"Did I just see your friend driving away?" she asked.

"Yeah," I said, and decided not to bother mentioning that I wasn't sure if he was my friend.

"What did he want?"

"He wanted to hang out. I just didn't feel like it."

G. Clara nodded, then sank into a kitchen chair. "Wow. Long day. I feel like a cup of tea. You?"

I was startled by the suggestion. "Is that a trick question, G. Clara?"

"No. But . . . after everything that's happened . . . and Noah's told me some things, I'll be honest . . . I'm kind of curious to see you in action."

I shrugged and filled her kettle. "You want your tea leaves read?"

G. Clara let her hair down. "Actually, it might be interesting to see you do your own."

"I've never done my own."

"You ought to," G. Clara said.

"Why's that?"

"It's like how they make therapists go through therapy. You need to know what it's like for the person on the other side."

"Then someone else ought to read my leaves," I said. "Not me."

"I'll read and you'll interpret, then. Since I don't know all of the symbols like you do."

While we waited for the water to boil, I prepared a loose-leaf cup for each of us and listened while she told me the story of her day. Some dumb kid had thought he'd needed to grease a pie pan, and his group's pie went flying halfway across the cooking room when they'd pulled it out of the oven. She didn't tell me the kid's name because she didn't want to embarrass him, she said.

"They're lucky no one got hit with it," she concluded. "Pie filling is pretty damn hot when it comes out of the oven."

"Well, at least everybody learned something. Isn't that the point?"

G. Clara shook her head and closed her eyes as I poured the water over our tea. I decided not to ask if she *told* her class you don't need to grease a pie pan. I wasn't sure most high school kids who don't cook at home would know that intuitively.

G. Clara kept her eyes closed until the cups were ready.

After we had finished drinking, I quietly flipped and turned my cup. When I handed it to her, she took her glasses off to peer inside.

She squinted into the cup for a few moments, then looked at me.

"I think I see the Starbucks logo. Does that mean anything?"

"Ha-ha," I mumbled.

G. Clara stuck her face back into the cup. "No, no. Really. Here's something. A wreath, I would say. Or maybe I should just say circle. Do you want to look at it?"

"Tell me what you think it is. You're the reader."

"Well, I said it looks like a wreath because it's leafy. But everything is going to be leafy, right? So . . ."

"Just go with your instinct."

"It's a wreath, then."

I sighed and settled my elbows on the table, my chin in my hands.

"A wreath is sorrow. Sorrow over a loss."

G. Clara put down the cup and slid her glasses back on.

"Jimmy?" she said. "You're sad about Jimmy?"

I shrugged.

G. Clara thought for a moment. "I think Jimmy and something else along with him."

"Maybe," I admitted. "Although it feels selfish to be sad about anything else, considering."

G. Clara nodded, and then thought for a minute.

"To see things—to *really* see things—means you have to sacrifice the way you *want* to see things."

And then we were both quiet. I thought I heard one of our

kitchen mice scratching around, deep in the farthest cupboard, where G. Clara kept the brown rice and buckwheat that nobody ever ate. I strained to hear it, but then concluded I hadn't heard it at all. I'd just wanted to think about something other than what G. Clara was saying.

She picked up the cup again.

"I see a cobweb. Stretching all along the side of the cup."

I could've said something snarky then, about cobwebs being symbolic of our house. But I remembered a more official meaning, from *Cosmos in a Cup*. It was supposedly a very lucky and relatively rare symbol.

"It symbolizes protection," I said. "Protection from negative forces."

G. Clara was still squinting into the cup. I wasn't sure if she heard me.

Maybe the cobweb was both of those things: my home with G. Clara and the protection it provided me. Protection I hadn't really recognized.

But that tea-leaf-reading book that G. Clara had brought home in a box of tag-sale books—it had drawn me back into this house's dusty warmth. Awakened my inevitable "gift"—or burden?—as gently as it could. Maybe it was for that purpose that G. Clara had first carried it home years ago, without exactly knowing it.

"That's you," I said.

G. Clara smiled weakly. "I'm a cobweb, then? Or I'm a spider?"

"Neither," I whispered.

G. Clara flushed slightly, stood up, and looked toward the window. Looking for a distraction, I guessed. She's never comfortable taking a compliment.

"Oh! My African violet," she said.

She grabbed a glass from the sink—Noah's orange juice glass from this morning.

"African violets are good for a forgetful old lady," she reminded me, rinsing the glass and then filling it with water.

"Because they don't like too much water. They like to dry up some. That's how I've kept it alive since 1994."

She poured the water into the dish below the flowerpot. The glass, once an old jelly jar, was crisscrossed with lines in diamond shapes. As G. Clara tipped the glass back up, it sparkled for a second in the light from the kitchen window.

When she was finished, she sat across from me and took up my cup again. "I'm sorry. Where were we?"

Right where we want to be, I thought. But I didn't want to embarrass her again.

"We were done with mine," I said. "Now let me read yours."

AUTHOR'S NOTE

My first introduction to tea-leaf reading was in 1999, when my husband (then boyfriend) and I visited his grandmother Ruth in Tucson, Arizona. My husband remembered her doing readings when he was a kid, and asked her to demonstrate for me. We used Lipton tea from a torn teabag and poured from a teapot with no strainer. "I see a lot of dogs," Ruth said of the clumped formations in my cup. "You must have good friends." I would later learn that she said this to almost everyone, in almost every reading she gave.

We didn't get to see Ruth that often, because we lived on the other side of the country, in Massachusetts. But from that time until her death in 2007, whenever we'd visit, we'd ask for a reading. Sometimes she seemed embarrassed by the request, and often seemed to rely on stock predictions. *(It looks like you're going to get your wish. But not exactly in the way you wanted it . . . It looks like you're going on a trip . . . probably going home . . . I see a lot of dogs . . .)* But almost every time, she'd look deep into the cup, her eyes would light up, and she'd say something that would later turn out to be uncannily prophetic.

Most memorable to me was a time she said, *I think you're going to have a dispute about a pet. But it's not really the pet's fault.*

A few weeks later an eccentric neighbor of ours started coming unhinged because our cat was sneaking onto her porch and eating her cats' food. She'd call us up to scream about how mean our cat was to her cats. She was going to call the pound, she said, or take our cat "for a ride" if he kept coming onto her porch.

One of the last times we saw her, Ruth gave us a small, battered paperback—*How to Read Tea Leaves,* by Joyce Wilson, published in 1969—and told us we could keep it.

My husband and I dabbled in tea-leaf reading a few times over the years, occasionally consulting Ruth's old book. Eventually, that book would be my inspiration for Marnie's fictional *Cosmos in a Cup.* In fact, the title comes from a passage in Wilson's book.

While I started with *How to Read Tea Leaves,* I consulted several other tea-leaf reading sources as I wrote this book: *The Art of Tea-Leaf Reading,* by Jane Struthers; *Reading Tea Leaves,* by a Highland Seer, with an introduction by James Norwood Pratt and an afterword by John Harney; and *Tea Leaf Fortune Cards* by Rae Hepburn.

Readers who explore this topic will find that there are many different ways to read a cup, and that Marnie's approach (outer rim as the present, bottom of the bowl deeper into the future) is just one of many.

ACKNOWLEDGMENTS

Thank you—

To my editor, Dan Ehrenhaft, for his insight, patience, and enthusiasm.

To everyone at Soho who worked so hard on this book.

To Laura Langlie, for being an awesome agent.

To Ross Grant, for his encouragement after reading the first fifty rough pages of this book, and for all of his support while it was being written. I hope there are moments here that capture a bit of Ruth's spirit.

To Danny Arsenault and Jennifer Purrenhage for their help with the tea leaves and teacups.

To Emma Arsenault for reading early pages and offering gentle suggestions.

To my fairy scientist Eliza, whose imagination inspires me every day.

THE CURIOUS ART

OF

TASSEOMANCY,

OR

DIVINING THE FUTURE THROUGH
THE READING OF TEA LEAVES,

A PRACTICUM TO ACCOMPANY
THE LEAF READER
BY EMILY ARSENAULT

Use one teaspoon of loose leaf black tea for every cup of hot water. The Asker should drink the contents so as to leave the dregs of tea and about half a teaspoonful of liquid in the cup.

She should then take the cup in both hands with the handle pointed to her heart and rotate it on a tilted axis three times, clockwise. Then, she should very carefully invert it over the saucer, again, with the handle pointing to her heart. After about a minute, she should make three full counterclockwise rotations of the cup on the saucer, gently tap the bottom of the cup three times, and flip the cup to reveal the symbols within.

Symbols near the bottom of the cup represent the more distant future; the side, events not so far distant; and near the rim, events which may be expected very soon.

Though not every cup will have a clear message, if the Asker concentrates on the revelation of future events or the answer to a particular question throughout the reading process, her sincerity will be rewarded with the clarification of that which is unknown.

SYMBOL KEY

A

ABBEY, future ease and freedom from worry.

ACORN, improvement in health, continued health.

AIRCRAFT, unsuccessful projects.

ANCHOR, success in business and constancy in love.

ANGEL, good news, especially good fortune in love.

APES, secret enemies.

APPLES, long life; gain by commerce.

ARCH, a journey abroad.

ARROW, a disagreeable letter.

ASS, misfortune overcome by patience; or a legacy.

AXE, difficulties overcome.

B

BADGER, long life and prosperity as a bachelor.

BASKET, an addition to the family.

BAT, fruitless journeys or tasks.

BEAR, a long period of travel.

BEASTS, other than those mentioned, foretells misfortune.

BIRDS, good news if flying.

BOAT, a windfall for the Asker.

BOUQUET, one of the luckiest of symbols; staunch friends, success, a happy marriage.

BRIDGE, a favorable journey.

BUILDING, a removal.

BULL, slander by some enemy.

BUSH, an invitation into society.

BUTTERFLY, success and pleasure.

C

CAMEL, a burden to be patiently borne.

CANNON, good fortune.

CAR, approaching wealth, visits from friends.

CART, fluctuations of fortune.

CASTLE, unexpected fortune or a legacy.

CAT, difficulties caused by treachery.

CATHEDRAL, great prosperity.

CATTLE, prosperity.

CHAIN, an early marriage; if broken, trouble is in store.

CHAIR, an addition to the family.

CHURCH, a legacy.

CIRCLES, end of a cycle, beginning of another; no going back.

CLOUDS, serious trouble; if surrounded by dots, financial success.

CLOVER, a very lucky sign; happiness and prosperity.

COFFIN, sickness or sign of death of a near relation or friend.

COMET, misfortune and trouble.

COMPASSES, a sign of travelling as a profession.

COW, a prosperous sign.

CROSS, a sign of trouble and delay or even death.

CROWN, success and honor.

CROWN AND CROSS, signifies good fortune from death.

D

DAGGER, favors from friends.

DEER, quarrels, disputes; failure in trade.

DOG, a favorable sign; faithful friends.

DONKEY, a legacy long awaited.

DOVE, a lucky symbol; progress in prosperity and affection.

DRAGON, self-delusion.

DUCK, increase of wealth by trade.

E

EAGLE, honor and riches through change of residence.

ELEPHANT, a lucky sign; good health.

F

FERRET, active enemies.

FISH, good news from abroad.

FLAG, danger from wounds inflicted by an enemy.

FLOWERS, good fortune, success; a happy marriage.

FOX, trickery or a trickster.

FROG, success in love and commerce.

G

GALLOWS, a sign of good luck.

GOAT, a sign of hidden guilt.

GOOSE, happiness; a successful venture.

GRASSHOPPER, a great friend will become a soldier.

GREYHOUND, a good fortune by strenuous exertion.

GUN, a sign of discord and slander.

H

HAMMER, triumph over adversity.

HAND, to be read in conjunction with neighboring symbols and according to what it points to.

HARE, a sign of a long journey, or the return of a friend.

HARP, marriage, success in love.

HAT, success in life.

HAWK, an enemy, danger.

HEART, pleasures to come.

HEAVENLY BODIES, SUN, MOON AND STARS, signifies happiness and success.

HEN, increase of riches or an addition to the family.

HORSE, strength.

HORSESHOE, a lucky journey or success in marriage and choosing a partner.

HOURGLASS, imminent peril; time to finish a project.

HOUSE, success in business.

HUMAN FIGURES, must be judged according to what they appear to be doing.

J

JUG, good health.

K

KANGAROO, a rival in business or love.

KETTLE, death.

KEY, money; success.

KITE, a sign of lengthy travel leading to honor and dignity.

KNIFE, antipathy, revenge, or fear; a medical procedure.

L

LADDER, a sign of travel.

LEAF, a sign of impending change.

LEOPARD, a sign of emigration with subsequent success.

LETTERS, shown by square or oblong leaves, signifies news.

LILY, at top of cup, happiness; at bottom, anger and strife.

LION, greatness through powerful friends.

LYNX, danger of divorce or breaking off of an engagement.

M

MAN, a visitor arriving; if the arm is held out, he brings a present.

MERMAID, misfortune, especially to seafaring persons.

MONKEY, the Asker will be deceived in love.

MOON (as a crescent), prosperity and fortune.

MOUNTAIN, powerful friends; many mountains, powerful enemies.

MOUSE, danger of poverty through theft or swindling.

MUSHROOM, sudden separation of lovers after a quarrel.

N

NUMBERS depend on symbols in conjunction with them.

O

OAK, long life, health, profitable business, and a happy marriage.

OBLONG FIGURES, family or business squabbles.

OWL, an evil omen, indicative of sickness, poverty, disgrace; a warning against commencing any new enterprise.

P

PALM TREE, good luck; success in any undertaking.

PARROT, gossip.

PEACOCK, the acquisition of property; also a happy marriage.

PEAR, great wealth and improved social position.

PEDESTRIAN, good news; an important appointment.

PHEASANT, a legacy.

PIG, good and bad luck mixed: a faithful lover but envious friends.

PIGEONS, important news if flying; if at rest, domestic bliss and wealth acquired in trade.

PINEAPPLE, wealth and luxury; friends with money.

PISTOL, disaster.

R

RABBIT, fair success in a city or large town.

RAT, treacherous servants; losses through enemies.

RAVEN, death for the aged; divorce, failure in business, and trouble generally.

RAZOR, lovers' quarrels and separation.

REPTILE, quarrels.

RIDER, good news from overseas regarding financial prospects.

RIFLE, a sign of discord and strife.

RING, marriage; and if a letter can be found near it, this is the initial of the future spouse.

ROOSTER, arrogance.

ROSE, a lucky sign betokening good fortune and happiness.

S

SAW, trouble brought about by strangers.

SCALES, a lawsuit.

SCISSORS, quarrels; illness; separation of lovers.

SERPENT, spiteful enemies; bad luck; illness.

SHARK, danger of death.

SHEEP, success, prosperity.

SHIP, a successful journey.

SNAKES, a bad omen; caution is needed to ward off misfortune.

SPIDER, a sign of money coming to the Asker.

SQUARES, comfort and peace.

STAR, a lucky sign; surrounded by dots foretells great wealth.

STEEPLE, bad luck.

STRAIGHT LINE, a journey, very pleasant.

STRAIGHT LINES, happiness, and long life.

SWALLOW, a journey with a pleasant ending.

SWAN, good luck and a happy marriage.

SWORD, dispute; a broken sword, victory of an enemy.

T

TIMBER, business success.

TOAD, deceit and unexpected enemies.

TREES, a lucky sign; a sure indication of prosperity and happiness; surrounded by dots, a fortune in the country.

TRIANGLES, always a sign of good luck and unexpected legacies.

U

UMBRELLA, annoyance and trouble.

UNICORN, scandal.

V

VULTURE, bitter foes.

W

WAGON, a sign of positive change.

WALL, misunderstanding; a physical or mental barrier.

WHEEL, a journey with a positive outcome.

WINDOW, consider a different perspective; psychic ability.

WOLF, an enemy; a greedy or vicious adversary.

WOMAN, pleasure and happiness; if accompanied by dots, wealth or children.

WORMS, secret foes.

WREATH, a ceremony to come, a wedding, a graduation, a funeral; a symbol of loss, grief, or death.

Z

ZEBRA, travel and adventure in foreign lands.

For more visit SOHOTEEN.COM